KILLER ON THE ROAD

Also available from
Stephen Graham Jones
and Titan Books

The Only Good Indians

The Lake Witch trilogy
My Heart is a Chainsaw
Don't Fear the Reaper
The Angel of Indian Lake

I Was a Teenage Slasher

The Buffalo Hunter Hunter

The Babysitter Lives

KILLER ON THE ROAD

STEPHEN GRAHAM JONES

TITAN BOOKS

Killer on the Road
Paperback edition ISBN: 9781835415825
E-book edition ISBN: 9781835415832

Published by Titan Books
A division of Titan Publishing Group Ltd
144 Southwark Street, London SE1 0UP
www.titanbooks.com

First Paperback edition: June 2026
10 9 8 7 6 5 4 3 2 1

A CIP catalogue record for this title is available from the British Library.

EU RP (for authorities only)
eucomply OÜ, Pärnu mnt. 139b-14, 11317 Tallinn, Estonia
hello@eucompliancepartner.com, +3375690241

Set in Adobe Caslon Pro by Richard Mason.

Printed and bound by CPI Group (UK) Ltd, Croydon, CR0 4YY.

for my brother Spot,
who I can talk trucks with for days

0

"THANKS FOR THE ride," the hitcher says, climbing in from the sheeting rain.

"What's the old joke?" the driver says, clocking his mirror to ease back up to speed. "I ask you—no, you ask *me* if I'm a serial killer, and I say no, I'm not worried about that. The chances of two serial killers randomly being in the same car are through the roof, right?"

"Something like that," the hitcher says, taking the towel the driver's dug up from behind the seat, nodding thanks over it.

The driver clicks his headlights from bright to normal then back again, trying to see through the rain.

"More like I should ask if you know how to handle a submarine," the driver says, easing them ahead.

"Biblical out there," the hitcher says, strapping his seatbelt across.

"Belly of the whale," the driver says back.

"You don't listen to talk radio, do you?" the hitcher asks, squinting through the blurry windshield at the road ahead of them.

"Maybe I do?"

"Good," the hitcher says. "Me too. Can't get enough."

"Or maybe I don't."

"Me either. Hate it. Talking heads, floating voices. Puts me on my meds."

"You're medicated?"

"Not right now, don't worry."

The driver considers this for a handful of seconds.

"Just to be transparent here," he finally says, and pushes his hand down alongside his seat, comes up with a chunky snub-nose.

"I get it," the hitcher says. "Road can be a dangerous place."

"I don't usually do this," the driver says. "Pick someone up, I mean."

"And I usually don't manage to catch a ride when it's raining," the hitcher says.

"Firsts for both of us, then."

"Just two killers heading west."

The driver chuckles, likes that. Switches hands on the wheel and looks over to the hitcher. "Confession time," he says. "My radio's actually on the fritz—why I stopped for you. So you can help me stay between the lines. Know any scary stories to keep us awake?"

"Work for my supper, got it," the hitcher says, scooching down in the seat for a comfortable position then straightening back up.

"I'm driving either way, man," the driver says. "Just"—easing over for a whirr of the rumble strip on the shoulder—"am I over here or not, right?"

"I could drive, you want," the hitcher says. "License is good and clean in Wyoming."

"Thanks, of course, but . . . you know."

"I get it, yeah," the hitcher says. "So, a story . . ."

The hitcher narrows his eyes to dredge the right one up.

"You heard the one about the guy picks up a girl who turns out to be a ghost?" he asks.

"You telling me I'm talking to a ghost?" the driver says, very ready to thrill a smile up.

"There's the one about the vampire thumbing rides at night to get his dinner."

The driver lifts his revolver again, makes like he's peering into the back of the cylinder, says, "And here I am without my silver bullets."

"Think that's werewolves," the hitcher says, folding the towel that wasn't folded before. "You know about the lot lizard who kept working after she was dead, and ended up getting pregnant with something?"

"Sounds like a cautionary tale," the driver says, raising his hand to shield his eyes from a bright car on the other side of the divided highway.

"Here's one," the hitcher says. "You hear it everywhere, last year or two."

"Everywhere like . . . hobo camps?"

"If this was 1932," the hitcher says with a tolerant smile. "Rest stops, truckstops. Lock-up. Tunnels when it's raining like this, or under bridges."

"This isn't the lot lizard one?" the driver asks, his disappointment nearly theatrical.

"Better," the hitcher says. "It's one of us—dudes looking for rides. Deal is, this Bucketmouth guy climbs in like I just did and after a while he asks you if you'd rather be dead or missing a finger."

"He just asks it out of nowhere?" the driver says. "Out of the blue, like?"

"Kind of a conversation killer, yeah."

"Is Bucketmouth his name?"

The hitcher shrugs sure.

"Finger, obviously," the driver says. "You've got ten fingers but just one life. Easy call, especially if it's hypothetical."

"Thing is," the hitcher says, "it's not. He'll give you a knife or something to cut it off if you can, then he makes you sit there while he takes it and"—miming a tiny cob of corn—"he eats the meat off it while you watch."

"A *cannibalism* story," the driver says, his lips peeled back from his teeth in appreciation.

"Except this one's true," the hitcher says, and opens both his hands, presses them into the dashboard for viewing, all his fingers there through his fingerless gloves, except . . . the pinky on the left.

The driver jerks the car over, away from this, the tires thudding over the reflectors embedded in the shoulder, then he flutters his right hand over his beating heart.

"I'm awake now," he says, making himself breathe big in and out, the seatbelt tight across his chest from all his moving around.

The hitcher chuckles, his hands still pressed onto the dash.

"You've done this before, haven't you?" the driver says at last.

The hitcher unfolds his pinky finger, waggles it.

"What if you really met this guy, though?" the driver asks, undoing his seatbelt to reset it, guiding the strap back down to the buckle, having to dig and adjust to find it. "No, no—what if it's *you*, and this is how you prep me for what's about to happen?"

"Already had my finger for the day," the hitcher says, looking at all his own, still spread out perfect on the blue vinyl of the dash.

"Not me," the driver says, and presses the snub-nose barrel of his revolver against the hitcher's pinky where it connects to the hand, and pulls the trigger.

The sound in the cab of the car is massive.

The driver drops the revolver to press this finger to the dash, catch it before it can fall into the floorboard. The hitcher reels away, pushing hard with his feet, his butt climbing the seatback, but then he realizes: the *gun* in his lap.

He fumbles it up, trying to hold it and stop his new stump from gouting blood up into the headliner.

"You, you, you," he says, and pulls the trigger at the driver again and again.

There was only the one bullet.

The driver lifts the still contracting finger up like thanking the hitcher for it, then inserts it neatly into his mouth, rotating it a little on insertion like getting it just how he likes it.

"Where you headed, mister?" he says as if starting them over, dialing them back to when the hitcher got in. His words a bit muffled by the finger in his mouth, but it's only the pinky.

The hitcher doesn't respond, is still climbing his seat.

"What?" the driver answers in his own voice, leaning forward over the steering wheel, the raw end of the finger still protruding from his lips. "You mean this *isn't* the highway to hell?"

He laughs and laughs about this, then sucks the finger all the way in.

The hitcher fumbles at his door handle but the lock sucks down.

He elbows the window but is wearing so many layers that they pad his blows.

"*What the fuck are you?*" he screams to the driver.

"Bucketmouth, evidently," the driver says around the thick finger. "I know I don't get to, like, select my own name, that's not how the big machine works, but what does Bucketmouth even *mean*?"

He leans forward to inspect his mouth in the rearview mirror, work it open and shut a couple times to confirm that it's just a normal mouth. Then he sees something that needs attention at the base of his jaw on the right side. He angles his head over so his fingertips can pinch up a skin tag.

He tugs gently on it, then harder, longer.

His whole face peels off, leaves just muscle and fat and tendons and dripping blood, and something cloudy and viscous coating it all, like the saliva of someone who's been sucking on a Vaseline lollipop.

He inspects himself in the mirror again from all sides, nods that he likes this, yeah. This is good.

He tosses the face he just peeled to the hitcher, who flinches away hard enough that the back of his head shatters the window out at last. The interior of the car swirls into a madhouse, burger trash and receipts and emptied-out Fritos bags whipping around everywhere, then sucking out into the night.

"What are you, man?" the hitcher says, weaker.

"More like *who*, sir," the driver says, unlocking the doors with his master control and then reaching across the hitcher to pop the door open, push him out, leave him rolling in their lane, the headlights of the semi behind them coming on fast and unavoidable, the horn blaring at what probably looks like a trash bag of something. At least until it goes under the wheels.

Alone in the front seat, the driver looks in the rearview again, winces when the headlights behind him turn sharply away. Then he angles the mirror onto himself, says, "Bucketmouth?"

He shakes his head in wonder then turns his functional radio on, hums with the Roger Miller coming through, and clicks the headlights off, slips ahead, into the darkness.

1

THERE MIGHT HAVE been a better way to do it, Harper knows.

Also, she could have packed.

And, just spitballing, but what if she'd thrown less of her mom's precious collector's plates across the living room? What if she hadn't lifted the couch up by one end and, in trying to send it flying after the plates, jammed it against the ceiling?

No way was she taking back what-all she'd said, though.

On Harper's list of things she hates now and always will, forever amen, around number six or seven would be people simpering back after a big blowup, saying how they didn't really mean to say that.

What they mean with that, actually? It's not that they hadn't meant to say that, it's that they got pissed enough that they said what they really meant, and now kind of wish they could reel that back in, do you mind? Can we all just forget, pretend that never happened, keep moving forward?

No, Harper tells them in her head. No do-overs, no takebacks.

As of two months ago—graduation—she's eighteen, so doesn't have to play nice anymore. Granted, there's her little sister Meg to keep in mind, who in a perfect world wouldn't have been watching this big blowup from the hallway, but . . . had Harper had anybody watching out for *her* when she was in seventh grade? No. It was just and only her, twenty-four/seven, and she made it through . . . not completely unscathed by Mom, but she wasn't a smoking husk, either. Not yet, anyway.

But she could have packed.

When her mom disappeared back down the hall, came storming back up with Harper's laundry to throw at her on the porch, yeah, it wouldn't have been terrible to have held onto some of those dirty clothes. But it had felt so good too, hadn't it? Flinging it all over the front of the house, screaming how this was a clean break, that she didn't want any reminders of this place, that she didn't need any of them, that this podunk Wyoming shitkicker town wasn't going to hold her back anymore? That she had better opportunities anywhere than this. That her friends were her real family anyway.

That last part . . . Meg hadn't still been listening from the living room, had she? Because she didn't mean it *that* way. Her and Meg would forever be sisters. Just, Harper could not stay in that house even one second longer. Sorry, Meggie. But if Harper made it this long, so can she, right? Anyway, it's not like Harper can take a little sister along. Really, it's just her for this big exit. Those friends she calls family *would* be there for her, but two of them have already zipped their sleeping bags together and taken off for Yellowstone to work for the summer, one of them's blasting off for college in Salt Lake next month, doesn't need this kind of distraction, and the other one, her many-times ex Dillon, they aren't exactly talking, and probably won't be until the ten-year reunion, which Harper does *not* plan on attending. So there.

In ten years she's going to have a room above a bar in Seattle or Los Angeles, her right arm's going to be full-sleeve, her left arm waiting for her thirtieth birthday, and she's going to wear mostly leather vests, keep her hair always pulled back unless she's shooting pool and doesn't want the night's mark seeing her eyes.

Her mom isn't going to have any idea where her daughter is, either. Guaranteed.

Meg? Maybe she can know, sure. No reason to hide from her. But, too, Meg'll be in college by then, or just getting done, Harper can't math it out perfect. Maybe Meg'll even have found the perfect guy or girl by then. They'll backpack through Australia, send Harper postcards with spiders and snakes and kangaroos on the front, not the elk and bears and cowboys of idiotic Wyoming.

Harper kicks a rock ahead of her, tracks its vaulting gallop down the asphalt into their shared future. Hers and the rock's.

Her one consolation for the moment is thinking about her mom trying to work the couch down from the support pillar it is now. It's up there tight. When that puffy arm had caught against the ceiling, Harper had backed off, given it her shoulder, all her hundred and forty pounds plus whatever her rage came to, but the couch hadn't had even one ounce of budge in it. She'd backed off then, stood in the soft rain of the popcorn acoustic and sparkly glitter scraped off the ceiling.

In fifth grade, her and her dad had blown that ceiling up there together, the air compressor over by the back door in the kitchen so they wouldn't all asphyxiate, and her mom had said no glitter in the living room, but Harper's dad had let her sneak a handful into the mix anyway, and it had been beautiful, like twinkles of secret gold.

This of course being five years before Mom ran Dad off.

That of course, Harper figures, being pretty much the official beginning of the end. The last good summer.

Write it in your memoir someday, she tells herself, and passes the rock she kicked. She doesn't kick it again.

It's hot now but this is Wyoming in July. Come dark there'll be a chill. Which is why she's not going to be outside. Also, if things go right, she's not even going to be in Wyoming anymore. Maybe if she runs hard enough, if she never looks back, she can forget she's even from this place at all.

And she's *not* fucking crying, okay?

"Happy last summer before real life," she says to the idea of her mom. "Thanks for all the laughs, it was a riot."

A big rig grinds past her—the on-ramp to the interstate is right there—and she hunches her shoulders against the dust and sound it's dragging then sneaks a peek at the back of the trailer. Just to see.

Her dad, whatever trailer he was dragging that week, he would always draw a rough circle in the grime on the back of it, lower right, then lick a different finger, dab some hashmarks in for the idea of numbers. A short slash and a long slash, then—careful not to cut a piece of pie from this circle—and . . . it was a clock. It was supposed to be his way of telling all the tourists on his roads that he was on a schedule, that he had places to be, that he had a family to be getting back to, that he didn't have time for RVs drifting from this lane to that, for sports cars passing on the right side, for minivans flipping lanes to get to the next tourist attraction twenty seconds sooner.

That's Harper's first tattoo, so far: the round, slightly oblong face of a clock on her right scapula. She'd told the guy to just put the hands pointing at whatever time, it didn't matter. It wasn't about the time. It was about who she was. It said she had places to be, thanks. Places very much not here.

Another thing that's going to be out here on the road with her tonight, she knows, is stars. Wyoming stars, which she has to admit she might come to miss someday. Lying under them she's going to be eleven years old again in the living room, the ceiling above glittering and sparkling.

Too late, just for the gesture of it, just to show she's committing to this enterprise, she hikes her thumb up for the trucker's mirrors but he's already hauling his big wheel over to the left, reaching for a lower gear, to ride the on-ramp into America proper.

When the truck doesn't slow, Harper lowers her face, thrusts both hands into the kangaroo pocket of her pow-wow sweatshirt—Meg's, oops—and stifflegs it under the eastbound then westbound bridge to make that big left onto 80 as well.

In her head she does her blinker, and, coast clear, swings her right leg around, pivoting on her left foot, taking that important first step away, into something better, something real. Something not here.

2

BECAUSE THE STATIES will stop to have words with you for hitching on the actual interstate, the ramps are where all the rides are, Harper knows. Well, the ramps are what work when your mom might be cruising slow through all the pump islands of town.

That's the way it always works with her mom: I hate you I hate you I hate, followed by I'm sorry I love you come back you're the most important thing in the world I could never lose you please.

So: the ramp, which is just a ramp by name, not by actually angling up or down more than three or four feet.

Because West Laramie's a blink-and-miss-it joke, Harper's the only one sailing her thumb out at five thirty in the blazing afternoon. Which is good. In her current state she doesn't need any Bobby McGee tagging along.

The first big rig that rumbles past has too much speed to waste it on a runaway who's probably a minor, and the second and third rigs—a Mack cabover, a Freightshaker like her dad's—both already have riders perched up in the passenger seat. Yeah, one of those riders is a dog, one's a woman her dad would have called a seatcover, and all the trucks had sleepers she could have napped in just fine for three hundred miles, but screw it.

Is it the big stenciled feather on her back that's warning the drivers off? Are Indians automatically trouble? If so, then it's good she stole Meg's sweatshirt, isn't it? Otherwise the drivers would have to wait to ditch her until they saw her hair, her skin, her face.

I could be Mexican, though, Harper says to those drivers, her eyes slit hard at them. Except this is Wyoming, yeah. And except for this big feather on my back. More like a bullseye.

Thanks, Mom.

If these drivers knew her dad had been a gearjammer *and* white like they maybe are, would they be lining up to give her a ride? Probably to the first exit, yeah. Where they could turn around, trash their schedule to deliver this little girl back to where she belongs.

Screw that noise.

An hour later Harper is sitting by the last reflector pole down the ramp, her back to Laramie, her face west, west, always west. Now she's thinking it would have been nice to pack some clothes and *also* her headphones, wherever they are.

Big gestures don't always involve forethought, though. And anyway, it's not like this is the furthest away she's ever made it, right? Her junior year she made it all the way down to Colorado before a waitress called her in for approaching trucks in the back row. According to the cops, that waitress maybe saved her life.

Her comeback when the cops told her that: What life?

The younger one told her yeah, she'd been seventeen once too.

When tires finally crunch onto the shoulder behind her, Harper hauls herself up, no smile, ready to give whatever bluff or attitude she needs to make this work out. Maybe even a smile. Extreme circumstances call for extreme measures, all that.

It's an old long Thunderbird, faded red with a vinyl roof peeling away in a thousand tiny curls of white.

Her eyes flash to the car's rearview first of all. It's how she's trained: will there be an eagle feather there, or some baby moccasins, a little beaded headdress? All of those would be acceptable, as would a twirling iridescent CD, meant to scatter radar guns. What'll send her scampering for cover will be a dreamcatcher. What's there in this Thunderbird is a cross that's really purple yarn wrapped around and around two popsicle sticks, with a secret and surely meaningful strand of yellow or gold in there.

Don't run, don't run, you need this, Harper tells herself, even though her genes have been programmed to know the church is the boogeyman for Indians—it's the hand that grabs you by the scruff while the other hand's already drawing back in a fist.

The passenger door opens, takes forever to *stop* opening because this car is long enough to be a train, practically, and both the passenger and the driver get out that side. For safety.

Harper, her face pleasant, hair threaded behind her ears, tries to see into the backseat. No one. Good. This can work.

The woman approaches first. She's got this long skirt and sandy-colored beehive do under a scarf—she should be wearing cat-eye glasses, Harper thinks. Next is the acne-scarred white man putting his sports jacket on, trying to guide his combover back into place and get his glasses resettled on his face.

The woman leads with a bottle of water fresh from a cooler, with a glow-bracelet threaded through the label for increased visibility at night.

Shit.

Do-gooders. Holy rollers.

Harper takes the bottle, twists the cap off and takes a polite sip.

"Do you know where it is that you're going, dear?" the woman says. This is probably their script: the woman carries the conversation load when the hitchhiker is female, so as not to spook her. Or maybe it's to establish sisterhood or be a mother figure.

The question is a loaded one, of course.

"To hell?" Harper says, to just get it over with.

The man looks back up the on-ramp, his cheeks crinkling around his eyes, his chest thrust out from the way he's stretching his shoulders back, his hands wrapped into thumb-swallowing fists from the strain.

"Next hundred and fifty miles are—they're like the Bermuda Triangle for travelers, do you know that?" he says, finally bringing his pasty face around to Harper.

"Thought it was the Snow Chi Minh Trail," Harper says right back. It's what her dad used to call 80 in the winter.

"He's talking about all the people who go missing, dear," the woman says. "You've seen the posters in the windows at the gas station, haven't you? Not just . . . *walking* people either. Drivers too."

"Just because people don't call to check in doesn't mean they're missing," Harper says. "Just means they don't want to get found."

"No, I mean—" the woman starts, then starts again: "One of the young women from our congreg—from our flock, she's kind of a data expert, see, it's her job, and she's identified this stretch of interstate as statistically more—"

"Thanks for the water," Harper says, being sure they can tell she's already looking on down the road. "Don't worry, I recycle." She tips the bottle off her forehead, saluting them bye, but they're on a mission, are blind to any and all social cues.

"Just last month," the man says with apologetic finality, guiding his hair into place again, passing a slick photograph to Harper.

She doesn't take it but she can't help but clock it.

It's the head and shoulders of a dead man in the dry grass of what's probably the ditch—no, this is deeper into the BLM wasteland, isn't it? Harper can tell from the snow fence this man's been leaned up behind, that's tilting him forward. His eyes are gone, probably taken by birds, and his mouth has been hollowed out as well, and his skin's been baked to leather. In the winter he'd be a corpsicle, but in summer like this he's just a mummy.

Harper sucks air in through her teeth, almost a hiss. It's not so much from the shock of seeing this with no preparation, it's from—it's stupid. Right after her dad didn't come back from his last run, this was where she'd spent all her time: studying what photos she could find of unidentified men found in proximity to the interstate. At first she'd been able to eliminate some of them by hair length, but after a couple of years her dad could have grown his hair down to his shoulders. So now all she had was facial hair versus no facial hair. Her dad had none when he left, and had always been against it, said it creeped him out when he could see it out the bottom of his eye. This dead guy maybe had the same hang-up. Clean-shaven.

"You okay, dear?" the woman asks.

"Scared straight, ma'am," Harper says. "Thanks, thank you. Wouldn't have a sandwich for a lonely traveler now, would you?"

Ten minutes later, the Thunderbird people gone, Harper bites into the first of the three sandwiches she was able to talk them out of. It's pimento cheese, which is paste with chunks in it that are a slightly different temperature, or texture. After two normal chews and four longer, slower ones Harper gags it out, thinking of that dead guy's dry, empty, open mouth, damn those holy rollers to hell.

"That won't be me," she says, making it so by saying it out loud.

And it isn't her dad either, she adds, in secret.

3

TWO AND A half sandwiches in her kangaroo pocket now, Harper finally just decides to stand, hoof it. She's got the glow-bracelet on her wrist, right? Doesn't that make her practically bulletproof?

Half a dozen steps later, another set of tires crunches in behind her.

Harper cringes, doesn't need any more salvation, fuck you very much. But, at the same time, she knows she probably should load up on water, if there's water to be had. And maybe a handful of tissues too, since she's now committed to walking away from all indoor bathrooms.

She turns, her most pitiful face on like a mask, and it's—it can't be. Cropped-short orange hair in the passenger seat, a perfect white smile over the steering wheel. *Kissy and Jam?* Who are supposed to be in Yellowstone for the whole summer, chasing wolves and tagging bears?

Harper holds her arms out so they can see how flabber-gasted she is, how out of the blue this is, and then she holds them there a bit longer, shoulder high, her face trying to maintain the same shocked expression. But she's processing now: if they were in town for the day, for the weekend, for whatever, then . . . they were in stealth mode? not looking her up? avoiding her?

What kind of bullshit is that supposed to be?

Jam slithers up from the passenger side of the blocky-old four-door used-to-be-white Forest Services looking truck—*Park* truck, Harper's just now registering—crosses his arms over the roof and flops his head over to the side like to see Harper better, or slower, make this moment last.

"We leave for two months and you're already sacrificing yourself to the interstate gods?" he says.

"*Harper!*" Kissy yells from behind the wheel, tapping the horn three times in celebration, the third time long and loud.

Harper has to smile.

Her hands thrust back into her sweatshirt pocket, she sashays up to Jam's side—short for 'James' since junior high—and leans in to hug him, reaches past him to hold hands with Kissy, which has been her name since forever, for obvious reasons.

"Figured you'd be pregnant already," Harper says to her.

"Not for lack of trying," Jam says around the back of his hand and not even close to a whisper, and Kissy hits him in the hip with the side of her fist.

"There's bears up there!" Kissy says, about Yellowstone.

"Bears and pic-a-nic baskets, yeah," Harper says, looking down the ramp to a clump of three choppers riding in formation. "Y'all are going back?" she says into the cab real casual, trying not to load it with anything.

"We swung by your house," Jam says, quieter, shrugging it true. "Your mom was, um, redecorating?"

"She'll be moving on to my room next," Harper says, rolling her top lip in between her teeth. "Now that she can do what she wants with it, I mean."

"I'm sorry," Kissy says, batting her eyes like she's a deer in a Disney movie. The bad thing about Kissy, which is maybe the good thing too, is that she's put together just like the cartoon Pocahontas in the movie Harper took Meg to last week: impossible cheekbones, bustline that won't quit, shampoo commercial hair. Never mind that she's not enrolled at Wind River, or anywhere. On all her applications she checks the ethnicity box she has to draw in, "Cherokee Princess." It kind of fits, sick as it is. It makes her everybody's grandmother, just, when that grandmother was hot.

"You look good," Harper says to her. "Pre-pregnancy suits you."

"This is all I've got cooking in me," Kissy says back, extending her middle finger slow like a bun rising in an oven.

"I've missed this," Harper says. "Been kind of a long summer."

"Tell them where you went looking for her next," a voice calls over the backseat, even though the backseat's . . . empty?

Harper lowers her eyebrows to Kissy about this but is already stepping back to look through the rear window.

Dillon, kicked back across the bench seat, his down-at-the-heel boots chocked up on the passenger side armrest.

"We thought y'all might be . . . back together," Jam says, as apology.

"And he's going back to the Park with you now?" Harper says.

"I was worried about you," Dillon says. "I know how you can be. I mean, if anybody does."

"You fixed my mom's couch, didn't you?" Harper says to him, disgusted.

"I did," Jam says, raising his hand to take this heat. "We didn't have loverboy with us yet then."

"That's one name for hi—" Harper says, looking up the ramp and catching almost immediately on the side-profile of her mom's pale Buick, cruising out from under the bridge like she gave the car some pedal a quarter mile back, is just riding that out in silent mode.

Harper rolls to the truck, flattens herself against it, and, easy as anything, Dillon slips the door open, pulls her in, his hand to the jut of her right hip, his other hand guiding her head below the level of the window.

"She's stopping, she's stopping . . ." Kissy announces, tight to the rearview, her foot revving the engine even though they're not in gear.

"Shit shit shit," Jam says, bouncing in his seat, drumming one hand on the outside of the door.

"Go already!" Harper says from the floorboard of the backseat.

"She'll know," Dillon says, and then kicks the door open decisively, takes one step out into the grass, and lets loose with a harsh arc of pee, leaning his whole body back from it.

Halfway through, his staged emergency over, he looks up like just seeing the Buick up there. He turns to it, waves big, probably some other part of him waving as well, and Harper's mom puts her foot to the gas now. When Dillon leans back in, breathing hard with excitement, Kissy passes a baby wipe back to him.

"You can just pee any time like that?" Jam says, impressed.

"Never knew that about you."

"Full of piss and vinegar, my mom always said," Dillon says, leaning back to zip up. "That's half-true, anyway."

"You could have faked it," Harper says. "She can't see detail that fine all the way from up there."

"That *fine*?" Dillon says after a beat.

He balls the wipe up, tosses it into the grass.

"Listen, thanks," Harper says to Kissy and Jam, her voice ramping up to goodbye—no way does she need to be taking any road trips with her ex, thank you—"but y'all probably need to be getting back to—"

"Ho," Jam says, his hand cupping the side mirror, holding it steady against the engine's vibrations. "You weren't the only rabbit hiding in this ditch, were you?"

All of them look back, and, goddamnit: it's Meg, standing from the drainage part of the ditch she'd evidently ducked down into at the last moment, probably after sneaking out the backseat of their mom's Buick at the gas station—oh, of course: she saw the Park truck, knew it from Kissy and Jam stopping by, and . . . shit. Here she is, right where she should never be.

She raises a hand hi, her smile sheepish, seed heads floating all around her.

"Caught," Kissy says, and before Harper can say anything the truck is reversing *up* the down-ramp, one tire on the shoulder, one on the blacktop, Dillon standing on the running board, his arm wrapped around the window post as easy as anything. Which Harper kind of hates, since it's kind of precisely what she used to love about him—how he doesn't have to think about complicated dangerous scary stuff, just does it like it's the most natural thing ever. In another era he would have stepped up onto a moving train just the same, never had to look down at tracks or the big steel wheels or anything.

Kissy stops right alongside Meg.

"What the hell?" Harper says to her.

Meg shrugs, her lips covering her new braces.

"Mom thinks you're sleeping in the backseat, still?" Harper goes on, trying to make her eyes hot and mad, not about to cry from seeing Meg.

"You broke my plate too," Meg says with a shrug, and Harper has to concentrate to keep all these plates spinning in her head. But then it slows enough for her to see it: the one Meg got off that infomercial because the dog on it looked like Sheba, her dog that had got parvo two summers ago. Harper had camped in the backyard with her and Sheba for four nights until . . . until.

"Shit," Harper says, and reaches through the window to pull Meg's head to her shoulder. "Shit shit shit, girl. I'm sorry."

"I tried to put it together, but Mom—Mom—" Meg says, which is the last thing Harper hears before the world becomes sound and stinging gravel: a shiny Kenworth's taken the left onto the ramp fast to keep its momentum, really dive down onto 80, but that means it's riding the bright white line of the shoulder. The one their truck is straddling.

The Kenworth's air horn opens, splitting the afternoon in two, filling all their heads with instant panic, with certain death, and then Kissy straightens her arms against the steering wheel and stomps the pedal in.

For a moment, a lifetime, the truck stands there on its one spinning tire, Jam screaming, his left hand pushing up into the headliner like that can possibly save him, that Kenworth's grill filling all their mirrors, its horn filling all their heads, but then the Park truck's one spinning tire catches and they bolt forward, and it doesn't matter that Harper is trying to clutch onto Meg, to keep her safe. It doesn't matter because Dillon's stepped back onto the running board, is cupping her body with his, holding her and Meg both safe. Just another thing he does so natural, without having to even think about it.

Goddamn him.

By the spit-out of the ramp they're doing forty, the tired engine chugging, smoke billowing behind them, and a half-mile later they're up to a shuddering unsteady sixty, the truck's absolute limit, and then Kissy is crying and driving and trying not to hyperventilate.

"Any . . . *time*," Dillon says through the open window, still riding the running board, and Kissy eases them off the next ramp, the one that's all motels and truckstops.

The Kenworth slams past, at speed now, its air horn blasting the whole way.

"I-I think I prefer bears," Jam says, trying to smile, his eyes shiny.

Kissy glides them into the scrub nobody cares about and leans into the steering wheel, her hair draping down through the shifter and blinker and whatever.

"Thank you," Harper says to Dillon, over Meg's head, and Dillon shrugs like it was nothing, is already stepping down, looking ahead, tracking that Kenworth.

4

IT TURNS OUT that the Park truck Kissy and Jam are driving is why they're in town. Just for the day. Yellowstone is getting a new fleet, selling off the old, and Kissy's dad always needs another. Donny, their legendarily gruff supervisor, had given them eighteen hours to Laramie and back for show and tell—breakfast cleanup to last call—to see if her dad wanted the truck.

Turns out, he didn't. The arrowhead emblem on the door is cool and distinctive, especially half-faded like this one's, but Park trucks have spent their lives grinding down two-tracks in first gear, are better left to that than trying to come to town, put on a suit and tie.

"So . . . you were here all day today?" Harper says.

"That's what you get from that?" Dillon says, impressed.

"Family *lunches*," Jam says, emphasizing the plural. "As in, over at my mom's, then my dad's, then Kissy's parents?"

"Good to eat something that doesn't taste like smoke," Kissy adds, guilty. "But two lunches probably would have been enough."

"What was the fight about this time?" Dillon says to Harper.

"Usual," Harper says, eyeing the interstate, all-too-aware

Meg is right there listening. "It's good that it's almost dark."

"True that," Kissy says, patting the truck like the sad thing it is. "Old Whitey here kind of has . . . *overheating* issues."

"Interested?" Jam asks, playing. "Our other buyer turned out to be actually smart."

"I mean," Harper says, about it getting dark. "Just—we're already on trucker radar, right? That little stunt on the ramp? All the drivers headed east on 80 know to be on lookout for a truck with a big stupid arrowhead on the door."

"As in, they want to be sure we make it to our destination?" Jam says, innocent and hopeful as ever.

"As in we're number one on the shit list," Dillon says.

His dad's a driver as well. It was the first thing that brought Harper to him.

"Meaning?" Meg asks, reminding Harper that her little sister was too young to ride the doghouse with her dad on his short runs.

"I think what Harper's saying," Kissy says, drilling an index finger theatrically into each of her temples and closing her eyes to better focus her psychic powers, "is that . . . a revenge-minded semi or two might be razzing us."

"Two inches away at eighty miles per hour," Dillon says, slamming his open hands past each other to show, the palms scraping. "Horn blasting, bombs flying."

"*Bombs?*" Kissy says.

"Bottles of pee," Harper fills in.

"Fun," Jam says. "Who needs amusement parks when there's the Wyoming interstate?"

Harper studies the truckstop across the field.

"Y'all can drop me at Rawlins," she says. "That's where you

turn up to the Park, right? What, hundred miles?"

Kissy gives a tolerant smiles, says, "Harp, we're not just going to—"

"And you," Harper says to Meg. "You're calling Mom from that phone."

She points and they all follow that across the field to the payphone koala'd onto the side of the truckstop. The lights glow on over it just then, like Harper staged this.

"But—" Meg tries, only to be stopped by Harper's serious eyes.

"I can't take you with me," Harper says. "I don't even—I don't even know where I'm going. It's not safe."

"For you?" Meg sort of objects.

"For *you*," Harper says. "Why'd you . . . I mean, Mom likes you. You're the good daughter."

"And that's better?" Meg asks, her chin pruning about . . . probably about "expectations," and it being so impossible to live up to them. With their mom, you've either already let her down, or you're soon to.

Harper pulls Meg to her, rests her chin on top of her head and blinks fast.

"Listen," Jam says, "let's *all* go back. We can sleep in my mom's basement. We'll tell Donny the truck overheated. He'll understand."

"He'll understand that we're lying," Kissy mumbles sheepishly.

"But nobody'll be walking on the shoulder of 80 at *night*," Jam says to her, importantly.

"I've *got* this," Harper says, showing off her useless glow-bracelet.

"That a deterrent or a target?" Dillon says.

"And you're not going to be late because of me," Harper adds, argument over, then turns to Dillon: "And—mister smartass, you can stay with her until my mom picks her up?" With Meg.

Dillon just watches Harper's eyes about this.

Finally, "Can we talk?" he asks, tilting his head out past where the group can hear, his bangs falling into his eyes, which is *another* thing Harper despises about him. For reasons.

They walk out, Harper's fingers trailing out of Meg's until the last moment. It almost feels wrong to Harper, not leaning into Dillon. But this isn't old times. This is new times.

"What?" she says to him when she can.

"I'm not letting you do this either," he says. "You're right about it not being safe for Meg. But it's not safe for you, either."

"You don't get to say what I do and don't do," Harper says back.

"I'm saying this as someone who cares about you. It's not—I mean—"

"You're trying to protect me because I'm a girl," Harper tells him. "Thanks. Not insulting at all, Dillweed."

He flashes his eyes up to her about this use of her old name for him.

She glares it true, lets the ghost of a smile curl her lips.

"My brother's shop's in Rawlins," he says. "We all ride there together. Hour and a half. If you still want to get out there, start walking, then I take that old Camaro he has, bring Meg back myself."

Harper looks past him, to Laramie. To the idea of it. Then she comes back to Kissy and Jam, Jam with his hands on an imaginary steering wheel so he can re-enact Kissy's slow-motion facial expressions with that Kenworth bearing down on them. Meg's laughing, her braces flashing, her hand coming up to cover her mouth.

"We can't make them late, deal?" Harper says to Dillon.

"Think I want to single-handedly bring down the national park system?" Dillon says back with a smile.

"And we're not even close to getting back together," Harper adds, just to be sure.

"Wasn't even considering that," Dillon says, falling in behind her. "I hate everything about you, remember?"

Harper hip-checks him, doesn't look over.

5

THEY'RE ON THE road exactly two and a half miles before the first rig steps up onto the highway stripes, brings its passenger-side front fender close enough to the truck that Kissy reaches out with her hand to push it away, which results in the Park truck drifting onto the right shoulder. To prove this actually just happened she holds her now-grimy palm out to all in the cab.

"Shit," Jam says to Harper. "You weren't joking about them hating us now, were you?"

"That a bird?" Meg says, directing them all to the road ahead of them.

"Crow," Harper says, watching it because Meg's right: it's a big black bird flapping up from the road, into the dusk, but . . .

"What's it carrying?" Dillon says.

"Roadkill," Kissy says, thoroughly grossed out, at which point the crow wheels back over the road, away from a pair of smaller birds divebombing it. The result: whatever it had in its talons, it's falling now. Not like a flattened snake or the rubbery intestines of a deer, either. More like it's caught an updraft swirling up from the heat the asphalt's radiating, but its weight is still pulling at it, so it's just drifting. Down, down . . .

Onto the windshield.

Jam screams loud enough for all of them, is pushing back, over the seat.

It's a face. The skin of a man's white face, which isn't a thing Harper's ever considered before, or considered having to see. It's a mask, she realizes, the backsides of her own cheeks crawling. Just look through the eyeholes, line the mouth up so you can speak through it.

"Shit," Dillon says.

The truck whips from side to side, not quite enough to tip over at sixty, but it is top-heavy with its gone shocks and spongy tires, so, nearly enough.

Harper holds onto the back of the front seat and reaches forward like to touch this face on the glass, says, "Do I know him?"

"What?" Kissy says, and, on automatic, just using her palm not her fingers, like that'll mean she's touching this face less, she does the wipers.

The face slides with the wiper to the side of the windshield and then the wind has it, is flopping it over to the side mirror on the driver's side.

Kissy dives away, isn't interested in driving anymore, just needs distance from this.

Harper surges over the seat to take the wheel but it's a short-term fix. In the moment of stillness she has, she looks over to the face on the rearview—just skin and blood, mostly—and says, "Combover."

It's the guy from the Thunderbird. She can tell from the pastiness, from the acne scars, from the bags under the eyeholes.

And then he's gone, slipped behind them.

Everyone but Harper turns to track the face.

"Kissy, Kiss, brakes . . ." Harper says, way too calmly, about the ten-wheel dumptruck they're about to drive up under.

Kissy moves back over, takes the wheel, veers them away from that certain death and into another: the splatty gravel of the shoulder, then the slick grass of the ditch. After flattening two mile markers, she finally slows them to a ragged stop, their headlights splashing out into the pasture, everyone breathing hard.

"I saw—I saw my life flash before my eyes," Jam says, laughing with nerves. "It was mostly sex scenes."

"I'm *done* driving," Kissy says, turning the key back and stepping out all at once, Harper just managing to reach through the window to grab her shoulder, pull her back from the rig slamming past deep in the shoulder, a hairsbreadth from clipping their cocked-out rear bumper.

Kissy stands with her back to the truck, Harper's hand holding her there, and cries in a breathless way, her whole body shuddering. Jam slithers up from his window, walks across the cowl at the back of the hood, drops down by her, pulls her close.

"Got her?" Harper says.

He nods.

"Harp?" Meg says.

"I don't know," Harper says, and checks the front rearview for headlights before stepping out, whipping around the front of the truck to stand in the ditch, think.

Dillon's there waiting for her.

"You knew that . . . him?" he says.

Harper waggles her uncracked glow-bracelet, says, "He gave me this."

"Guess he stopped to help someone else too," Dillon says. Then, a beat later: "Hey, your friend's back."

Harper looks up.

The crow. *A* crow, anyway. Just perched on a fencepost, an eyeball in its beak, hanging by the pulpy stalk. The stalk is longer than Harper would have guessed. It makes her aware of her brain in a new way, like it's thick with cords waiting to be pulled.

"They're close," she says, casting around the pasture.

"They?" Dillon says, ducking from the bird flapping up, coasting over them nearly at head-level to settle down on the cab of the truck.

"We need a—" Harper says, is cut off by Dillon slinging a rock at the crow.

It doesn't connect, but it's close enough that the crow squawks back, having to spread its wings for balance, its meal of eyeball falling away.

An instant later the rock connects with the hefty grille guard of a Volvo rig barreling past at ninety. The rock comes back like birdshot, takes the rear window of the Park truck out in an explosion of glass.

Harper's already running for the cab, dragging Meg out.

"You all right, you all right?" she's saying, patting Meg's shoulders, checking her face.

Meg, half in shock, touches her own face, looks back to the truck. Her hair sparkles with pebbles of glass.

"*Stupid!*" Harper yells back to Dillon.

He licks his lips, doesn't look away.

"What the hell was that?" Jam says, side-hugging Kissy, walking her around the front of the truck.

One side of his face is sparkling, too. Then, kind of all at once, bleeding, a hundred little pinpricks welling blood.

Kissy looks up, sees it, wants to wipe the blood away but it'll cut her hand.

"Shit," Dillon says, turning around, sick with himself.

"We're going to get you home somehow," Harper's saying to Meg, both of them on their knees now, Harper pinching the glass from Meg's hair.

Meg nods yes, that, please.

"You shouldn't have followed me," Harper tells her.

"Do you think it's my favorite place, there with her?" Meg says back, a tear slipping down her face.

Harper tilts her face back to keep from crying then turns to Dillon, snapping his fingers back to all of them to get their attention.

"What?" Harper says into the quiet he's made.

"Your friend with the face," he says, directing them to taillights out in the pasture. "Who used to *have* a face. Was he driving a mid-seventies Ford? Red?"

"Thunderbird," Harper says, standing to see, a passing rig throwing her shadow out ahead of her then ripping it away.

6

WITH KISSY IGNORING everything to try to pincer as much shattered glass as she can from Jam's face, Harper stations Meg by the fence, well away from the road, and forges out into the pasture with Dillon, walking in the tire tracks the Thunderbird left. She doesn't want to, but she has to see, too.

"What happened?" Dillon says.

"Nothing good," Harper says back.

The Thunderbird is maybe a hundred yards out, still idling and in gear, only the parking lights on. It's pushing against a tall weathered snow fence that's not giving, just groaning and creaking, like still complaining about being rolled into. Meaning the Thunderbird was hardly moving by the time it nosed out this far.

Harper and Dillon stop a few steps out, look to each other for confirmation that they're doing this.

"Remember," Harper says. "One of them won't have an eye anymore."

"And the other's missing a face, check," Dillon says, taking the driver's side, leaving the passenger for Harper.

"I just *saw* them," Harper says, stepping ahead, careful of making sound, like that might spook the Thunderbird, send it flapping deeper into the scrub.

"Maybe you should let me—" Dillon warns, to the open driver's door now. "Empty," he calls across the roof to Harper. "Gone."

"Got somebody," Harper says back, wrenching the passenger door open and trying, through the open window, to hold the beehive woman steady. She flops half out so Harper has to catch her.

Harper looks over the woman's shoulder at Dillon, reaching in over the bloody white bench seat to twist the ignition off, moving carefully so as not to leave any fibers or skin that might incriminate him.

The Thunderbird keeps right on idling.

"What the hell?" he says, holding the key up to be sure he's actually got it.

"Old car, worn out key," Harper says, obviously, then: "Little help, please?"

Like that Dillon's to her, already guiding the woman back into her seat.

She's the one with the missing eye. The crow probably sat right on top of the door, right in the open window.

"Impact broke her neck," Dillon says, nodding to the awkward bulge on the side of the woman's neck. The bulge that has to be bone. The skin around it is discolored.

The woman gasps a ragged breath in.

"She's paralyz—she can't move!" Harper says, not sure where to hold her, how to hold her that won't hurt her worse.

"So where's the driver?" Dillon says, standing to cast around in the darkness. "He just leave her here?"

Harper registers Dillon walking around the trunk to reach in the driver's side again, pull the headlights on. They light the snow fence up, and a little brush past it, but don't show any driver stumbling around out there, his face removed.

"He's out there somewhere," Dillon says. "Shit. What do we do?"

He turns to Harper, and she one-hundred percent knows he's doing what he always does: using her like an external conscience. He doesn't want to go crashing around in the dark for the rest of the night, looking for a man with no face, but if she says to, he will.

"I don't—" Harper starts, and then a red bubble slowly expands over the woman's dry lips, goes back down before it can pop. "We need to—we need to get help," she says, reaching in to . . . she doesn't know: put a pillow behind the woman's head? clear her airway somehow? raise her feet above the level of her heart?

Then the one eye the woman has left opens, wheels around in terror, settles on Harper and Dillon.

The woman gasps, choking on her own blood, unable to change the angle of her throat. Harper reaches forward, takes her limp hand.

Dillon steps up onto the bumper, waves both arms to Jam and Kissy.

"Bring the truck!" he calls, just as another rig lays on its air horn. "Shit!" he says, jumping down, slapping his open hand onto the trunk, the car edging forward maybe three inches from his jostling.

The trunk opens too.

Dillon looks down into it, confused.

"Their *bags*," Harper says, nodding. "There's—we need to make a bandage, get something!"

Dillon hauls the one duffel out, closes the trunk just because that's what you do, and that last jostle is just enough to break that one important splinter keeping the snow fence upright, evidently.

Moving slow in the way of massive things, it leans back, the Thunderbird pushing it, pushing it, and then it falls all at once, in an exhalation of splinters.

The Thunderbird surges ahead over it, both doors closing when they encounter broken boards, and like that the big red car is easing deeper into the pasture, *with* the paralyzed holy roller.

Harper starts to run after but Dillon has her wrist.

They watch the car bump and roll, and then both step back when the next panel of snow fence falls over. And the next.

Like dominoes going either way from this one panel tipping over, the snow fence falls, and falls, dust sighing up into the air.

"It wasn't us," Dillon says.

"It was us," Harper says, and turns back to see if headlights are slowing on the interstate.

They aren't.

"We've got to—" she says, and, holding Dillon by the hand, pulls him away from this.

THEY WALK BACK up on Kissy and Meg calling out into the pasture for Jam.

"What?" Harper says. "You were supposed to stay together, I told you to—"

"He took the, you know, the *wipes*," Kissy says. "Three lunches in one day, plus the trauma of—?" She does her fingers around her face to show what she means, why Jam is out there looking for something to squat behind.

Harper looks out into the darkness but not very hard, has no desire to see Jam's head at stomach level.

"How's his face?" she asks.

"I still love him," Kissy says back.

"Were they out there?" Meg says.

Dillon shifts the big duffel to his other shoulder, says, his eyes skating away from Harper's, "Just the car."

Harper blows air out her nose at this. Is he protecting Meg from getting a version of what they just saw, or does he really want to have never been out there, should the law come asking how two hundred yards of snow fence got knocked over? To say nothing of the two corpses sunrise will reveal. The same way he's always been easy with dangerous things, lies have always been second-nature to him too. Just the grease necessary to get through the day in one piece. Which wasn't reason *one* why they're not together, but it was pretty much three through ten, anyway.

Still, Harper lets it slide, doesn't want Meg thinking about the one-eyed beehive lady out there, paralyzed and choking in the passenger seat, her big red car nosing forward for a gully, a creekbed, a sudden canyon.

The headlights are on, though, Harper tells herself. That means the taillights will be a flare for the rest of the night. Once they call this in, the Thunderbird will be easy to find, provided its battery lasts.

"Any time, James!" she calls out into the darkness.

"Pinch it off!" Dillon adds, needlessly. Grossly.

Maybe two minutes later—six rigs, only three of them spattering gravel at the Park truck—the shape of Jam totters up from the bushes. He's buttoning his shirt. Harper doesn't ask.

"My turn!" Kissy says and bounces out past him, taking the baby wipes he's holding up like a baton to pass to her. But he's at the end of his leg of the race, too, is weak, spent, half-gone.

"Does it hurt?" Harper asks when he's close enough.

He looks up to her, his eyes startlingly white in that half-mask of blood.

"I'm sorry, man," Dillon says.

"I just want to get back on the road," Jam says with considerably less humor than he's been having so far.

One quick pee later, Kissy's back.

"Was that all the snow fences falling down?" Meg asks, still looking out into the pasture.

"What's in the bag, big man?" Jam asks Dillon.

Dillon looks to Jam about this—big man?—but just shrugs, sloughs it off his shoulder, into the bed of the truck.

"Bibles and pimento cheese sandwiches," Harper says.

"So we're robbers now too?" Kissy says.

"Too?" Harper says.

"Let's go," Dillon says, checking the road to step around to the driver's door.

"Whoah, whoah," Kissy says. "Donny—like, our boss—he says only Park personnel can drive Park trucks."

"Like he'll know?" Harper asks.

"Not your ass," Jam says, delicately touching a pebble of glass from his top lip.

"Then you," Dillon says to Jam. "Can you see good enough with . . . all that?"

"He forgot his license," Kissy says, face down to deliver this news.

They all look to Jam about this.

His defense: "I—I haven't needed it all summer! It's . . . it's at the bunkhouse, I think. Top drawer. I'll just run up and get it right quick." He laughs about the hopelessness of this and rubs his top lip again, gingerly.

"He can't drive," Harper says. "He can barely see."

"I've got it," Jam says, swallowing loud as if with resolve. "It's just my face that's hamburger, not my eyes."

"But what if we get stopped?" Harper says. "You don't have a license."

"Said the church mouse," Kissy says.

Dillon sputters an accidental laugh about this—it's an old joke, that Harper's always on the straight and narrow—but he holds his hands up to show how not-involved he is with this.

"I think it's choirboy," Jam says. "Church mice are, like, poor, aren't they?"

"It's altar boy," Harper says. "And I'm not one."

"Altar girl?" Meg tries.

"You're not involved in these deliberations," Harper says, flashing her eyes at Meg.

Between headlights and air horn blasts, they load up.

Jam adjusts the rearview, sees himself at last and sags back, lets a deep cough out. The gagging kind.

"You're not going to throw up, are you?" Kissy says from the passenger seat, trying to distance herself from him. "Are you throwing up? Tell me if you're throwing up."

Jam shakes his head no then is throwing up over his knees, into the floorboard.

"Window, window!" Dillon says to Kissy.

"Think you already took care of that," Kissy says with a protective glare, about the back window.

"This is like an afterschool special," Harper says. "Reasons not to run away, one through five."

"How much longer to Rawlins?" Kissy asks, still holding Jam's head so it's pointed more out the window than in.

"Ninety miles," Dillon says, standing up a bit through the broken back window to catch a breath.

"Ninety miles," Harper repeats kind of hopelessly. "So we're . . . like three miles from Laramie? Four? Where's the next turnaround?"

"Emergency or civilian?" Dillon asks.

"What, are you a robot now?" Kissy asks him.

"I don't want to get stopped without a license," Jam explains. "Civilian."

"Highway 12," Dillon says. "Four miles, five."

"That Herrick one?" Jam says, maybe done puking. "That's —Sand Creek, right? There's no phones there, man."

"Hunt Road, then," Dillon says. "We can call in from that gas station. Fifteen minutes. Well, twenty at fifty-five. If it's open, I mean. Sound like a plan?"

"You really are a map," Meg says up to Dillon.

"My dad said if I was going to ride with him, that meant I was the navigator," Dillon says with a shrug. "I took it serious, I guess."

"You have to sit down in the seat," Jam says back to him. "One of us up here doesn't have his license with him, remember?"

"We don't need to get stopped," Kissy seconds.

"Unless we want, you know, *medical help*," Harper mutters. "Or want to report a wreck with fatalities."

Dillon slides back down, clearing the chance of glass out of the way.

"Nice air freshener you got in here," he says to the front seat.

"My own personal blend," Jam says back, lowering the truck into gear, his foot on the brake, eyes in the mirrors.

"Twenty minutes," Harper says to Meg, and pulls her close, holds her there.

7

***THREE* MINUTES LATER**, maybe not even that, Kissy is enumerating the night's bullshit so far: Harper's big blowout with her mom, Kissy and Jam finding their best friend in the world in the ditch waiting for a serial killer, all three of them kidnapping a minor—"Do you think your mom's reported her missing?"—all the truckers in Wyoming targeting the Park truck for destruction, a human *face* on the windshield, and then two missing Bible-thumpers, a quarter-mile of snow fence knocked down, and a boyfriend who looks like he cut himself shaving a hundred times in a row.

"I miss anything?" she asks, eyes glittering over the back of the front seat.

"That the truck's overheating," Jam says, studying the gauge. "If that counts."

"Shit," Harper says, slumping further down into her seat.

"Turn the heater on," Dillon instructs. "That pulls the heat from the engine."

Almost instantly the cab is muggy hot, tastes like antifreeze.

"Welcome to hell night," Kissy says, giving up.

"Up here," Dillon says, pointing, and Jam coasts them into

the pullout he means. It's nose-to-tail with sleeping truckers, sleeping rigs.

He kills the truck before Dillon can stop him and they all just sit there.

"Should we—" Meg says, trying to figure out the best way to say it: "Should we have left a little pyramid of rocks on the side of the road back there? For the ambulance to find?"

"I could have hung this on a mile marker," Harper says, holding her glow-bracelet up. "Also, I could have *looked* at the mile marker."

"The one Kiss ran over?" Jam asks, trying to grin and immediately wincing from the effort.

"It's not all on you to save the world, to think of everything all the time," Dillon tells Harper.

"I'm the big sister," Harper says, and pushes her door open before he can come back with anything.

The night air is crisp, and sticky with diesel exhaust. One or two of the rigs are idling. Harper can feel the steady grumble in the asphalt. It's comforting, reminds her of childhood.

"There bathrooms at this one?" Jam asks, kicking his door open as well.

"Again?" Kissy says.

"Ammo dump," Dillon says, looking around at all the sloshing-full plastic bottles.

"Say what?" Jam says, not making the connection.

"Where you store your pee bombs," Harper says, already bored with it. "No, no facilities, Jam. Sorry."

"World's full of facilities, man," Dillon says, opening his arm to the big, dark night.

"You just wanted to look at your face, didn't you?" Meg says, taking a chance—being the kid, talking with the adults. Or, the closest thing to adults.

Jam looks away instead of answering. It's how Harper knows Meg was right.

"Is it drying into a scab?" Harper asks Jam, her right hand lifting not exactly to touch his face, more to almost touch it, like to pad it with a cushion of air.

Jam flinches back all the same, his arm coming up to protect.

"Sorry," Harper says.

He shakes his head no, not to worry about it. But he's not smiling anymore either.

"We should get some water," Kissy steps in to announce in her perky way. "For the radiator."

"Where?" Jam says, holding his hands up. "This isn't a rest stop. It's just a . . . is there some cool trucker word?"

"Hunh," Dillon says, then to Harper, "What *are* these? Nap trap or something?"

"We can call them whatever we want," Harper says like it even matters, leaning over the bed of the truck. "Swingout, how about?"

"Park 'n' nod," Meg says with authority.

"Park 'n' nod," Harper agrees without hesitation.

"Y'all making that up?" Kissy asks.

Meg shrugs and they all turn their heads to the buttery line of running lights coming on, outlining the cabover and trailer of a rig in front of them. Instant Christmas.

"Somebody wants us off their lawn," Dillon says, smiling in appreciation. "Flashing the porch lights at us."

"Shhh," Harper says to all of them.

The lights glow off in what Harper can tell is a surly way.

"It's like we're sneaking into the cave with the bears that want to eat us," Jam says, the ghost of a smile at the corners of his mouth now, his teeth seeming larger for some reason—maybe because they're so white in all that red. Harper wants to smile with him. She wants to smile just because he still *can* mile.

"He's just trying to sleep," Dillon says about the afterimage of the yellow lights still burning in all their eyes.

"Or she," Kissy says.

"Hungry, M?" Harper says to Meg.

Meg shrugs.

Dillon holds his eager hand up.

"I *know* you're hungry," Harper says, and hauls herself up into the bed of the truck, pulls the duffel bag over.

"You sure?" Kissy says, standing on the other side of the bed now. "This like breaking and entering?"

"They're both dead," Dillon says. "Think they can spare us a . . . what was it? Cold grilled cheese sandwich?"

"Pimento," Harper corrects.

"How do you know they're both dead?" Meg asks, not letting that slip past.

Harper rips the zipper down all at once so Dillon won't have to answer.

The duffel isn't Bibles and ziplock baggies.

Clothes? Not even folded?

Dillon steps up with her, the truck shifting with his weight, and Jam comes around to the bumper, his fingers nervous on the top of the tailgate. Harper looks up, finds Meg watching through the missing rear window.

"What is it?" Kissy says.

"Men's clothes, I think," Harper says, and starts pulling them out.

She's right, but that doesn't mean the clothes make sense. There's grimy hitchhiker gear but there's a pinstriped suit, and then a bright yellow sweater vest of all things—

"Easter egg disguise?" Dillon asks about it—and, pulling hard, a thick leather biker jacket, patches all up the left arm.

"These don't—" Harper starts, trying to make this make sense. "The guy who was in the car, he was . . . he didn't dress like this."

"Probably Goodwill stuff to like pass out on the road to people, yeah?" Jam says. "Didn't you say they were good samaritan types? Fairy godmothers of the interstate?"

"Ding ding ding," Dillon says, dropping the sweater vest back in.

Harper pulls it up to her face, smells it.

"Thrift store stuff usually smells like formaldehyde," she says. "It's that spray they use to delouse or whatever."

"What else?" Meg asks.

Harper pushes all the clothes out and to the side, reaches in for . . .

"Baby food?" she says.

Meg reaches above her, clicks the cargo light on over all this.

Baby food jars, yep. Probably twenty of them, each wrapped in rubber bands to . . . to keep them from breaking against each other?

Harper lifts one to inspect, shakes it, the contents runnier than apple sauce or strained carrots are supposed to be, and, and—

She flings it away.

It lands on the motorcycle jacket.

Delicately, Dillon two-fingers another jar up, holds it to the cargo light.

Swimming in the murky suspension is an eyeball.

"Holy shit," Kissy says. "I was just joking about the serial killer thing."

Harper passes Dillon another jar.

Finger.

The next jar is a finger as well, then a stubby thumb, then what looks to be an ear, maybe.

"What the living *hell*, Harp?" Kissy says. "I thought you said these people were proselytizing or whatever?"

"Some gospel," Dillon says, lining the looked-at jars on the rail of the bed.

"He was just . . . normal," Harper says. "Stupid and nothing and normal."

"I'll tell you what happened," Jam says, nodding with this, figuring it out as he goes. "They were pretending to be helping hitchhikers. Really they were . . . doing this. But they tried to do it to someone who didn't like it. Bam, justice."

"Guess that tracks, yeah," Dillon says, impressed.

"Then he's still out there," Harper says, looking behind them.

"Who?" Meg asks.

"Whoever cut that guy's face off," Jam says with more certainty.

Harper nods, keeps nodding.

"We can't keep this," she says about the bag, the clothes, the jars.

"It's proof," Dillon says.

"It's in our possession," Kissy says.

Jam says, "We can give it to the first cop—"

"I'm not riding with it anymore, I mean," Harper says. "I can—Meggie and me can get out here, if y'all want to keep riding with that."

Meg nods, agrees.

"This an Indian thing about . . . about associating with a corpse or something?" Jam asks, and Kissy looks in for the answer too, which is like seconding that stupid question.

"It's a human thing," Harper says. "But yeah, Indians like us, being a subset of humans, we don't like riding around with pieces of murdered people. Bad karma."

"Isn't karma Buddhist?" Kissy says.

"Shh," Harper tells her. "You're on our side here."

"Well then," Dillon says, upping this ante by rolling the wheel of the lighter already in his hand somehow.

"He's right," Kissy says to Harper. "We can't just leave it in the trash."

"We can leave it by the fence," Jam says, pleading. "We can tell the cops it's three posts down from the exit, whatever."

"Fire is burial," Meg says then, just out of nowhere. "That's a Viking thing."

"*What?*" Jam says to her.

"Let her," Harper says.

"It's the only burial they'll get," Meg says, shrinking under the attention.

"And the oracle has spoken!" Dillon announces, way too loud.

Harper shushes him back down to their level.

"I mean, I guess I don't want to get caught with that stuff either," Dillon whispers, "right?" With that he hauls the duffel over, pushes the line of jars back into it.

"These too," Harper says, picking the strewn-around clothes up like a load of laundry, working them into the bag Dillon's holding open.

The trash barrel closest to them is full but Dillon stands in it to pack it down. Harper smushes the duffel down in after.

"Anybody want to say anything?" Dillon says, holding the lighter to the corner of the bag.

"That we're destroying evidence, yeah," Jam says.

"Good riddance," Kissy says with a sneer.

"Do it," Harper says.

Dillon lets the flame catch, then when it's too slow he simply lights the trash under the bag. A flare later the duffel is enshrouded in flames six feet high. Then ten.

The jars pop in muted succession.

"Smells like cinnamon?" Meg says.

It does.

"Must be what that water in the jars was," Harper says.

"Freak," Kissy says, disgusted.

"Freaks *plural*," Jam corrects. "It was a man and a woman, right?"

Harper nods, lost in the dancing flames.

"Truck's cool enough now, I bet," Dillon says, leading the group back to their parking place.

Harper's the last to fall in, and then the first to look back.

"Shit," she says.

They all turn around.

Shit is right.

The trash in the fire is floating out, lighting the dry grass, is already spreading too fast to ever hope to stomp out.

"No no no," Dillon says.

"Go, go!" Kissy says, and pushes Meg into the front seat, Jam climbing in behind the wheel.

"What do we do?" Dillon says to Harper.

The fire is licking at the tires of two of the rigs, is going to be under all of them inside a minute.

"We can't let them burn," Harper says, and takes off running to the closest truck, the ones the flames are already to. She hauls herself up with the grab bar, slams her open hand on the window until the light inside comes on.

"Fire, fire!" she screams, and then is running to the next truck.

She looks back and Dillon is running the other way, waking the truckers parked at the other end.

Harper falls in the gravel, rises, stomps hard on the diamond-plate step of the next truck, comes up slamming her hand on the window again. When the light doesn't come on she closes her eyes and crashes her elbow through the glass, reaches in, pulls hard on the air horn strap in the ceiling. There's enough pressure that it bellows, splits the night with sound. Ahead, taillights are coming on.

From around the seat she's leaned across, a man in a pushed-up sleep mask and ear plugs rouses, tire beater in hand.

"Fire, fire, fire!" Harper yells, and then is gone, stepping back down into a field of flames. She steps ahead and draws back from the heat, is about to try another way when the Park truck skids in beside her, the rear passenger door opening, Dillon in back.

"C'mon, c'mon!" Kissy's yelling, the tired engine of the Park truck bogging down from how far she has her foot in it.

Harper looks back to all the trucks with fire already under them and then she lets Dillon pull her into the bed, wrap her in the biker jacket she must have forgot to burn.

"Oh no," she distinctly hears Dillon say, as Jam's accelerating them up the ramp.

Harper looks to where he's looking: a tanker truck, its lights still off, a beagle jumping at the driver's window, the driver probably conked in back.

"No, we've got to—" Harper says, trying to fight out of the jacket, save that truck, that dog, this pullout, but Dillon bundles her tighter, saves her from herself.

With a touch of distance, the pullout, glowing, is almost beautiful. Until one of the truckers, half-asleep and panicked, tries to grind his rig out of its slot but catches on the rear bumper of another rig, pulling it with. And then they both shake when a rig slams into them from behind. Another's trying to climb the grass up to the asphalt but its front tires are on fire, and now it's rolling over sideways, so slow, back into the flames.

Thirty seconds later the tanker truck explodes.

It's a perfect orange mushroom cloud.

Harper turns away from this, stares ahead, numb.

"It wasn't our fault," Dillon says.

"Then whose was it?" Harper asks back. "There somebody else back there setting fires?"

She thrusts her hands into the pockets of the jacket, feels a cool lump in there, through the fabric—biker jackets are made of pockets—and pulls her hand out fast, shakes it like she might have caught something.

"What?" Dillon says, suddenly there, all around her.

She shakes her head no, no, pulls forward, away from him.

The cargo light is still on, making her shadow crisp.

There through the center hole of the spare tire is the eyeball the crow dropped, staring back up at her.

She reaches up, clicks the cargo light off.

8

"THEY'RE GONNA LOVE us even more now, aren't they?" Kissy is saying through the missing rear window. "All the truckers?"

Harper blinks, her hair stinging her face, the tall collar of the leather jacket held tight around her neck.

"Let's—" Dillon says, and guides her through the window into the rear seat, an awkward process since standing up higher than the cab delivers them to the sixty mile per hour wind. He follows, settles in right beside her, Kissy wriggling back into her place in the front seat. It's what micro people like her can do.

Harper holds her hand out to Meg and Meg melts through the window more than really crawls, as *kids* can do.

"Dad," she says.

Harper pulls her close. She can't stop thinking that either: their dad could have died just this way. From stupid kids playing with lighters.

"He wasn't there," Harper says.

"He who?" Jam says to them in the mirror.

"Nothing," Dillon says, though Harper knows he knows, is probably thinking about his own dad right now. Harper wonders if he's on a run right now. Could he have been back there?

No—why pull over for some shut eye so close to home? That'd be a dick move, even if it is just Dillon waiting for him at their trailer.

"My elbow matches your face now," she says ahead to Jam, hiking her arm up to show, except it's the elbow of a worn-out leather jacket now.

"Hilarious," Jam says, switching from his left hand on the wheel to his right hand at the top of the wheel. It's as close as he can come to turning his back on everyone in the cab.

"She's just joshing," Dillon says, some bite to his tone.

"It's not her face," Jam says back with just as much conversation-killing bite.

"Here," Kissy says, scooching over to him, opening the wipes.

Jam draws away and raises his right shoulder higher, keeping it between her first-aid and his raw skin.

"I just want to get the blood off," Kissy says. "It's not even cut on this side, is it?"

"Music?" Harper says hopefully.

Kissy slides back to her side, thumbs a cassette in on the way. Gordon Lightfoot. "Not mine," she assures them all.

"Yellowstone approved," Jam adds.

Kissy narrows her eyes at him about this.

"Whoah," he says back, and pulls hard onto the shoulder without losing any speed.

They all look back, and *whoah* is an understatement: one of the rigs made it out of that pullout. But now it's trying to outrun its own flames—it's trying to put them out with speed. Its trailer is burning down to nothing, must be wall to wall with cardboard boxes—shoes or VCRs or linens. The rig slams past like the Park truck's standing still, leaves big black flakes swirling in its wake.

"What if he'd been hauling corn, right?" Dillon says.

Harper looks over to him.

"Popcorn," he says, forcing a smile.

"Or chickens," Jam says. "I could go for some fried-right chicken."

"Pigs," Kissy says like a challenge.

"Mmmm," Jam says, stabbing his arm out his window, plucking imaginary strips of bacon from the wind.

A mile later, in the eastbound lanes, it's all blue and red sirens whining in on this explosion.

"Where they coming from?" Dillon says, in wonder.

"Laramie too, I bet," Harper says. "Just, we can't see those."

"We—we can't call that wreck in now, can we?" Kissy says.

"Why not?" Meg asks.

"Because we need to never have been here at all," Jam says, a step ahead.

"He's right," Kissy says.

"But it was an *accident*!" Dillon says. "And we tried to—"

"We left the scene," Harper says. "It's what guilty parties do."

"This doesn't feel like a party," Meg says.

"The jars," Harper says then. "We have to tell them about the jars anyway, don't we?"

Jam cocks his face into the rearview, says to Dillon, "The two people doing that are . . . you said dead, right?"

Dillon nods.

"Then we call in about whoever did that to them," Harper says.

"It was probably self defense," Kissy says.

"Cutting someone's face off is self defense?" Harper says back.

"Maybe that was the birds," Meg says.

Harper shakes her head in disgust, tracks one set of blue and red lights, pushing hard to catch up with the rest. "This is probably how Bonnie and Clyde started out," she says. "Mickey and Mallory."

"That old movie with Arthur in it?" Kissy asks, not following.

"She's talking about Mickey and Mallory," Dillon says. "From last year? That guy from *Cheers*? Jam?"

Jam flashes his eyes into the rearview like caught, then, slowly, and with not much confidence, he nods.

"Your mom hated that movie," Kissy says.

He nods that she did, yes. Obviously.

"She loved it," Kissy says. "She wore that KISS makeup for Halloween, even."

Harper looks from her to Jam, isn't sure what's going on.

"*Shit!*" Jam says then, banging the heel of his right hand on the steering wheel. "I just figured out what those jars were. Y'all've heard of Bucketmouth?"

"Bucket-what?" Harper says.

"Like the fish?" Dillon says. "Isn't that what they call bass?"

"Bass?" Jam says, turning his actual eyes to the backseat for this.

Dillon shrugs, says, "Fishermen call largemouth bass bucketmouths. Smallmouth are . . . yeah, *bronze*backs. You don't know this? Thought you were mister anglerman?"

"There's mostly trout at the Park," Kissy says.

"Catfish are mudcats," Dillon says, listing. "Crappie are speckled perch, and my dad calls steelhead—"

"Why 'Bucketmouth,' though?" Jam's saying, adjusting the rearview to not miss a single thing Dillon's saying.

"Because their mouths are, you know, *large*," Dillon says obviously. "But they're bass, right? A bass eats everything it can long as it's flopping or twitching or chirping, doesn't worry about it till later, just scoops it up, lets digestion do the rest."

"Hunh," Jam says, nodding with this explanation. Liking it, it seems.

"Why does this matter?" Harper asks. "We just burned down a pullout, and now we're talking about fish?"

"Just wondering," Jam says, angling the rearview mirror back to normal. "Nothing."

"You figured out the jars, though?" Dillon prompts, then, for Harper: "That relates to . . . what just happened."

"What we just *did*," Harper corrects.

Kissy is just watching Jam.

"Oh yeah, the Bucketmouth story," he goes on, switching hands on the wheel like this is a Sunday drive they're on. "He's this, like, highway boogeyman, I don't know. You really haven't heard of him? If he eats a piece of you, he can turn into you, something like that. Don't remember exactly. I was thinking that maybe he keeps jars in a bag like that the same way James Bond might keep a suitcase of disguises."

"Quick change," Dillon says, nodding with this explanation. "Let me just nibble on this ear right quick."

"Gross," Meg says.

"To us, yeah," Jam says.

"You're really saying that this, this urban legend or whatever,"

Harper says, "that those body parts in cinnamon water back there were from that? *For* that?"

"For *him*," Dillon corrects.

"Then we destroyed all his shit," Kissy says.

"Unless he thought ahead, buried some along the way," Jam says.

"Buried *jars* along the way?" Kissy says.

"This fencepost, that utility pole," Jam says with a shrug about how obvious this is. "It'd be smart, wouldn't it?"

"It'd be stupid," Harper says. "It would mean he's running up and down the same stretch of highway over and over, asking to be caught. That's the problem with these bullshit campfire stories. Apply logic and they're not so scary anymore. The only monsters out here tonight are us. Ask that guy whose truck blew up back there, if he's even still alive. Ask him if he's more scared of this Bucketmouth or of stupid kids with matches."

The cab is quiet for a quarter-mile after that.

"Don't take Harp to the carnival," Dillon finally says. "She spends all her time popping little kids' balloons."

Harper elbows him.

"It's more fun to believe!" he says, protecting his ribs now.

"Bullshit monsters digging jars up from the ditch don't make the world better," Harper says. "They just let you put off the world you're actually living in a little longer."

"Not much longer . . ." Jam says then, leaning back to get a showy angle on the temperature gauge. "Where's the next place we can stop?"

"Still Herrick," Dillon says, leaning over the seat to see the needle. "We're not exactly making great time."

"Herrick's not a place," Harper mumbles. "It's just an exit."

"That gas station on 59," Dillon says then. "Hunt Road."

"You are a robot," Meg tells him.

"Don't talk to him," Harper warns.

Dillon robot-dances his arm out beside him as best he can in the limited space, does his jaw up and down like it's on pistons. Meg smiles and Harper has to look away.

In the front seat, Kissy, on her side of the bench seat, is still studying Jam.

"What?" he finally says.

"You didn't use any wipes," Kissy says, holding them up.

They all look to her, Gordon Lightfoot crooning about sundown but seeming to listen too, while he strums his 12-string.

"What do you—?" Jam starts, but Kissy's already there: "Nature called back there, or nervous squirts, too many lunches, whatever, right? I get it, whatever, who cares. But . . . but—"

"She said 'butt,'" Dillon leans over to say to Meg.

Harper shushes him, is watching this closely.

"—but you didn't use any of the wipes, did you?" Kissy finally completes. "I know how thick this was when you went out there. It was the same when you handed it to me. And you're never, shall we say . . . thrifty, are you?"

"Dry run," Jam says. "False alarm. 'There I sat so broken-hearted—'"

"You were gone *forever*," Kissy says, throwing the wipes into the floorboard in a huff.

"Sorry?" Jam says, mostly for Dillon and Harper and Meg, Harper knows. To get them on his side.

"What are you saying, Kiss?" she asks.

"What drawer were you talking about, where your driver's

license might be?" Kissy says then, her voice ramping up into a real fight.

"I think that's where it is, geez."

"No, I mean—are there dressers or nightstands at the bunkhouse I don't know about? Because we all use footlockers, Jam. *Trunks*."

"We work at Yellowstone, right? That's why we have this truck?"

"Nobody who works there calls it 'Yellowstone,'" she says. "'Yellowstone' is a dirty word. It's the Park, Jam. The *Park*."

"Listen, I don't know what you're—" Jam says, reaching across the seat to help her down from her indefensible position. She shies away hard, offended.

"Who are you?" she says. "What is your name even short for? Tell me that."

"My name?" Jam says, letting his foot off the gas.

"Just tell us your full name, yeah," Harper says. "Don't look in your wallet either."

"He doesn't have his license," Kissy says, watching him so closely now.

"You're buying into this?" Dillon asks Harper, a little awed. "You think . . . what? He told us that Bucketmouth story because he's actually Bucketmouth? *Jam* is Bucketmouth?"

"*Why won't you let me see your face?*" Kissy screams then.

"Because it's fucking ruined!" Jam says right back. Then, right to Kissy, "Here, you want to see? You really want to see?"

He jerks the wheel over and stomps the brakes, locking the rear tires up. The truck skids and fishtails, rocks and almost rolls, comes to a harsh stop half-in half-out of the ditch, the harsh scent of burned drums and hot rubber washing in through the missing back window. The truck sputters out and the headlights dim a notch, are shining across the two lanes of the westbound, are in the sky by the eastbound, like searching for something up there.

"C'mon," Jam says, opening his door without looking, storming around to the front of the truck—the headlights.

"What the hell is this?" Dillon says.

"Kiss, don't—" Harper says, reaching over the seat for Kissy, but she's already got the door open, is rounding the front of the truck as well, isn't going to let this die.

She comes back for the wipes, holds them up to all in the cab like proof, slams the door after her.

Her and Jam meet in the headlights, are two glowing angels.

Harper opens her door to go up there with them but a station wagon whips by honking, startles her back.

"Just let them," Dillon says, his hand around her wrist. "You know how they are."

"Harper . . ." Meg's saying, her tone rising into panic.

Harper moves over to her, leans ahead to see what's happening at the front of the truck.

"She's—she's gotta be wrong," Harper says.

"About Jam being Bucketmouth?" Dillon says with a smile.

"About Jam not being Jam," Harper says, no smile at all. "When would it have even happened, this big switcheroo?"

"While he was . . . using the facilities," Meg says quietly, and sort of with a gulp.

They both look to her, and then, with different eyes, over the hood again.

"But it probably takes a while," Harper says, mostly to herself.

"What takes a while?" Dillon asks.

"Bucketmouth," Harper says. "After he—he eats a finger, an ear, whatever. It's got to take a while for him to . . ." She does her fingers over her face to show what she means.

"How long was he out there in the bushes?" Dillon says back, not looking away from Kissy and Jam in the headlights.

Kissy has a wipe stretched over her finger now, is pointing that finger up to Jam's face delicately, like a girlfriend, but then the light isn't right. He switches sides with her and they lower down to the driver's side headlight, disappear except the glowing haze of their hair.

"I thought it was the other side of his face," Meg says.

"It was," Harper says, and then jerks back hard when Kissy is pushed up and away, her feet not in contact with the blacktop for maybe a whole second.

It's timed perfectly for the next rig slamming past—probably the last one to pass the pullout before it was blocked off.

It doesn't just hit her, it *bursts* her, and, because Harper's looking right at her, is trying to reel her back in just by not breaking eye contact, she has to see it in high detail: the round passenger-side headlight carving Kissy's face into a clean half-moon, the bumper passing through her like she's a Jell-O sculpture, Kissy's left shoe flinging up alongside the fender for an impossible snapshot of an instant, before the front tire grabs it, pulls her under.

What sticks for Harper is the look on Kissy's face. It's not satisfaction for having been right about Jam not being Jam, and it's not the surprise and shock she would expect. It's the same look Kissy had when they were seventh graders, using her mom's old Polaroid camera to take pictures of each other jumping into the swimming pool at the Y, before the lifeguard cued in, made them stop.

In one of the Polaroids that turned out, Kissy had a look on her face, in her eyes, like she knew the cold dunk that was coming, but she wasn't scared of it, she was ready for it. She couldn't wait.

That's how she looked in that last split instant, her full head of hair lifted all around her.

And now—now it isn't just seventh grade that was gone, it's all the grades since, and all the grades to come. Not college, none of them are thinking more school, but jobs, and marriage if her and Jam made it that far, kids even, grandkids. Checkers at the grocery store giving her the eye when she's not looking, wondering how killer she must have been twenty, thirty years ago.

But she still would have been just as killer, Harper knows.

She's Kissy.

No: she *was* Kissy.

Now she's a scream welling up from Harper's . . . from her soul, her core, whatever's most secret and pure at the very center of her. It's like—it's like Kissy was a *part* of her, a part now being ripped away at eighty-five miles per hour, a part that's now just a breath of red mist hanging in the halogen light, a breath of red mist and a long strand of black hair hanging there.

The part of her mind that's off to the side, that's not building a shriek and pushing it out, it's whispering to her that she's never been this close to death, has she? Sure, on runs with her dad, she's seen a rig blow its driver's side front tire, step over the line, onto a little Datsun or Toyota, but her dad would always reach across, pull her face into his chest.

He's not here now.

Harper can't turn away.

Kissy is . . . she's gone, she's dead, she's nothing. All her years of living, all her experience, all her bad jokes, that way she had of never remembering her jacket, even when it's cold, it's all gone in less than a tenth of a second. And the driver who hit her, he doesn't even have time to honk or brake or anything, maybe isn't even aware he's hit anything. Any*one*.

Harper collapses over the front seat, her right hand reaching, scrabbling uselessly at the dash, her insides cold.

They get colder when Jam stands, wiping his face himself, carefully, dab by dab, looking at the wipe after each slow wipe then applying it again, stretching his neck to tighten his skin, remove each fleck of blood, each smear of red.

Slowly, all the blood and chunks come off, and his face isn't pebbled with glass at all. He's just Jam. But not.

He shrugs one shoulder about Kissy like what you gonna do, like she brought it on herself, then, moving heavy like this is the chore part of these proceedings, he reaches to the small of his back, comes around with a shiny snub-nose revolver that Jam definitely didn't have on him, either before or ever.

"Bucketmouth," Harper says, as sure as anything, and now Dillon, more aware of what that little pistol means for them, is bellowing her name, diving across the front seat to twist the ignition.

The Park truck rumbles to life.

Jam holds both hands up like impressed, like obviously outgunned. He smiles, cocks his head over, watching this small drama play out through the windshield.

"You killed my best friend, asshole," Harper says, and drops the transmission all the way into first just as Dillon, half in the front seat now, slams the accelerator down with his hand.

The Park truck burps forward, catches this Bucketmouth in the midsection, tosses him back into the shoulder like a ragdoll. He rolls through the glowing grass, all the dust in the headlights swirling golden over him.

The Park truck putters out from the effort.

"Shit, shit, shit!" Dillon says, fumbling up for the key again.

In the headlights at first it's just Kissy's bones and Kissy's shiny insides, splattered across thirty or forty yards of asphalt. Until Bucketmouth stands, unkinking his back, shaking his head like breaking cobwebs, like impressed that they actually *hit* him with the truck.

Then he holds his right hand up, opens and closes it in wonder, doesn't have the snub-nose anymore. He looks in his left hand. It's not there either.

He chuckles at how ridiculous this is and Harper turns the headlights off, his bright smile still burning into her eyes.

"He can't find it in the dark," she says.

"Go, go, go," Meg is saying from the backseat, quietly.

"Put it—in park," Dillon says, straining from his awkward position, legs in the backseat, body across the front, arms in the floorboard.

Harper does. Dillon grinds the starter, feathering the pedal. The battery drags, drags, and then, finally, the engine roars to life again.

"*Gas*," Harper says, an order not a request, and Dillon lays into it with his hand again. She waits until the RPMs are screaming to drop the truck into gear.

It surges forward and she clicks the headlights on an instant later, to see Bucketmouth go under the front bumper.

He's not there anymore.

What the tires are crunching through now, it's the bone parts of Kissy.

"Go," Meg pleas, her voice small.

They do.

9

WHAT HARPER CAN'T stop looping in her head is that Kissy didn't have to die. That her best friend could still be here—could still be up in the passenger seat, her hair casually, maddeningly perfect, her purse stuffed with a thousand things she was never going to need but had to have with her all the same.

It's so fucking unfair. It's so stupid.

How could Jam not be Jam? How could there really be monsters who can become other people just by eating a piece of them? What was Jam—no, *Bucketmouth*, what was he even hoping to do? Is that what counts as fun for him, fooling people into believing he's whoever he looks like? Does playing with his food make it taste better?

And, and: what about Jam, lying naked back in the bushes where the Thunderbird went through the fence?

They're both dead, Harper realizes.

It's like she has to keep telling herself that every few seconds. Because it won't stick, it won't stay real.

Kissy, Jam. They're not in the world anymore, and never will be again. Just like that.

"And all because they stopped for me," Harper says, wiping

her nose with the sleeve of the leather jacket, tilting her head back to keep her tears in. It doesn't work.

"What?" Dillon says, though he had to have heard.

He's at the steering wheel, Harper in the passenger seat, Meg between them, in some sort of shock. The backseat is a wind tunnel. Gordon Lightfoot's not singing about sundown anymore, but the *Edmund Fitzgerald* going down. It feels right.

"This can't be happening," Harper says. "People can't just change like that. This isn't *The X-Files*."

"Then," Dillon says, picking through all the bad answers, "then that would mean it was really Jam, wouldn't it? It would mean his switch flipped."

"He didn't have that kind of switch," Harper says. "That wasn't him. He would never . . . not Kissy. He would never hurt her. He wouldn't know how."

Dillon nods, knows.

"Then what was he?" Meg asks in monotone. It's how she deals, Harper knows. It's the flat affect she retreats to after a big blowout between Harper and their mom.

Harper doesn't have any answer to what Jam was. "Bucketmouth" doesn't seem like a legitimate answer.

"Two-thirty, two-forty . . ." Dillon reads aloud, not liking the truck's temperature.

"What'll happen?" Harper says.

"It'll seize, maybe crack the block," Dillon says.

Harper expected something like that.

"Good thing her dad didn't buy this truck," she says, forcing a single chuckle that feels more like a sob.

"If he had, we wouldn't be in it now," Dillon says back.

He's practical like that, always sees the straight line

between A and B, even if the rest of the alphabet is completely out of sight. Still, B isn't bad. You've got to get to B before all the other letters.

"Do you remember that first December?" she says across to him.

Dillon looks across to be sure, then nods.

It's where they met: December of their eighth grade year—one year ahead of where Meg is now. Dillon was already sitting on top of the apartments his mom was living at when Harper stepped out from the stairway, bundled up against the snow because she wasn't coming down until she saw her dad. But she'd thought it would just be her. She wasn't the only one with a dad slipsliding his way home for Christmas, though. She wasn't the only one who knew these apartments had a bird's eye perfect view of 80.

For four hours they sat up there hardly saying anything, just watching rig after rig lose it on the ice, their trailers coming around in slow motion, churning up snow and dark earth from the ditch. The first one that tumped over, Harper gasped, held her hands over her mouth, and Dillon had put his arm around her, and together, in secret, they promised that they didn't care if their dads made it home that night, that they didn't want them to, that they wanted them to be at a motel in Cheyenne or Salt Lake, warm and safe, watching *Law & Order* on the television. They didn't care about Christmas, they cared about forever.

By the New Year they were promising each other that it was the two of them against the world, that they'd found each other just like they were supposed to, they didn't need anybody else from here on out.

That was how Kissy and Jam had always been, too. Even when they were fighting.

Harper wipes her eyes with the sleeve of the leather jacket, which doesn't wipe shit away.

"I can't believe they're gone," she says, her voice hitching.

"What was he?" Meg says.

"Bucketmouth, I guess," Harper says. "He told us, right? Had either of you heard that story before?"

Dillon and Meg shake their head no.

"I know about that ghost girl who hitchhikes—" Dillon starts.

"Not her," Harper says. "She's just scary, not hungry. Why wouldn't we have heard, you think? We live right on the interstate."

"Maybe he's just getting to Wyoming," Dillon says.

"Or maybe everybody he tells the story to, he . . . you know," Meg says.

"Yeah, that," Dillon says. "He croaks them before they can spread the legend."

"Meaning we're still on his list," Harper says. "He can't let word of what he's doing get out. What he *can* do, whatever he is. But—there won't be any more drivers through there for hours, now. He won't be able to hitch a ride."

"So we're good?" Dillon says.

"We're in an overheating truck we don't own and we just blew up about twelve semis and we left a paralyzed woman to die in her car and I'm wearing some dead guy's jacket and we just saw our two best friends die and there's a killer after us who can change his face and likes to eat people," Harper says. "Yeah, I'd say we're great."

"Us, I mean," Dillon says. "December."

"Long time ago," Harper says. "I was thinking about . . . I guess Kiss and Jam's December would have been band camp, sixth grade, right? That's where they got together the first time?"

"Nerd alert," Dillon says.

"I'm in band," Meg says.

"Idiot alert," Harper says about Dillon. "And no, we're not together. I'm leaving, remember?"

"You're still doing that?" Meg says.

"Does Mom still live in Laramie?" Harper says back.

"I'm going with you, then," Meg says.

"Like hell," Harper tells her.

"That the only reason we're not getting back together, though?" Dillon says. "Because you're leaving?"

"Also because we're probably both dead by sunup," Harper says, wedging her knees up against the dash and holding her hair back with her hands.

"Both dead?" Meg says.

"Not you," Harper says. "You live, always."

"We need a code word," Dillon says. "For if he, you know." He holds his hand up with the ring finger folded down as if bitten off.

"He couldn't remember the bunkhouse," Harper says, nodding with this. "He gets the face, not the memories, has to make it all up on what he sees, or hears, what he can figure out. He knew Yellowstone because of the truck, but he didn't know what it was like to *work* there."

"Band camp," Meg says with finality. "We'll ask where Kissy and Jam fell in love."

"Band camp," Harper says.

"Nerd camp," Dillon says. "Sure. Comes up in natural conversation all the time."

"Temperature?" Harper asks him.

Dillon peers down, shakes his head no, does his lips like steam hissing out, and reaches down to see if he can open the heater up any more.

10

THEY HAVE TO stop at the exit for 12 whether there's anything there or not.

"Isn't there a creek around here?" Harper asks.

"We'd need a bucket, a hose, and it'd clog the radiator up besides," Dillon says. "You're supposed to use distilled water."

"And this matters to us because we care about this truck so much," Harper says back. "All we need is to get to the first phone."

"There," Meg says.

They're sitting at the bottom of the off-ramp. Under the bridge they can just see signs of life past the eastbound lanes. Not a payphone, but structures anyway.

The truck clatters and almost dies but Dillon feathers it and pats the dash lovingly, eases them under, to the lone light over past the eastbound lanes.

It's a house, some outbuildings.

"Salvation," he says, and coasts them in, past the house to the tanks up on ten-foot racks, all of it painted dull industrial silver, dust and seed heads painted right in with.

"Gas, gas," Dillon identifies, coasting past the tanks, then, braking: "Bingo."

"A hand pump?" Harper says.

"Cleaner than a creek," Dillon says, and puts the truck up in park.

"Turn it off?" Harper says.

"Got to cool it down first," Dillon says, and the way it works is Harper pumps the pump—it's greased, silent—and Dillon directs the thin, once-green hose over the steaming radiator slow at first, touching his palm to the cap over and over, Meg at the gas pedal to keep the truck alive if it tries to sputter out.

Twenty agonizing minutes later—long enough for Harper to cycle back into Kissy and Jam being the forever kind of dead about six times, and come back with a lump in her throat each time—Dillon can finally hold his bare palm to the steel cap.

He backs it off slow, one stage at a time. It hisses at the first stage, doesn't have any steam left by the second.

"If we put too much cold water in while it's still super hot," he explains, "it'll crack. Got to go slow . . ."

"Thanks, shop teacher," Meg says ahead to him, and Harper has to smile in spite of how many times she's cranked the hand pump's lever up and down already.

Dillon eases the water in a spurt at a time, letting the engine suck it up, massaging the top hose to be sure the thermostat's opening, narrating each step as he goes just like, yes, a shop teacher, and then the water's surging up out of the mouth of the radiator and Harper can stop pumping.

"Sounds better already," he says, patting the nose of the truck, easing the hood down and giving it his weight at the very end, trying to close it without slamming it.

"Sounds better for the *moment*," Harper says.

"Guys?" Meg says, and when they look back they see what

she means: the shirtless fifty-year-old man approaching with a shotgun.

"Whoah, whoah," Dillon says, stepping forward, hands high, directing the shotgun away from Harper, she's pretty sure.

"Got the gas locked up," the man grumbles. "Think I'm an idjit?"

"Just the water, just the water," Dillon says. "Truck was hot, we hung the hose back up, were going to leave some . . ."

Harper holds up all the cash she has on her: two fives.

Moving slow, she stuffs it into the wire hanger of the pump.

"Just water," the man says, lowering the shotgun. He sniffs the air, can smell the antifreeze now it looks like. "It's well water," he adds.

"Truck's older than me," Dillon says back with a smile.

The man looks up and down the truck.

"It's for sale," Harper says.

"No thank you, ma'am," the man says, then smiles and winks. "I hear it's got kind of a hot temper."

Harper smiles with him, flashes her eyes to Meg, which is the only reason she catches the slight movement behind the truck, coming in from the road.

"Hey—" is all she's able to get out before the blacked-out chopper, engine off, sweeps past at forty miles per hour, the helmeted rider swinging a chain or piece of wire, it's too dark to be sure.

Whatever it is, it takes the man's throat with it, leaves him standing there.

He fires one barrel into the dirt at his feet, and the other barrel into the top of his right foot, blossoming it up into hamburger meat that just keeps coming.

He teeters over, burbling frothy blood down his bare chest.

"Jam," Dillon says, backing off.

"Bucketmouth," Harper hisses.

She runs to the falling man but only gets her arms bloody holding him, can't do anything.

Out in the darkness Bucketmouth pops the clutch, the chopper's throaty exhaust filling the night.

He turns the headlight on, runs the face shield of his helmet up so they can see how perfect his Jam-face is, and stands on his left foot to spin a neat donut, swirl all the dust up into the air, exactly as Jam never knew how to. Then, still throttling high, he unplants his left foot, settles it on a peg, and accelerates right past them, swinging the—it's a chain, yes—swinging it at Dillon, who manages to slide underneath, but just barely.

The chain hooks onto the driver's side open door of the truck instead, Meg squealing back, and the sudden pull yanks Bucketmouth off the back of the bike, sends it careening off. It crashes into the house.

"You asshole!" Harper screams, running from the dead man to Bucketmouth.

On the way she picks up a stray piece of rebar, is already holding it behind her like a broadsword.

But then Bucketmouth looks up at her with Jam's face, says, "Harp? That you? What's happening?"

She stops, the rebar still cocked behind her.

At which point something sparks in the wrecked chopper. It's not an explosion, just a flare of flame that catches the dry grass.

When Harper comes back to Bucketmouth, he's gone again, just the helmet where he was.

The first place she looks is to the truck, but Dillon's already guarding Meg, a board in his hand, his eyes everywhere at once.

"We should leave," he says.

"And maybe we shouldn't, like, *stop* anywhere else?" Meg adds.

"First, this," Harper says, walking to the tumped over chopper. "We're not leaving another fire."

She kicks and stomps it out, then stares down where it was, daring it to come back.

"Let's go, let's go!" Dillon says to her. "He's still here, Harp!"

"How did he get here so fast?" she says back to both of them.

"Like that," Dillon says, tipping his head at the westbound lane, not exactly *jammed* with headlights, but there's a steady enough stream now.

"The eastbound lane's turning around," Harper says in wonder. "Because of us. Because we started that—because we burned his stuff, now they're all lining up to . . . he can refill his little jars."

"With us," Meg says.

"WE'VE GOT TO call it in," Harper says once they've merged in front of a little brown Audi, since none of the big rigs are even considering letting *this* truck have anything.

"Anonymously?" Dillon tries.

"I don't care anymore," Harper says. "We'll explain. We'll explain for five days, until they believe us."

"If we all have the same story," Meg adds.

"It's not a story," Harper says. "It's what happened."

"Think he's hitching to catch us?" Dillon says, clocking his mirror.

"Do I think it's a game to him?" Harper says. "Yes. That motorcycle was too easy for him. It didn't make us scared, the way he likes. I think—I think this is so easy for him, he likes to have fun. We're tonight's fun."

"That . . . that gas pump man," Meg says, her breath hitching.

"He was even—" Harper says, figuring it out as she goes. "When we thought he was Jam, he was telling us how he does it, wasn't he? The jars, the, the different faces he can put on. He said it would be smart to have buried them for emergencies. We didn't destroy his stash. We just burned what he was carrying around."

"They've got to be miles apart, though, wouldn't you think?" Dillon says. "How many people can he have bitten a piece off of?"

"Seen all the missing posters in the gas station windows?" Harper says.

"He's one guy," Dillon says.

"You're right," Harper says. "He's a monster, but he's also . . . human. Like us. We hit him with the truck. It wasn't a hard hit, but it knocked him down. He can be hurt."

"He *did* get back up," Dillon notes, slowing to let an Oldsmobile in, to keep an impatient trucker off its rear bumper.

"We've got to assume he's like us," Harper says. "Mostly."

"Because that's less scary?" Dillon asks.

"If he's not," Meg says, her tone half reverent. "If he's not, then he could be however old, couldn't he?"

"Y'all got some old Arapaho boogeyman stories about him, you mean?" Dillon says.

"Most of our boogeymen stories are about white men," Harper says back, holding her hand up for Meg to slap a sisterly five.

"He is white," Dillon says.

"For now," Meg says. "Temperature?"

"She likes doing just fifty like this," Dillon says, patting the dash with his right hand. With his second pat there's an explosion on the windshield. He brakes hard, the rig behind them having to lock it up as well, but then he raises his hand out the window for the driver to see all's well, eases up to speed again.

"Pee," he says, looking for the wiper knob.

Harper cranks her window up almost fast enough.

Once they can see again, Dillon lifts his finger to a new crack in the windshield. His finger comes away wet. He smells it, crinkles his nose.

"Baby wipe," Meg says, digging them up, passing him one.

"This night," Harper says.

"Maybe we should paint the door," Dillon says.

"Or abandon truck," Harper says.

"Some of us aren't as committed to thumbing it as you are," Dillon says. "I'm a dude. Picking me up off the side of the road is a risk. You're pretty. Both of you are. Picking women up is a chance for a good time."

"Fuck you and fuck that," Harper tells him.

"Just saying it like it is," Dillon says back.

"Don't listen to him," Harper tells Meg.

"Would you pick me or you up first?" Dillon says then. "Being honest, I mean. I'm in my Sunday best, you're wearing that sweatshirt."

Harper considers, considers, then looks away, doesn't want to talk about this anymore.

"*He's* not having any difficulty finding rides," Harper says. "He even got a motorcycle to stop."

"We don't know that," Dillon says. "For all we know, dude stopped to drain the lizard, got jumped by mister bloodyface."

"Jam," Harper says. "He looks like Jam now."

"As of ten minutes ago," Dillon says.

"How long do you think it takes him to change all the way?" Meg asks.

"I don't think you can watch it happen like a special effect," Harper says. "But, look away for a few minutes, an hour?"

"Shit," Dillon says. "He probably stuck around, ate a piece off that guy with the shotgun, think?"

It makes sense.

"Everybody," she says. "He's everybody. He could be anybody."

"Band camp, band camp," Dillon says.

Meg smiles from that.

"Don't," Harper tells her. "He's not funny."

"Just ruggedly handsome," Dillon says, making like studying his look in the rearview, then flinching back and jerking the wheel when another pee bomb explodes on the windshield.

Thirty seconds later, wipers waggling through the oily residue—"What was he *drinking*?" Harper asks—Meg wipes a dot of wetness from her cheek, then another, then pushes fast over the backseat.

The crack in the windshield is worse, now. Leaking urine.

"Will it cave in on us?" Harper asks Dillon, her hand to the escape lever the door handle is.

"Not just from the wind," Dillon says, pushing against the glass with his fingertips to test it for give. "They keep using us like a urinal, though . . ."

"*Stop, stop!*" Harper screams, hating the shriek in her voice, her arms locking her against the dash not because she told them to but because that's what arms do in situations like this.

Dillon stomps the brakes again, harder, sees what he was missing beyond the windshield: the ass end of a livestock trailer.

"No," he says about what he's seeing in the rearview, and Harper looks around, sees the cabover maybe a foot and a half from their rear bumper, the driver leaned over his wheel, waving his hand in front of his nose about the smell coming from the livestock trailer.

"Pigs," Meg says.

The rig beside them eases tire-deep over into their lane so there can be no doubts about whether this is intentional or not.

"I hate pigs," Dillon says.

The smell is so thick there's particles to it.

Meg, the only one of them thinking, dispenses three baby wipes from the soft bag, passes one each way and presses her own over her nose and mouth, draws deep through it.

Harper does the same. Dillon too, going by the gagging sounds over there.

"You're not throwing up," she instructs him, which is just the puke trigger he needs, evidently.

His vomit is thin, sprays around the edges of the wipe onto the wheel, the dash.

He cranks and cranks on his window, leans out, loses everything else.

The three trucks hotboxing them all lay on their air horns in celebration.

"Ditch, ditch," Harper says, and Dillon nods, steers them over and has to come right back: staties are spaced out on the shoulder to keep traffic moving. To keep cutters from cutting, causing more accidents.

"They knew," Harper says.

"Of course they know," Dillon says, still breathing in an upchucky way. "They can see everything from up there."

"And talk about it on the, on the radio," Harper says, and that's her limit: she's cranking her window down, puking down the side of the door.

When she comes back in, Meg's face is mummied with wipes, her back ramrod straight, like she's pretending to be somewhere else completely.

"Did you, did you cover the decal on your side at least?" Dillon asks.

Harper has to laugh. Her eyes are already crying from throwing up.

"They'll never know us," she manages to get out, and then Dillon's laughing as well and Meg's a mummy, not acknowledging any of this, and that's how they ride the next three miles out, until the exit opens up beside them like the gates of heaven.

"Hunt Road," Dillon proclaims.

"We've got to call," Harper says, hanging her head out the window for fresh air.

"On that phone?" Meg says, a wipe peeled hesitantly from her right eye.

The payphone line snakes back like a rollercoaster ride.

Akal Travel Center.

"The gas station is *open*, ladies," Dillon says, presenting it to them in all its ungloriousness.

He's wrong though, Harper thinks. It's not a gas station, it's a circus: with the interstate piled up for miles, this place is an oasis in the nighttime desert of Wyoming. All the truck parking is nose to tail, and rigs are lining both sides of the road as well, the ground shaking with idling engines, the air sticky with diesel.

Dillon cruises past, looking for parking. It's hopeless.

"I've been here . . ." Harper says, clocking the low red roof that's like a stubby Stuckey's. She turns to Meg all at once: "This is the place with those, you know—bathrooms."

"*That* place?" Meg says, bringing a wipe back up to cover her mouth.

"I'm sure they're better now," Dillon says, pointing to the Women's line with his chin. It's snaking down the aisle, out the door, either merging with or intersecting the payphone line.

"Shit," Harper says.

"Exactly," Dillon says back.

11

WHERE THEY HAVE to park is a good quarter mile up Hunt. To try to avoid getting walled in by truckers with a score to settle, Dillon turns the headlights on and eases them deeper out into the pasture. That way if the rigs want them they'll have to chance their tires finding a soft spot, which will be an instant tow-truck situation, and on a night when all the tow trucks in Wyoming are already tied onto something.

"Wait," Harper says twenty steps from the truck, and goes back for Kissy's oversize purse. "I gave all my money for the water," she explains.

"What about . . . you know," Meg says.

Harper tracks where she's looking: the shotgun guy's blood on her leather sleeves, splashed on the thighs of her jeans.

"Will this night never end?" she asks.

"Sand," Dillon says, and works some up from the grass—dirt, anyway—cups it to Harper's arms, gets off what he can. Because the blood on her legs is still tacky, the dirt just sticks, but at least it just looks like grime. Somewhat.

"You didn't pack any extra clothes for the road?" he asks.

"Let's go," Harper says, hooking Kissy's heavy purse on her

other shoulder, threading her hair out from under the strap.

"We should, you know," Dillon says, "split up."

Harper looks to him about this, brows furrowed, eyes waiting.

"They saw us puking our guts up out the window?" he says with a shrug. "They know there's a dude, an Indian girl, and a kid."

"Truckers don't need that decal on the door to ID us anymore, you mean," Harper says.

"He's right," Meg says.

"Well I can't stop being Indian," Harper says, and, to Meg: "And you can't grow up in thirty seconds."

"But we can stop being three," Meg says.

"Can it not just be over with them already?" Harper says. "What, are they elephants, they hold a grudge forever?"

"Elephants do that?" Dillon asks, falling in behind her.

"They remember things," Harper says, not looking over to him.

"We did catch some of them on fire," Meg says.

"They know that was us already?"

"What's CB move at?" Dillon asks. "Speed of gossip?"

"What do y'all want in there?" Harper asks. "Kissy was . . . I guess they just got paid."

She has to blink fast to keep from thinking more about Kissy.

"How much does she—did she have?" Dillon asks.

Harper slows, digs into the purse, past the weatherproof journal—Kissy was always the romantic—past the Park ID badges, past the economy size box of rubbers, past the *extra* baby wipes, into . . . at last: the wallet.

"Pay day," she says, fanning out six twenties, all facing the same way like fresh from the bank.

"How about we each get our own stuff?" Dillon says. "Less suspicious."

"No magazines," she says, passing him a bill.

"I mean . . ." he says, squinting a guilty squint. "Probably not, yeah, but what if they've got the new—"

"Okay, okay, your money," Harper says, and gives a twenty to Meg as well.

"That enough?" she asks her.

"We need gas?" Meg says back.

"Five-eighths," Dillon says. "They must have filled up in Laramie. But, if I had some *more* money, I could buy water for the radiator, should we need it before Rawlins."

Harper gives him another twenty, hates the way she's calculating "forty" in her head, and trying to figure how far that'll get her, food and bed and the rest of her life-wise.

"We're still going to Rawlins?" Meg asks.

"Our best chance," Harper says.

"My brother's shop is still there," Dillon says. "Meg's ride home."

"I'm not going home," Meg says.

"His Camaro," Harper says. "Yeah, that. Good."

"Were you thinking of just sticking your thumb out, starting here?" Dillon asks.

Harper looks to the line of headlights trailing west, shrugs.

"You've got the truck," she says. "Laramie's closer than your brother's shop. I can get off here, you keep asking."

"I'm not going home if you aren't," Meg says again.

"Rawlins," Dillon decides out loud, pulling ahead to

singleton it into the travel center, and then he turns around to deliver the last of it: "More time to talk you out of this, bring you home with her."

Harper shakes her head, impressed with his hopefulness.

"Why's he even try?" she asks Meg.

"He's not that bad," Meg says back.

"You're looking at him with junior high eyes," Harper says, watching Dillon push his way through the glass doors. "Wait till you've dated a few of him, you'll see."

"You've only dated one of him, right?"

Harper can't argue with that.

"I'm still not going home," Meg says, walking ahead to be one-of-one as well, not one-of-three.

"Why do *I* even try?" Harper says to herself, and tracks an ambulance screaming down the eastbound lane, lights flashing.

Does it mean they found the shotgun man, the original chopper guy, the Thunderbird woman, the Thunderbird man with his face peeled off, Jam minus one finger and all of his life, or does that burning pullout just need every paramedic in Wyoming tonight?

"I'm sorry, Dad," Harper says, and blinks that away as best she can, turns to the lights of the store, pushes her way in as well.

AKAL TRAVEL CENTER is wall to wall bodies. A morgue shuffling around for salt and sugar, their mouths hanging, eyes shell-shocked, hair every which way.

Standing in the forever line for coffee, breath mints wrapped in her hand for everyone who's been puking, Harper watches two guys Meg's age load their forty-four ounce fountain drink cups up with candy bars before filling them with a revolting mix of root beer and Sprite.

Over the aisles, because he's tall and obvious, Dillon is easy to track. At first he's trying on sunglasses, leaning down to look in the little square of mirror, but then he spots the magazine rack right there and's squeezing in to scope for anything archery related, as if he doesn't already have every single article of every single issue for five years back memorized.

"You're supposed to be eating," she says to him, evidently out loud enough that the trucker in front of her looks back, delivering his scent back to her. "Not you," she says, eyes either burning or moldering, she's not sure.

"You my dietician, darling?" he asks, the fluffy lap dog in his arms waking.

"Forget it," Harper tells him. "I was talking to someone else."

The dog rouses more, dredged up to awareness by . . . its nose? Oh shit, its nose, definitely. It's keyed on the blood Harper's slathered in. The dog leans far enough out of the trucker's arms that it gets its tongue into contact with the sleeve of Harper's jacket, which dials its yapping up to frantic, desperate, want want want.

She turns away but the walking dead are slowing to look. And not just at the dog. At the girl in the bloody jacket.

"What are you wearing?" the trucker asks. "A slaughterhouse?"

"Ketchup," Harper says, loud enough for all. "My burger exploded."

"Burger?" he says, his mouth cracking into a devious smile. "There's not a decent eat-em-up for—"

"Little America," Harper says, holding his eyes steady in hers.

He shrugs like sure, whatever, cups his hand over the dog's muzzle, getting it shushed, and steps ahead with the line but isn't turning around to face forward yet. The rubberneckers waiting for a dog attack—it would have been more like t-ball practice with a stuffed animal—go back to their browsing.

"Sorry about Sheba here," the trucker says, lifting the dog to show who he's talking about. "She is an animal, though. Got instincts."

"That's her name?" Harper says, casting around for if there's any chance Meg might have heard this. A random dog named after the dead dog you still carry a torch for, that's something. Especially when you just lost that dog's collector plate.

"My little queenie, yes'm," the trucker says, roughing up the hair between Sheba's alert ears. "Funny thing about her, too. Turns her nose up at ketchup. Kind of spoiled for a canine, you ask me."

"A dog that doesn't like spilled human food?" Harper says.

"Depends if it's *from* a human or not," the trucker says, letting Sheba reach across for Harper's sleeve again.

"Allergic," Harper says, trying to keep her jacket away from the dog's nose.

"To questions, yeah," the trucker says, then grins without parting his lips. "You, you know, working?"

When he asks it, Harper's narrowed in on the sunglasses rack again, is finally keying on what Dillon was doing—looking for a *disguise*. But then the trucker's words and meaning finally process, and she hears what he evidently thinks she is.

"What makes you think that?" she asks, giving him her full and undivided attention.

"Knew a girl looked like you," he says with a shrug.

"Oh," Harper says. "This skin, this hair?"

"Close enough," the trucker says.

"I'm not her," Harper says evenly, so there can be no misunderstanding.

The trucker does his shoulders like he had to ask and Harper tries her best to stare literal daggers into the craggy back of his neck.

"Don't mind him," the man behind her says, his voice both low and booming somehow. "Been a while since he stumbled into a rainbox, I'd say. We might should pass the hat, take up a donation."

The trucker in front of her comes around like filling his mouth with something smart to say about who does and doesn't need a shower, but then he swallows it back down, lets his eyes keep roving across the store, his lap dog growling for him, because he knows better, apparently.

Harper looks behind her and then up and up again to the driver. She can always tell who drives for a living, who doesn't. It's not about what they're wearing—some truckers are rhinestone cowboys, some go commando in gym shorts and flip-flops—it's how their eyes focus, like they can see all of America from their rocking chair. Like they're seeing it all for the hundredth time.

"Maybe it's the dog," she says.

The tall driver shrugs maybe, sure.

"John Henry," he says by way of greeting, smoothing both his bushy red-grey muttonchops with a single huge hand.

"Ava," Harper lies. It's her mom's name, the first that came to mind. "And, John Henry like the song?"

"You a little young to know something that antique?" John Henry says.

"There an expiration date on Johnny Cash?" Harper says back.

John Henry grins wide, his eyes crinkling up from it. He says, "You're maybe thinking of Big Bad John, little miss. But thank you. Either Jimmy Dean or Johnny Cash'll get you where you're going, I figure."

That's the thing about truckers: they know every song that's ever gone out across the FM or showed up on cassette.

"Which way you headed, you don't mind me asking?" Harper asks.

"To my bunk if I can ferret it out in the dark," John Henry says. "But my schedule, that's going straight to hell—pardon my language."

"This isn't Sunday school, last I checked."

"Lot more beef jerky than I remember, if it is," he says back, nodding over to the rack of plastic bags.

Harper looks, comes back.

"Why's everybody coming back this way, you think?" she asks, just an innocent traveler.

"Spot of trouble up the road a bit."

"Trouble?"

He gives her his full and unfiltered attention, says, "Some semi-pro kids torched a pullout up towards Love Town."

"Anybody di—any fatalities?"

John Henry shrugs, is watching her closer now.

"They catch them?" Harper asks, just a concerned citizen

now. "Those pickup truck kids?"

"How'd you know they're in a pickup?" John Henry says, stepping back to better appraise her. Maybe check if she fits a general description.

"You *told* me," Harper says, insulted. "That's what my dad meant when he'd say 'semi-pro,' anyway. What?"

"Your father drives?"

"He had me talking on the CB before kindergarten."

"What was your handle?" John Henry says friendly-like, sidling back in now that Harper's not the one who lit that pullout up. "This would have been . . . ten, fifteen years ago?"

"You coming through here a lot back then?"

"I've been everywhere, man," John Henry says with a grin—another lyric.

"I supposed to say I used to be Teddy Bear?" Harper asks with the same grin.

"Jackson Street 229," John Henry says back, the address from that song, and somehow neither one of them break down in tears, standing there.

"I'm not on the air anymore," Harper says, "haven't been since . . . for years." Then, taking a flier: "Ever hear the term 'bucketmouth' through the static?"

"You're not even twenty, are you?" John Henry asks.

"Not certain where I heard it."

"Think that's one of the old ones," John Henry says, rubbing his scratchy-sounding chin.

"Something with a fish?" Harper tries.

"Somebody who moves their mouth like a fish on shore, I guess," John Henry says, stepping ahead with the line. "Far as I recollect, it's a motormouth on the citizen band, not giving anyone space to even lay their twenty down, deal in to the chatter. Opposite's a . . . it's a sandbagger, yeah. That's what *my* dad called them. Just listens in, never says not word one."

"It's not talk radio," Harper says.

"Copy that," John Henry says, watching her eyes. "Short stuff? That your handle back then?"

"It was a long time ago," Harper says, looking around for Meg. "Galaxy far, far away from where I am now."

"None of my business, of course," John Henry says, "but which way you headed tonight?"

"Was Cheyenne," Harper says. "See my aunt. I guess not anymore."

"Rodeo Town," John Henry says for her. Then: "Coming from Yellowstone?"

"I wish," Harper says, then, with no hesitation, "Salt Lake," and logs that info: Ava is headed to Cheyenne, out of Utah. And she stopped for a sloppy burger at Little America, which she guesses makes her a Little American. "We're in a brown Audi?" she adds. "Seen us out there scurrying around?"

"Like a prairie dog amongst the buffalo . . ." John Henry says, nodding solemnly ahead that it's her turn.

Harper steps forward, fills her cup hot to the brim. The coffee's burned, she can tell from the smell, but still, it's coffee. She's trying to get her lid on without collapsing the side of the cup when a commotion at the register makes her look up.

It's the boys with the candy-filled cups. One of them's spilled his all over the counter, making a mess and blowing their scam. The other's light on the balls of his feet, ready to blast out of this place, keep running all night.

"Idiots," Harper says with a smile—that's her and Dillon,

four years ago—and turns away taking that first careful slurp, which is when she sees Jam's red head at the mostly-plundered beef jerky rack. He's following his finger down to the bigger bags at the bottom, but when he leans down for one the two peanut jugs he's already hugging to his chest go tumbling down to the loud metal shelving.

Not Jam. Bucketmouth. *Here.*

He gathers the peanuts with the beef jerky, feels enough eyes on him that he stands wheeling his face this way and that, already chewing a long pink piece of taffy that's hanging limp from his mouth like a severed tongue.

In a single desperate step Harper's standing back in front of the fountain drinks, her breath deeper than she means, her coffee splashed onto the front of her pow-wow sweatshirt, the lapel flap of the leather jacket, the tops of her thighs.

"Ma'am?" John Henry says, because she's pressed right up against him.

"Sorry," she says, and curls around him for the other side of the store, the other side of the world, wherever, please. Just away, away, away. She lifts a camo cap from a hanging string of them, pulls it down low over her eyes, shoves the tag up by her temple.

Calm, calm, she tells herself.

At which point Dillon stands from the magazine rack, waving a magazine for Harper like he's just found buried treasure: the new issue!

"No," Harper says, pleading with him to be anybody but who he is, but he's tall, he's waving that magazine, he's the same Dillon as ever.

Bucketmouth zeroes in on him, bites his taffy off, lets his

jerky and peanuts and candy bars slide down his front. He steps over them, looks around, finds Harper in a mirror almost instantly.

He tracks down from the reflection to her, says, "Wait, wait, shouldn't *I* be wearing the camo here?"

He steps over, pulls the same camo cap up from its hanging strip of plastic and seats it on his head, trying to keep both Dillon and Harper in his line of sight. Except they're opposite each other—on either side of him.

A passing clerk with a dolly of water bottle cases says, "Sorry, sir, but you have to pay for that before—"

Bucketmouth steps forward with no hesitation, launches her into the medicine rack. Lip balm and aspirin explode all over the aisle, and one of the shelf's metal fingers pokes up through the clerk's cheek, has her hanging there, mouth open.

"Just stay there," Bucketmouth says, holding his hand out to keep her there, still trying to track Dillon and Harper both.

Finally he just shakes his head no, admitting he can't do this.

"Didn't mean for it to come to this already," he says, and steps forward, to the books-on-tape display, hauls Meg out into Harper's view, her throat in the crook of his arm, her fingers pulling uselessly at his forearm. Then he turns around so Dillon can see who he's got, too.

"No!" Harper barks, stepping forward, into this.

The crowd parts for her.

Bucketmouth smiles, nods yes to her, yes yes yes, and takes one of Meg's wrists, struggles her skinny arm up and up until her hand is at his chin, her fingers in front of his theatrically snapping teeth.

"Hey," one of the register clerks says, stepping forward, and, without even looking back, Bucketmouth frees up his snub-nose and points it back at him.

The clerk stops, dutifully raises his hands, and when Bucketmouth comes back around to Meg, six of the customers standing close to him are looking at him over the barrels of their pistols.

"Oh yeah," he says, holding his up, finger very clear of the trigger, "this is Wyoming, isn't it?"

Moving slow, he reaches across to the shelf opposite him and Meg, drops his pistol into a large plastic jug of loose jaw breakers.

"Better?" he says.

Slowly, reluctantly, the six other pistols lower, most of them finding holsters.

"I just wanted some chips!" Bucketmouth says then, loud, to everyone, still holding Meg. "Maybe something to drink?"

A bottle of orange juice slow-rolls out to his foot. He laughs a sick laugh.

All Harper can think: Meg, Meg, Meg.

"*I know who he is*," she says then, loud enough for the whole store as well. All eyes settle on her.

She looks from face to face, to be sure she has every trucker's attention, every armed customer's eyes, and then she finally settles on John Henry, his cup of coffee raised to his mouth.

"He's—he's that one in the Yellowstone pickup!" Harper says all at once, the words tumbling from her mouth too fast. "The one who started the fire!"

Bucketmouth looks at her, dumbfounded, then around to all the glowering faces.

He takes a step back, says, "It's her, it's her! I saw her get out of that truck."

"Where's it parked, then?" Harper says, stepping forward again.

Bucketmouth glares at her.

"It's a quarter mile down Hunt," she says. "Back in the pasture. We saw you get out of it, followed you in."

"Just for the hell of it?" he says back. "This what you do?"

"We thought the two of you were up to something," Harper says. "Gonna rob the place, maybe."

"I saw it out there," a voice confirms. Trucker probably. "That one with the arrowhead on the door, right?"

Bucketmouth turns to Harper about this, thins his lips in appreciation, says, his last try: "*Two* of us, you say?"

Harper reaches into Kissy's purse, says, "My sister you've got there, she saw your girlfriend throw these away in the Ladies'."

Going just by touch, she extracts Jam's and Kissy's Park badges. The ones with their faces on them. She steps forward, sets them on the chest-high shelf Bucketmouth parked his pistol on.

"I saw her leave them in the trash when—"

John Henry sets his coffee down and steps forward, peels the two badges up with a kind of brutal formality, the same way a professional wrestler might walk into the ring with the whole coliseum watching his every move. The first badge is Kissy's. He compares it to both Harper and Meg—both of them together aren't half the Cherokee princess Kissy was—and then it's Jam's badge.

He holds it up alongside his angle on Bucketmouth.

"That was *particularly* careless, what you did to my brothers back there," he says, his voice somehow leaning forward, into this.

"You don't, it wasn't, I've got—" Bucketmouth says in Jam's voice, with Jam's mouth, and John Henry just shakes his head no, steps forward.

Bucketmouth swings Meg around like a shield but then a log of Copenhagen arcs up behind him in a fast, short swing. It connects with the back of his head and Meg pulls free of his arm, falls to her hands and knees, is already scrabbling away.

John Henry's big hand lifts Bucketmouth bodily from the floor by the scruff, which is when the clerk finds his voice again: "*Outside!*"

John Henry looks over to him and, hands still up, the clerk says, "Please?"

The mob of truckers scrum around Bucketmouth, deliver him through the door, the cowbell above the door dinging over and over, and Harper finally finds Meg in all the bodies.

"We've got to—" she says, and the two of them hold each other up, walk down the closest aisle, grabbing random chips and peanuts on the way. Passing the register, Harper lays all three of her twenties down, keeps walking.

12

"WELL," DILLON SAYS, shifting in the driver's seat of the Park truck, "Think it's safe to say he's not going to have the same face anymore, yeah?"

They're up on 80 again. Harper's just staring at the tail-lights of the camper in front of them. Maybe it got turned around at the burning pullout, or maybe they're letting traffic through. Does it even matter?

Where Dillon found her and Meg was walking alongside the westbound interstate.

On the backseat are the two cases of water bottles he stood in line for, because all the gallon jugs were gone. On his face are the surfer sunglasses with neon-yellow arms he's disguising himself with. Never mind the arrowhead on his door, under the crusty puke.

"They're going to hate us even more now," Harper says.

"Once they figure out it was us, you mean?" Dillon says.

"It *was* us," Harper says.

"Jam really was in this truck," Dillon says, trying to get their defense in order. "That part wasn't a lie."

"I'm the one who wanted to burn those jars," Harper says.

"You can't blame yourself for everything, Harpo," Dillon says.

"Don't call me that."

"Were y'all ditching me back there?" he asks back, leaning forward to rest both his forearms on top of the steering wheel, his posture all about how the answer doesn't matter either way.

"More like saving you," Harper says.

"Without saying goodbye."

"Thanks for the water," Harper says, taking another drink.

Meg isn't drinking hers, is just sitting there.

"Do you think it's over now?" Harper says to Dillon.

He shrugs, checks the mirrors.

"He didn't look like that guy with the shotgun," he says.

"He probably can't do it too many times," Harper says. "At that—in the gas station. Before he saw us. He was getting all the snacks he could. I think he needed to replenish."

"Calories," Dillon says, liking that. "Growing a new face that fast, it probably leaves you hungry like football—like two-a-days."

"More than that."

"You ever do two-a-days?"

Harper takes another drink, holds it in her mouth and closes her eyes.

"Think he has to pick people who are the same height as him?" Dillon's saying. "What about hair? teeth? scars? tattoos? What if he bites a piece off that big fucker who was carrying him outside? Will he be that big, or just have the same face?"

"How far to your brother's shop?" Harper asks, too drained for these mental calisthenics.

"Seventy, seventy five miles," Dillon says.

Harper slumps down in the seat, leans her head against the window for about two seconds, since the Park truck's about as smooth as a rollercoaster grinding up and up. Kissy's dad was smart not to buy it.

"Maybe they killed him," she says, leaving a lot of silence afterward for someone, anyone, to agree. "Maybe Bucket-mouth's dead."

"Hey . . ." Dillon says instead, letting off the gas so the rig already passing them can pass them faster.

It's a white-on-red Kenworth cabover done up with the BJ McKay swooshes coming up from the nose, around the sides—what her dad always called Irish eyebrows, which has to be racist, Harper suspects.

Her and Dillon watch it with the kind of awe you save for a blue whale, cruising past your kayak. No, it's more. They watch it like a dragon slithering past through the air, flying low, still crackling from having slipped from its world to this one for a moment.

"What?" Meg says in her scared voice, when Harper and Dillon can't even conjure words.

"You're too young," Harper says, watching that truck's tail-lights, now.

"That monkey I smell?" Dillon asks, sniffing at his open window.

Harper can't help but smile.

"Kissy saved us back there, didn't she?" she says once the truck's past.

"Jam too," Dillon says.

"What are we going to tell his mom?" Harper asks.

"We need to make it through ourselves first," Dillon says.

"He's dead," Harper says. "Bucketmouth. Gotta be. John Henry killed him."

"We never got to pee," Meg sneaks in like an apology.

"Some of us might have found a tire to water," Dillon confesses, shrugging like sorry it's so much easier for him and his kind.

"Yeah, well, some of us maybe didn't," Harper says. "Where's next?"

"Arlington," Dillon says. "Few miles up. But that little gas station's never open."

"Next?"

"Wagonhound, I think?" Dillon says, switching hands on the wheel to better focus on the map in his head. "Twenty minutes. There's a rest stop there, south side? We used to, um, go there, remember?"

"That place," Harper says.

"That place," Dillon says.

It's where they used to sit and park facing west and dream of being anywhere else. It's the first place they ever left a rubber's square package torn open at the corner, never mind all the truckers grinding past, all the senior citizens walking their dogs, all the sketchy men and women standing in the blasting wind like they can outlast it.

You can't outlast it—this is Wyoming—but you can roll the windows up with someone you love, or think you maybe love. Someone you love for however long this moment lasts. And when you're done, there's anonymous restrooms right there.

"Hold it?" Harper says to Meg.

"I'm not five years old," Meg says back.

"I've got to go too," Harper says, and tears open the barbecue chips she knows she's going to hate.

"Whoah, whoah, *down* . . ." Dillon says, talking quiet for some reason, using his flattened hand to show them what he means, what they need to do.

Harper and Meg scrunch down and Dillon pulls Harper's camo hat off her head, tries to fit it onto his own. Then—Harper can only tell this because she's known him so many years—he settles in behind the wheel in what he thinks is a different way. In what he thinks is the way someone not named Dillon might drive.

"What?" she whispers up to him.

"Shh, shh," he says, smiling the fakest smile, moving his upper body ever so slightly with some beat he's pretending to hear.

Slowly, and partially because Dillon's slowing even more than he did for the *BJ and the Bear* truck, a car passes them. Harper can tell it's a car because a rig would be looking right down at her, and a pickup's roof would be cresting through the window past Dillon.

"It him?" Meg says, ready to panic.

"La la lala la," Dillon sings, not not *not* looking into the left lane.

Finally Harper peeks up, sees the trunk and rear window of a Buick with a single driver, a woman. Same off-white as a certain Buick she knows. Same NATIVE PRIDE bumpersticker. Same nine-foot whip antenna coming up from the right rear fender, arcing forward to the front fender like the feather in a Robin Hood hat.

"Mom?" she says. "What's she doing here?"

"Shh, shh," Dillon says, trying not to use his lips, and then the Buick slows, falls back beside the Park truck.

"Oh shit oh shit oh shit shit shit," Dillon says.

"Duck, duck!" Harper tells him from the floorboard.

"Can't look, can't look," Dillon says through his teeth, at which point an air horn blasts at this Buick slowing down in the passing lane, clogging up traffic, slowing down commerce, blowing everyone's schedules right to hell.

The Buick accelerates—Harper can hear it, knows that rattly exhaust—and in thirty seconds it's passing the camper in front of them, is mostly hidden by the Mack riding its bumper.

"Why is she all the way out here?" Harper says to Dillon. "She never comes out this far!"

"Because of, um . . ." Dillon says, taking the hat off to adjust it out to his size, not looking at Meg but definitely meaning her.

Of course. Harper's not worth the gas it takes to scour the interstate, but, Meg? Their mom'll burn tank after tank, chasing her. She's the last chance to get it right, isn't she?

Harper guides Meg back up onto the seat with her.

"Can he, you know," Dillon says, looking over under his new brim to catch Harper's eye, "do you think he can, like, change into a woman? He sounded like Jam, didn't he? That mean he can sound like anybody?"

Harper stares at the bumpersticker of the camper still in front of them. *rv there yet?*

She shakes her head, wondering what this night can possibly still hold, which is when Meg, without looking over, says in her small, little sister voice, "What was the fight about anyway?"

Harper winces inside, lowers her face, studies the floorboard between her sneakers.

Dillon, who's not completely clueless, thumbs Gordon Lightfoot back in, leans against his door, turns the camo hat around so the wind whipping at him won't pull it out the back window.

IT HAD STARTED out as a good day. Good enough.

The night before, Harper and Meg had watched a baseball movie from the grocery store's rental rack. Not because either of them cared even one little bit about baseball, and they weren't watching for Charlie Sheen or that blond guy from *LA Law*. It was Omar Epps. He'd been in a football movie the grocery store had too.

The baseball movie had been funny, but it could have played on mute and that would have been just the same. Her and Meg were entranced by Omar Epps, giggling to rewind it, play his scenes again in slow motion, even though that made tracking lines roll up the screen and, according to Meg, stretched the videotape out for the next viewer.

When their mom had come through the room on the way to the store for spaghetti noodles, she'd scooped the tape case up.

"It rewound?" she said, holding it up.

Harper was lying on the couch with the fingers of her left hand spread out above her, so she could tap each hard fingernail with her right fingertip. At first she'd been humming a tune to it, but now she wasn't sure what exactly she was doing, really. Just nothing.

"It's still in the VCR," she said without breaking her rhythm, whatever her rhythm was, or was going to be.

Her mom shook the case and held it there like waiting for Harper to rise, fill it.

"Can we get another tonight?" Harper asked instead, finally looking over, doing her eyes all big like Kissy's.

"Ninety-nine cent shelf?" her mom said back.

"As always," Harper said back, turning back to the deliciously spread fingers of her left hand.

"Are you on something?" her mom asked.

"Life," Harper said. "Want some, or you already used up what you had?"

"I don't have time for this, Harper," her mom said, tossing the tape case onto Harper's belly. "Unless you want to make dinner?"

"Not hungry."

"You don't work tonight?"

Harper turned her left hand around so the palm faced her now, said, "Are my hands like Dad's, do you think? Where do I get them?"

"The tape, please," her mom said.

"So we *can* get one?" Harper asked back.

"Not something stupid this time, right?"

"Are you watching with us?"

"Not if it's stupid, I'm not."

"Don't worry about it, then," Harper said, studying the ceiling now. The field of glitter.

"I still need to take that one back, though," her mom said.

"We'll just watch it again," Harper said. "Late charges are the same as renting another, so it'll be like we rented something else."

"*Harper*," her mom said.

Harper turned her head to study her mom, and thought what she always thought: *me plus twenty, minus happiness.*

"It's the same ninety-nine cents, Mom," she said. "Why's it some big hairy deal?"

"Because—because watching the same movie when you could be watching something else, that's not . . . it's like throwing money away."

"Throwing a dollar away."

"Dollars count."

"But it's the same dollar, isn't it? Whether we rent something new or watch this one again?"

"Nobody does that."

"Here," Harper said, and straightened her legs to uncrumple a lone dollar from between the two fives in her pocket. She dropped it on the table like cleaning her fingers of it. "Better?"

"No," her mom said. "It's not about the money."

"So every dollar doesn't count? Is this a new kind of parenting, where you contradict what you were just telling me? Am I learning a lesson here?"

"You already know how to be a smartass."

"Obviously."

"Are we really going to do this again, Harper?"

"Do what? We just want to watch the movie again. Meg fell asleep, missed how it ended."

"I heard the two of you in here," her mom said. "There was no sleep happening."

"We like baseball," Harper said. "It's our new favorite sport. We might go pro. Are you going to crush our dreams before they even start?"

"I'll believe that when I see you playing."

"Is it such a big crime to want to watch it again?"

"It's not using your time well."

"Mom, I go to work, I do my job, I pick Meggie up from school when I can to help you out. All work and no play—"

"Relax, sure. You're doing a good job of it right now, looks like."

"Past tense. I *was* doing it just now."

"Watching the same movie two nights in a row, Harper. You can't see how that—it's going nowhere."

"That's what this is about? Really? My future? My decisions? Is it five o'clock already? That's lecture time, right? Shit, where's my notebook, I need to write some of this down, see if it's the same list as last time . . ."

"You don't get *that* from me," her mom said.

"What?"

"That attitude."

"Survival mechanism."

"And watch your language in this house."

"Because it's such a special, special place."

"This is my punishment. Ungrateful daughters."

"Singular, Mom. It's just me saying this."

"Training your sister to."

"She's checked out on my headphones, which I *let* her borrow this time."

"You don't even see how much she idolizes you."

"Smart girl," Harper says.

"With limited role models," her mom says right back.

"And that's *my* fault, that what you're saying? Dad didn't come back because I didn't win the science fair, or dominate in basketball?"

"No, I'm just saying that if you would—"

"Go on, you're getting there."

"Harper."

"No, please, please, I know it's coming, Mom. I'm like Dad. I just want to take enough deliveries to pay the bills, never make any extra."

"Anything that was said between him and me is still between him and me."

"I think the confidentiality on *that* one's expired, Mom, thanks. And when I say that I mean thank you so much for running him off, saving us from his bad influence. I probably never would have graduated if I'd had him here at home. Know what? I bet Meg doesn't even get braces if Dad's still around. I bet the macaroni wouldn't have burned to the pan last night if—"

"Not so loud," her mom said, stepping closer, her lips just opening enough to let her words out now. "Your sister will hear."

"*Meg! Meg, come here!* See, nothing. Or, do you want to take this out onto the lawn like last time? Give the neighbors the Mom and Daughter show again?"

"I don't know what to do with you anymore. I really don't."

"Nothing, Mom, I want you to do nothing with me, how's that? I want you to let me and Meg watch whatever we want to tonight."

"I don't care what you watch."

"Then why are we having this discussion? There's no judgment going on, is there? It's just a stupid baseball movie, Mom. Geez."

"It's not that."

"You hate Charlie Sheen, then? What?"

"Just give me the case thing. We can forget about this. Just eat dinner and go to bed."

"But we want to *watch* it, Mom. Again. Your stupid senseless daughters want to ruin their minds with the same movie, did you forget?"

"I don't have time for this, Harper, I've got to get—"

She brushed past Harper but Harper beat her back to the couch, stepped back holding the case high.

"*Harper*," her mom warned.

Harper stepped back again and it was far enough that the case bumped into the open-faced china hutch filled with commemorative plates. They both looked back, tracked the very top one wobbling on its wooden stand, then tipping, tipping—

Harper lunged forward, caught it with both hands, the case falling underfoot, but she had enough momentum that she tapped the plate she was saving into another one that hadn't even been in danger.

It held its shape for a moment just like a cartoon, then shattered, fell down the front of the hutch. Her mom turned around, stared at the ceiling for serenity.

"Mom, I didn't—" Harper said, holding the good, *saved* plate out, but her mom came around so fast, so mad, that her lead hand sent the plate flipping away.

They both watched it go end over end, hit the wall behind the TV, shatter.

"Have I forgot to tell you how fortunate I feel that you've stayed here so long after graduation?" her mom said.

"So long?" Harper said, incredulous. "I know, right? Two months? Oceans have risen and fallen, all the stars have shifted into different places—"

"You make it feel like a lot longer," her mom said. "Theatrics like this."

Harper refocused her eyes trying to mentally digest this, then she shook her head, smiled, stepped over to the sacred fucking china hutch of idiot plates.

"Theatrics?" she said. "You mean like *this*?" She took one plate from high, sailed it across the room.

"That the best you've got?" her mom said. "Breaking things I care about? Do you think this is where that starts? Do you think you haven't been blundering into—"

"What, it's almost dinner?" Harper said. "Here, let me set all the plates out, *Mom*."

Before she could stop herself, she was grabbing onto the back of the hutch, planting a foot on the wall, and pulling everything down.

It fell and fell. The crash was tremendous, sent all the dust on the back of the hutch airborne, where it stayed.

They both looked through it upstairs, to the chance of Meg having heard that. She had to have.

"Feel better now?" her mom said, her voice level and pointed. "Think it hurts, that you're really getting to me with this pathetic outburst?"

"I. Just. Want. To. Watch. That. Movie," Harper said. "*Again*."

"Where?" her mom said, looking around. "Living room's kind of upside down now, isn't it?"

"Not yet," Harper said, which was when she stepped up to the arm of the couch, dug her hands underneath, and lifted it as hard as she could, trying with everything she had to flip it as well.

Her mom stepped back, expecting the couch to come her way. When it didn't—couldn't, was too tall to go end over end—she just shook her head, said with mock wonder through the falling ceiling texture, "Look, Harper. The stars you and your dad planted, they're all falling down . . ."

"*I hate you!*" Harper screamed. "I hate you I hate you I hate you! You ran Dad off—"

"He just didn't come back."

"—you try to control every part of my life! I wish you were dead! I wish you'd left instead of him! Then I could, then I could, then I could watch the same stupid movie every night of my stupid life! And get nowhere and become nothing and maybe, maybe, be happy!"

Her mom stepped back, opened her hand, presenting the front door as if it had been there all along. Harper stormed through it, not giving her mom the satisfaction of even slamming it, and was standing on the front lawn opening and closing her hands for control when a load of her own laundry hit her in the back.

"Don't say I didn't give you anything, dear," her mom said from the porch.

"You've given me more than enough," Harper said, and started picking her clothes from the grass. Halfway into it though, she bubbled over, slung them back up at the house. "I don't want anything to remind me of my life here," she said.

"You'll be back," her mom said.

"Bye, Mom," Harper said, already leaving. "Thanks for everything."

Which isn't exactly what she tells Meg.

What she tells Meg, Dillon still taking great pains either to not listen or to pretend not to hear, is that it was about that Omar Epps movie.

"I never even saw the first one," Meg confesses.

"Not worth it," Harper says. "He's not even in it. I don't even know why you make a movie without him in it."

Meg smiles into her chest and finally opens her water bottle, takes a drink.

"That'll help you not have to pee," Harper says.

"Pee on you," Meg says, shouldering Harper.

"Ladies, ladies," Dillon says. "Don't make me pull this car over, now."

Harper looks out the window.

"That black dude really better looking than me?" Dillon's half-whispering to Meg, in some way distant part of the truck. Harper places a barbecue chip in her mouth, closes her eyes to get past the taste, and ends up looking at the back of her hand, the fingers spread.

Her mom, she knows. That's where she gets her hands.

She can tell by the way they destroy everything they touch.

13

DILLON'S RIGHT ABOUT the little gas station at the Arlington exit: dark windows, no action.

"They could be cleaning up, night like this," he says.

"I never even turned my—this, on," Harper says. She holds her wrist out, the glow-bracelet circling it. "When we were walking," she clarifies.

"I still saw you," Dillon tells her, trying to overpack it with meaning, she can tell.

"It's not about 'look at me,' it's about 'don't not see me,'" Harper says, ignoring his subtext. "Those Bible-thumpers, they were trying so hard to save me. If I'd have just, I don't know, let them? Then y'all never pick me up. Meg walks home. None of this ever happens."

"Why stop with that?" Dillon says, turning Gordon Lightfoot down. "If your mom hadn't royally pissed you off. No, no. If *Major League II* hadn't been on the shelf for you to rent. No, no, if—"

"You know *Major League II*?" Harper asks.

"Just because we're not together right now doesn't mean we don't still watch the same movies," Dillon says. "Right, Megalator?"

"We were never dating," Meg tells him, her lips pressed together so she won't quite smile. She can't hide her dimples, though.

Harper elbows her.

"You're going to make me pee," Meg warns.

"It'll smell better than the throw-up in the floorboard," Harper says.

"And the throw-up on the doors," Dillon adds.

"And the eyeball in back," Harper says, only cueing in a moment later to Dillon and Meg, both turned to her about that. "That lady from the Thunderbird," she explains, and bursts her hand over her own left eyeball to show.

"It shot out?" Meg says, not wanting that to be true, Harper can tell, but thrilling from it all the same.

"Oh yeah, that bird had it in its beak . . ." Dillon fills in, nodding.

Harper holsters that hand-pistol into a different pocket of the leather jacket, comes out with . . . a baby food jar?

"No," she says.

"That's where that one went," Dillon says.

"I've had this all along?" Harper says.

"Motherfucker," Meg says.

"Language," Harper tells her.

"She's right," Dillon says.

"Throw it out?" Meg says.

Harper cranks her window down, turning the cab into an instant tornado. Well, into even more of a tornado. At the last moment, though, her hand out in open space, she doesn't let that little glass jar go.

"What are you—?" Dillon says.

"Last time we tried to get rid of evidence, bad things happened," Harper tells him, concentrating like doing math.

"So now we've got *two* eyeballs with us?" Meg says.

"From different people," Harper says.

"I don't think that makes it better," Dillon says. "I think maybe that makes it worse, even."

"It's evidence," Harper says. "Jam was right. . . . It was Jam, wasn't it? Or—"

"Why didn't we need proof before?" Dillon says.

"Because we hadn't blown any trucks up," Harper tells him.

"That looks more like one eyeball to me," Dillon says, about the jar Harper's still got pincered up like the worst show and tell.

Harper considers this, considers it some more, then flops over the front seat, bridges her body across the back and stabs her upper body into the bed, her hair whipping her face.

"More, more," she says to herself, and worms forward farther, can finally reach her hand through the centerhole of the spare, grab the only mushy thing there, her chest curling in, her stomach trying to gag those barbecue chips back up.

She collapses down into the backseat, her hair still sucking out the back window, getting a month's worth of split ends. Holding her breath and shielding the baby food jar from the wind, she holds her breath to crack it open, deposit the mostly dry eyeball in. The harsh scent—taste?—of cinnamon swirls through the cab, burns her eyes. She screws the lid back on tight and holds it there. Just in case.

"So now he killed the church lady *too*?" Meg says, turned around backwards in the seat to document this slimy little drama.

"I thought he was a hitchhiker the people from the

Thunderbird were *trying* to kill?" Dillon says.

"Because he was trying to kill *them* . . ." Harper completes. "Steal Combover's face or something."

"The face that was on the windshield?" Meg asks, halfway lost, it sounds like. Like Dillon, judging by the way his body's turned to Harper like a radio dish, waiting for her to beam an answer across.

Harper holds the bottle up, considering it. The eye she just dropped in, from the bed of the truck, is blue, is still floating down. The other, already settled, is brown, the white shot through with ruptured blood vessels.

"When—when Bucketmouth is telling the cops he doesn't know what we're talking about—" she starts.

"Just some crazy kids with their crazy stories," Dillon wedges in.

"—remind me we've got this. Proof."

"Because it's got only his fingerprints on it?" Meg says.

Harper makes a show of cleaning every bit of the jar's glass she can, lid too, then she pushes it back into the jacket's weed pocket like closing this discussion. She's nestled down into the backseat, her face just touching the fabric, when Dillon reaches back, grabs her shoulder to haul her up.

"What?" she says. "You the sleep police?"

"Glass," he says, and, her hands so light, Meg brushes the side of Harper's face then holds her palm up, the headlights behind them turning her hand into a rhinestone glove.

"Are we there yet?" Harper whines, and crawls back into the front.

BECAUSE DILLON'S GOT his window down again a few miles later, the lit cigarette from the trucker passing them arcs perfectly down into his lap in a puff of sparks.

Like he's supposed to, he stands up as much as he can without even thinking.

"The cherry, the cherry, get the cherry!" he's saying.

The Park truck dives hard to the right, is for sure about to go cartwheeling over the ditch until Harper lunges for the wheel, hauls them off the shoulder at way too steep an angle, which veers them sharply across the lane until Meg grabs the wheel as well, uncorrecting Harper's overcorrection.

As lightly as possible, the side mirror on the driver's side dings into the rig's trailer and comes off, goes under the big tires, is gone. And then they're going shakily straight again.

The camper behind them now flashes its lights at them.

Dillon sweeps the cigarette into the floorboard at last, retakes the wheel with his right hand, holds his left out and up to tell the camper they've got things under control now, thanks.

"They think we're drunk," Meg states. Just a fact.

Harper looks back to the camper people, their faces grim and expectant, their decisions about Harper and Meg and Dillon already made.

Harper waves to them anyway, shakes her head no, isn't sure what exactly she hopes to convey at sixty miles per hour. That all the truckers on this stretch of interstate tonight are waging petty war against the national park system? That maybe they should give her and her sister and her ex a break, since there's a face-changing finger-eating monster of a serial killer on their tail? Probably she should just lob her baby food jar out the back window, let it shatter on the camper people's windshield, hope that at least one of the two eyeballs will stick to the glass for a moment or two, maybe get across some shred—no, some *smear*—of what they're dealing with up here.

She turns back around, says to Dillon, "Maybe windows up?"

"You can handle the smell in here?"

"Better than dying," Harper says.

"Speak for yourself," Dillon says, cranking the stubborn window back up.

"That wasn't your dad, was it?" Harper says with a smile.

Meg looks over to him about this.

Dillon pinches the dead cigarette up from the floorboard, inspects it. "Not a Camel," he says.

"I thought he quit," Harper says.

"That was . . ." Dillon says, thinking back. "April? Think it was all some big April Fool's joke, really."

Harper thinks back as well, realizes she has the perfect image of Dillon's dad at graduation. He's way at the back, hunched behind a small tree, taking one last drag from his Camel before standing up to find his son, grey smoke trailing from his mouth and nose at the same time, like he's on fire inside, like his truck isn't the only thing that runs on internal combustion.

The problem with scratching open the graduation photo album in her head, though, it's that Kissy and Jam are there, Jam's mom and dad even sitting in the same row together for once, Kissy's mom looking more like she should be Kissy's sister, like always, gag. Crossing the stage for his diploma, Jam had stopped to raise his arms, celebrate the moment, his row screaming for him. Harper hopes he got to take that feeling with him. And—and she should read Kissy's Park journal when this is all over. She promises she will. This is the first time the two of them have been apart for summer since third grade. Did Kissy change, working up there? Was she becoming whoever she was going to be? Is it all going to be love poetry? Her writing her front name with Jam's last name?

Harper sucks her lips in, her eyes heating up. Which is when a cup splatters into their windshield, from the next rig passing in the left lane.

This time Dillon doesn't flinch, just clicks the wipers into their slow rhythm.

"Spit cup," he identifies for them, like they can't see all the Copenhagen grains wiggling against the glass like demon sperm.

Meg scooches over to Harper to keep away from the leaky crack.

"It's spit," Dillon says. "I think it's too thick to come through."

Meg looks over to him like is he for real, here.

"But good thinking," he adds.

"Temperature?" Harper asks.

He leans down to get a line on the gauge, says, "Hot but not boiling. Kind of like certain drivers . . ."

He straightens his back, strikes a Marlboro Man pose.

"Certain drivers of other vehicles," Meg adds, not able to contain her laughter.

Dillon playacts being hurt, says, "I mean, we can't all be Omar whoever, right?"

"*Epps!*" the girls say together.

For a moment it's almost like everything's normal. But then cop lights swirl on behind them, the sirens dopplering in.

"What was I doing?" Dillon says, looking down to the speedometer.

"More like what have we done?" Harper says.

14

DILLON HANGS THE passenger side of the truck deep in the ditch and the statie pulls in right behind, cocking his wheels sharply to the left at the last moment like they all do, so if their cruiser gets clipped it'll shoot back out into traffic, not plow over the officer writing the ticket.

"What do we say?" Dillon asks.

"Ten and two," Harper instructs, about his hands.

"What?"

"Otherwise he'll think you've got a weapon?"

Dillon places his hands high on the wheel, says again, "So what do we tell him?"

"That it wasn't us?" Meg tries.

"Except it was," Harper says. "It is."

"At least if we go to jail," Meg says, staring straight ahead, "at least Bucketmouth can't get us in there."

"He's dead," Harper says. "Those truckers back there, they—there were so many of them. And he was just . . . he was Jam. Jam couldn't even fight Kissy off, right?"

Nobody answers. Headlights stream past, all jostling into the passing lane to give this bad scene space, and the tension of just sitting there ramps up and up, punctuated by air horns marking the trouble this Park truck is in.

"Band camp," Dillon finally says across to the two of them like it's their rallying cry, their reminder of who they are—that they're *them*—and Harper and Meg repeat it in sequence, confirming that they're still them, and then the statie is shining his Maglite into the cab, all three of them squinting when it's their turn to get lit up.

"What's this about, officer?" Dillon says, both hands still firmly on the steering wheel, in the plainest possible sight.

"Trooper," the statie corrects.

Dillon nods yes, that.

"License, registration, insurance," the statie says.

"That's the thing," Dillon says, not looking over yet.

"You're employees of Yellowstone Park?"

"Well," Dillon says.

"No," Harper says. "It's not our truck."

"Ma'am?" the statie says, directing his light up to her and leaving her in that burning white brightness. "Little far from the reservation, aren't we?"

Harper manages to not say anything smart back, to just swallow all the comebacks and educational opportunities down.

"What were we doing?" Dillon asks, probably trying to draw the statie's attention.

"Whose truck *is* it then?" the statie asks, his light lingering on Meg now, his cop-brain probably calculating the extra time arresting a minor is going to carve out of his night.

"It's Yellowstone's truck," Harper says. Obviously.

"And you're driving it because?"

"Our friends who work at the Park this summer brought it

to Laramie for their—for her dad to look at it," Harper says. "He didn't want it."

"What friends?"

"Good ones," Dillon says.

"Dead ones," Harper adds.

In less than a second, the Maglite has a pistol under it.

"We were going to call you about that," Meg says, her voice flat. "The line for the phone was too long."

"It's the truth," Harper says, and holds her left hand up until the statie can settle his light on it. Moving slowly so he can follow, she dips it into the secret pocket of the leather jacket, births the baby food jar up, holds it between her fingers like the specimen it is.

"*Dash, dash!*" the statie commands, pointing there with his light and pistol both.

Still moving slow, Harper deposits the jar on the center of the dash above the radio, her wrist nudging the cassette back in on accident. Gordon Lightfoot swells up from the door panels like a surprise fourth person in the cab. One who nearly gets the other three shot.

Meg darts her hand forward, dials the volume knob down an instant before Harper can catch her hand, slow her down. You don't move fast around bears. It's not an Indian thing, it's a trucker thing, one she learned from making runs with her dad.

In response to Meg's sudden movement, the statie backs off a long step to better keep all three of them in his line of fire. His *potential* line of fire, Harper tells herself. Very, very hopefully.

"Look," she says about the jar, lacing her fingers behind her head, chicken-winging her elbows out. Meg takes her lead, does her hands just the same. Dillon keeps his on the wheel, tighter than tight, like if he doesn't hang on, he's getting sucked out the window, up into the sky. "*Look*," Harper says again.

Before the statie can, the mic clipped to his shoulder crackles open with static.

It's someone back down the road, reporting possible body parts in the westbound, and does anybody out here tonight know the difference in human vertebra and deer vertebra?

"That's our friend," Harper says. "Her name's—it was Kissy."

In response to that the statie works his left hand into his shirt pocket, shakes loose an ID badge, lets it unravel to the end of its forest-green lanyard.

It's Kissy's smiling face and unforgettable name twirling on the end of that string.

"You got called there for the disturbance," she tells the statie.

"We found the male as well," the statie says. "James."

"Was he . . . his face," Harper says. "Does he still look like his picture?"

"Is he still alive, she means," Dillon adds, covering, which is just getting them deeper into this, and not in a good way.

The statie is just watching them.

"We found his *badge*," he finally says.

"He's trying to trick us," Harper says to Dillon and Meg. "They already found him."

"I'm the one asking the questions here, ma'am."

"Was that a question?" Harper says. Then: "You found Jam—*James*, in the pasture by a place where a car punched through the fence. One finger missing. Or a tongue. An eyeball. Doesn't matter. He was dead."

"Save it for after I've Miranda'd you," the statie says. "Not that spontaneous confessions don't carry any weight in a court of law."

Harper shakes her head in defeat, amusement, hopelessness. It's maybe the most Indian gesture there is.

"*Look*," she finally says again, losing her patience. Because what her and Dillon did and didn't do aren't the most important thing right now. What's most important is that Bucketmouth is real, and really out there.

Slowly, moving like he knows this is a trick of some sort, the statie lights the baby food jar up.

Two eyeballs look back at him, sediment swirling all around them.

"They're not ours," Dillon says, like saying it just to be sure there's no misunderstanding. "I mean—*we* didn't do that. We just have them, we didn't, like, get them."

"We got one of them," Harper corrects. Reluctantly.

"I'm going to need the three of you to step out of the cab," the statie says. "*Slowly*."

"There's someone out here killing people left and right," Harper says. "This is—we found his trophies, his snacks, whatever. This is the last one left. At least until he makes more."

"Why did you even stop us?" Dillon says, and turns over to inspect this statie at last, which gives Harper a line on him as well, through the haze of Meg's flyaways.

"Cut yourself shaving, officer?" she says, about the . . . *is* that razor burn on his jaw? Sunburn? Acne scars inflaming all over again? And, sunglasses at night?

"*Trooper!*" the statie says, his trigger finger twitchy, his upper body angled over to the front, one foot forward like he's setting himself to absorb some recoil.

"Why did you pull us over?" Harper repeats, because that is the pressing question, suddenly.

The statie stares at her with his chrome eyes, stares some more, then comes back with, "We got a report of a truck matching this description. It was leaving the scene of a crime."

"Of a fire?" Harper says.

"I need the three of you *out* of the cab now!" the statie insists.

"You're right," Dillon says to Harper. "What's up with his face?"

Meg's crying now, her hands still behind her head, her whole upper body shuddering in a bad kind of sinuous rhythm like she's about to blow over, not be able to get back up.

The statie leans down to his shoulder-mounted radio rig, says, "All units be advised, I've got the operators of the truck in question—"

"What?" Harper says. "This is—he's talking like a TV cop, isn't he? Did you hear that on *Walker, Texas Ranger*?"

"'Truck in question?'" Dillon says, catching on.

The statie presses his mouth down to the mic, says, "I'm going to need backup at mile-marker, mile-marker—"

"Wait, wait," Dillon says, and takes his left hand off the wheel to open the door, speak to this statue man to man or some macho bullshit like that, and his pinky must be hooked into the handle when the statie takes a step farther back from whatever's happening here, and fires a warning shot over the cab, that report the exact sound of the end of the world.

Harper jumps in her seat, her hands still up, at least until she's pulling Meg close, like there's any way to protect a little sister from bullets, and Dillon rips his hand away from the door, to grab back onto the wheel.

There's no undoing this, though.

Especially since his pinky was already hooked in that handle.

With galloping through the ditch and all the other trauma this Park truck's suffered this night, not counting the hundreds of thousands of times it has to have been opened over the last however-many years, it . . . it—

Opens.

Harper surges over to try to grab it across Dillon, grab it and keep it in place, but it's like it's spring-loaded.

An old trucker trick is, if a state trooper stops you, and presumes to step up onto your running board to get face to face with you, and she or he elects to pull up with the mirror's strut instead of the grab bar, then all you have to do is pull the door handle back, just like Dillon just did on accident. Opening that door the statie's hanging on sends them tumbling, maybe teaches them about where it's okay to put their hands, where it's not okay.

This statie isn't hanging onto the truck's side mirror—this truck isn't that tall, and doesn't have a running board anyway—but still, he's familiar enough with this trick himself, evidently, knows that the driver's door opening means find the ground, set yourself.

He does. Except, already being a step back in order to keep his pistol and the Maglite between him and the cab, stepping back from that position—

His green on brown outfit lights up halogen hot, and before Harper can even breathe in, the ancient flatbed riding the white line clips him, after somehow *missing* the cocked-out nose of his cruiser. It takes Dillon's door with it in a scream of metal and sparks, slaps it and the statie into the front fender, and when that hundredth of a second is over, the statie's upper body is on the hood, his face to the windshield, opening and closing.

"*No!*" Harper screams, her hands still behind her head, Meg's too, so that when Dillon stands on the pedal, the truck fishtailing sideways in the slick grass, they sway over to the side window, Harper's leather elbow shattering it out.

For maybe a hundred feet, the statie's upper body and staring face rides the ditch with the Park truck, the spiral cable of his radio mic in the windshield wiper the only thing keeping him there, but his radio rig finally pulls free of belt and shirt, his body sloughing off, the radio staying with the wiper assembly, bouncing on the side of the truck now, on Harper's door, Dillon either screaming or moaning, it's hard to tell over the sounds she's pretty sure her own mouth is making. That her head is full with, full to spilling.

She sets the heels of her hands against the dash to try to make it through the Park truck fishtailing from side to side in the ditch, galumphing up and down over the dips and swells, eating up reflector poles, its headlights shining uselessly up into the sky when there's no weight on the front tires, then, on landing, showing only yellow grass rushing up under them. Dillon doesn't let up on the gas until Harper manages to reach across Meg, touch his knee.

It wakes him, sort of. He flinches, looks to her, then seems to become aware of where they are, what they're doing, how crazy and wrong and bad this is.

He doesn't brake, which would be disastrous in the ditch, but keeps the same speed, directs the driver's side tires onto the shoulder of the interstate, gravel spitting up into the wheel wells like machine gun fire, and then, using his blinker—blinkers still exist, the world is still real—he merges back into traffic. The missing sound of the grass brushing the undercarriage is a massive silence. It presses in all around Harper, takes her breath away.

The first vehicle to pass them is the little brown Audi.

The college freshmen in it all look over directly into the cab through the space where there used to be a door, and what they must see are three shattered people in a windstorm, their truck coming apart around them, the dome light on now because the door can't turn it off.

With his left boot Dillon pushes the plunger in that the door used to keep pushed, and the dome light sucks its light back in, giving them the darkness they need for what they're going through right now.

The Audi surges past.

Harper screams in frustration, bangs the sides of her fists into the dash over and over.

Sitting between them, Meg still has her fingers laced behind her head. She's crying, sobbing, too terrified to even process.

Harper reaches over, guides those chicken wings down, holds her hands over her little sister's until she becomes aware of something cold against her wrist.

The baby food jar.

Of course.

15

THE BIG RIGS are more spaced out now, this far from the fire. And the signs coming east out of Utah are probably flashing that the road's closed, so there's less people getting turned around for the night, coming back westbound.

Harper's standing at the front of the truck watching the interstate, her hands in her pockets, her hair still crunchy with glass from the side window.

They're at the Wagonhound rest stop. When she was a kid and her dad would stop here for her she would always think they planted these three brick buildings to commemorate the single windiest spot in all of Wyoming. Compared to riding in the cab of the Park truck now, it feels more like the eye of the storm: still, calm.

But when they leave, it all starts again, doesn't it?

Harper closes her eyes.

"No . . . no," Meg says from the backseat.

She's telling Dillon if the fuse he's popping out of the Park truck is the one for the dome light or not. Which means he has to now put that one he just pulled back in, and all he's using for pliers is two pennies pinched together.

Over the wall in the restroom that didn't go quite all the way up, Harper had been able to hear him next door, sobbing in his stall. And then punching it. Not about Kissy and Jam, she's pretty sure—they were always more competitors for Harper's attention than running buds—but that highway patrolman he didn't *mean* to kill.

He's got his brave face on now, though.

When the dome light casting Meg's blurry shadow onto the sidewalk blacks out like they've been waiting for, she calls "Good" to Dillon and he sits up at last. There are campers and RVs and station wagons and minivans scattered around every few spaces, the rigs farther out in their parking lot. Dillon eases up to the front of the truck, takes the time to balance the little glass fuse on the hood between them.

"Find a better station?" Harper calls over her shoulder to Meg. Moments later Gordon Lightfoot croons on, then becomes AM static going up and down with Meg's dialing.

"There's no good reception in Yellowstone," Dillon tells Harper, about the useless quest she's sent Meg on. "That's why there's cassettes in all the trucks, probably."

Harper looks down at the stained concrete she's standing on.

"They're going to shoot us on sight now, you know that, right?" she says. Obviously.

"Not you," Dillon says. "Me. I'm the one killed him."

"You didn't—"

"I don't open my door, he doesn't get hit. Case closed."

"Was he even really a cop?" Harper says, turning to catch Dillon's eyes, see if he's thinking the same thing.

There's grease on his cheek now, and the right side of his nose. She licks her finger, dabs at it, only succeeds in spreading it. It makes her laugh. The laugh turns into a sob. Dillon pulls her to him, presses her face into his shoulder.

"I miss them too," he lies. It's a lie she could kiss him for. It makes her shake harder. Makes her madder.

"It didn't have to happen!" she says into his shoulder. "They were just—they just wanted to bum around Yellowstone for the summer, maybe see a wolf or two, have some stories to tell their kids someday . . ."

"My dad always says that when your number's up, it doesn't matter where you are, what you do. It's just time."

"It wasn't *their* time."

"It's not ours either," Dillon says.

Harper pushes away from him, tries to compose herself, pretend she's a better, strong person. One who can handle all this bullshit.

"You saw that statie's face too," she says. "Tell me there wasn't something—"

"I was looking in the mirror right before," Dillon cuts in, the argument in his head spilling out into their discussion.

Harper steps around to see him head-on. "What are you—what did you see, Dill?"

Dillon gulps a swallow down, rubs the spot of grease on his nose worse.

"The headlights of that truck that hit him, they came *on*," he says. "They were—they were off when it was barreling down the shoulder, and then . . ." He poofs both hands open, does the soft sound effect: headlights where there were no headlights. "And—then I was looking right at the cop, where he'd been standing, and then, then right after, too. After it happened, the taillights blipped off."

Harper stares over at the interstate, her arms crossed, her brain cooking.

"And how do you hit the cop without hitting his car first?" he adds. "It's like . . . you'd have to *try*, Harp. And even then, you'd have to really know what you're doing, right?"

"What are you saying?"

"First, that I killed him," Dillon says. "Not you, not Meggie. Not Jam, not Kissy. I'm not running from that, understand. It's just a fact. I don't open my door—"

"On *accident*," Harper insists.

"If the door doesn't open, he doesn't die. But, second, I wasn't the *only* one who killed him. Now we just . . . we wait for the paper tomorrow, if we live til then. He had three kids, a wife, was probably paying for his mom's nursing—"

"If that trucker really took him out on purpose, it'll be on that, that drunk driving camera thing those cruisers have on the dash, won't it?"

"The one pointing over the hood, you mean?" Dillon says, lodging his objection. "But, yeah, it'll for sure have me opening that door." Like caught in that camera's eye, he re-enacts the middle and index fingers of his left hand popping that handle. "Then leaving the scene at a guilty rate of speed. There's even proof," he says, and steps back, unwinds the stretched out mic and radio from where it's hanging by the passenger side front tire, the wiper it's attached to bent out. He balls the radio up like trash, lobs it over the cab into the bed. Then, probably wanting to do good instead of bad, he tries to bend the wiper arm back to functional, but once a wiper's had torsion applied to it, it's never the same wiper. When it snaps off, he loses it for a bad few seconds, whips the hood with it over and over, chipping the paint, the rubber blade slinging out, losing itself in the faded black of the parking lot.

Harper hugs him from the back until he's calm, Meg watching through the windshield, the radio still pushing the same static now because Dillon's outburst has frozen her in her seat. She's not used to being around adult-sized men, Harper realizes. They're bulls in the china shop of her young life, bulls that can go red-eyed for any reason.

Dillon sags down to the ground, his head pushed into the crusty side of the truck, and Harper goes with.

"I would have stopped us too, if I were him," he's saying. "He was just . . . he was just doing his *job*."

"It's not on you," Harper tells him.

He turns around, careless of the seat of his pants on the asphalt, and stares up into the sky, his face greasy *and* wet now, his eyes blinking fast.

"I should—" he starts, swallows, starts again: "Y'all go on in the truck. Tell my brother you need the white Camaro. I'll, I'll *hitch*, I'll disappear. Or they'll catch me, and I was alone, I did everything, no accomplices. My mom left forever ago, my dad's on the road all the time. They'll believe anything of me."

"I don't give half a fuck what they expect you to be," Harper tells him, standing, looking around. "I know who you *are*. This isn't the end, not for either of us, and not for Meggie either. I won't let it be that. If we disappear, we disappear together, got it?"

Slowly, Dillon looks up to her.

"That doesn't mean we're back together," Harper says, her smile giving her away a bit.

Dillon pulls his lips in so he won't smile either.

"This truck is toast," he says, looking around for other options.

"I'm not becoming a car thief along with everything else," Harper tells him.

"Because that's the tipping point," Dillon says.

"I'm thinking it's more cumulative."

Dillon shrugs, can accept that. He lets her haul him up.

"You've got shit on your face," she tells him, touching her nose to show where.

"You've got shit in your hair," he tells her back, flicking it, her peripheral vision sparkling with glitter for a moment.

"The truckers know us by this stupid arrowhead," she says, nodding down to the passenger door they're standing beside.

"And the cops have our plates," Dillon says. "He had to have read them into the radio before coming up to the cab."

They nod, each knowing what they have to do.

For Harper, it's ducking back into the Ladies', making herself dig in the unmentionable trash until she comes up with a bottle of aerosol hairspray. Then she tears a blank page from the back of Kissy's journal, has Meg light a corner off the truck's lighter—it just takes breathing on it steady, not even really blowing—and then holding that burning paper in front of the faded arrowhead on the passenger side, shaking the aerosol can for one last prayer of a burst, and torching all of that decal off she can in the twenty seconds of hairspray left. The ash that's left smears wonderfully, looks like tar, or fiberglass bodywork in-process.

For Dillon, his part of it means wandering off, pinching a cigarette butt up from beside the trash and fake-smoking it until he can track who's driving alone, who's in the bathroom.

That plus a skinny dime for a screwdriver and he's walking back with a license plate tucked in the back of his jeans, under his shirt.

"Texas?" Harper says, fake-smoking that gross cigarette to cover Dillon at the bumper. "I thought we were trying to get people *not* to hate us?"

"Thought it matched the POS truck," Dillon says, and stands to appreciate his work.

"We're going to hell, aren't we?" Harper says, disgusted with how easy it is to flip a switch, be a criminal.

"Better later than now, right?" Dillon says.

"I still can't believe it, really," Harper says.

"That Kissy and Jam are gone?"

"That there are people, things, whatever like him."

"You mean he's not the only—" Dillon starts, but Harper's wide eyes stop him: a big rig's headlights are sweeping across them, the trucker gearing down to swing around but then just pulling through instead, making the circle, like he missed the spot he was aiming for. Like he was just . . . looking for someone?

"Probably just wanted to see if there was anybody here he knew," Dillon says with a smile.

It's what they used to do when they'd come up here to park: scope around for any familiar trucks or hats, then settle in to read the thoughts and lives of all the drivers coming through. Rigs and tourists and businessmen all. Dillon was especially good at the obvious emergency cases—the people hunched over, doing the peepee dance up the sidewalk.

Harper's specialty was making them all into rich snobs, looking down their noses at this grubby unclean place, the only facilities for miles in either direction—only port in a storm.

"Ex NASCAR driver," Harper says about that trucker. "He likes turning left, turning left."

"What is that, anyway?" Dillon says, that circling rig still in their conversational sights. "Rusty old Kenworth?"

"Peterbilt," Harper says. "281."

"Shit, girl," Dillon says, impressed. "Got diesel in your veins, what?"

"Their fronts look like faces," she says, "see? They were my favorite when I was a kid. My dad always pointed them out to me."

The truck's head-on to them again so they can see its headlights like two trembling eyes.

Dillon cocks his head over about that.

"Why is it—?" he says, and Harper finishes it in her head: Why are they seeing it from the front *again*?

Easy answer: because it's made the circle, is in the *car* parking lot now, is coming right at them, pouring smoke from its twin stacks, the asphalt trembling, the whole rest stop shuddering from this fundamental wrongness—from a rig pulling its long, empty flatbed up into the land of dog walkers and picture-takers.

"*Shit!*" Dillon says, diving across the hood, the Park truck already rumbling to life, because, because—Harper's coming around the passenger side fast and desperate—because Meg's behind the wheel, is at the key.

"Go go go!" Harper yells, waving her backwards, just running alongside like Dillon is, and Meg stomps the pedal an instant before pulling the shifter down into reverse.

The tire on Harper's side chirps back and takes the whole truck with it just a hair before the rig turns hard into where they just were, the curb nothing to it, the trash can even less.

"*Stop, stop!*" Dillon's screaming to Meg in some other part of the world, and Harper has the dim awareness of the Park truck crunching into the sloped-down nose of some little Chevy. She's mostly watching this antique Peterbilt slam into and *through* the camper parked three slots over. Almost immediately after that it rams the light blue work pickup parked on the other side, pushing it over until its passenger side tires catch on the curb. The work truck starts to roll over sideways, takes the front of the Peterbilt up with it and they stop together, the pickup dead on its side, the Peterbilt's ugly tough front bumper chocked up on the horizontal driver's side doors of the pickup, front tires hanging down in open air.

"Shit," Harper says.

She's only ever seen big rigs in the ditch, after the wreck, the crushed and broken cars all around. It's completely different, seeing it happen—a tank falling through the roof, from deep in the sky.

And this one's got reverse.

The driver grinds down and around to it and the drive wheels hitch and spin in the camper, pulling the front end back down with a ground-shaking clang, the pickup finding its tires again, its windshield finally blowing out like a soft exhalation of glass.

A man runs out from the bathroom, his pants clutched at his knees, and a woman is hustling two children away from this, and three or four drivers are prairie-dogged up from their front seats to get a better view of just what might be going on here, but more are starting their cars, stabbing their headlights out into a different future than this.

Harper looks across the front seat of the Park truck to

Dillon, standing by the steering wheel, his hand to Meg's shoulder, her face bloody from—from backing up into that little Chevy. Her head must have slung back from the impact and then whipped forward from the sudden stop, whipped forward into the steering wheel.

"A flatbed," Dillon says in wonder, and turns to Harper. "That's the same truck, Harp. Ninety percent sure. Hundred percent if there's statie blood on the front bumper."

"There is," Harper says, and eases the passenger door open to stand up onto the rocker panel, tippy-toe for an angle into this Peterbilt's dark cab. Before she can make even a silhouette out the rig bounces back and back, its empty forty-foot flatbed bowed up in the middle from no load, the rear bumper crunching hard into the restroom, shaking dust up from it, its low metal roof finding a new tilt, like the little building has just adjusted its hat.

The Peterbilt granny-gears it forward in a sudden hop, plowing into the work truck again, its drive wheels spinning in the trashed, bisected camper, and then it comes back harder, the flatbed's rear bumper gouging into the brick wall of the restroom now, pulling a section of it forward.

"He's not gonna stop," Harper says to Dillon and Meg. Meg grabs onto Harper's wrist. "We need to see what he looks like now," she says then. "That's—it's his secret power, right? That he can be anybody else?"

"Harp, no—" Dillon says, reaching across Meg for her, but Harper's already down and running.

Not letting herself stop to think about how stupid this is, she crosses the strip of parking lot at a leaning-ahead run, leaps up onto the empty flatbed and lands hard, rolls across that splintery rocking platform and flies halfway off the other side, only just manages to grab a dirty yellow cinch strap.

The Peterbilt stops and she knows she's in its side mirror.

She stands holding that four-inch strap for balance, feels like the smallest bullrider.

"Come out!" she calls to the cab.

The truck guns forward, trying to dislodge her, but she moves with it.

It tries reverse in as jerky a way as it can, knocking her down this time from the hard judder of the rear bumper cutting even deeper into the restroom now.

She gets back up, has that strap wrapped twice around her hand now, a suicide grip.

The truck stops, is in neutral, she can feel. At least until she lets that strap slacken the least bit, she knows. But then the truck, instead of trying to shake her, it turns off, easy as that. Like it knows when it's beat.

Harper lets the strap go, stands there waiting.

The Peterbilt's door opens and a man-shape stands up out of it, looking all around, one hand to the grab bar so he can lean out.

"Harper Harper Harper," he says, face still hidden in shadow. "Got to say, that little stunt back at the gas station, I wasn't expecting that."

"It didn't work, evidently," Harper says back.

"You are leaving quite the pile of bodies behind you, yes," he says. "You're all over the airwaves, did you know that?"

"You will be too," she says, then says his name out loud, like identifying him out in the open will give her some power over him.

He nods, shrugs, repeats it: "'Bucketmouth,' yep. Odd name, isn't it? But you don't get to choose. I don't *feel* like a largemouth bass, I mean. And it's not like this is fishing country, either."

"It's not about fish," Harper says, trying to get a line on Meg, make sure she's good.

"It's about something," Bucketmouth says. "Maybe you could cast some light on that?"

"Maybe you could tell me why you're even after us," Harper tells him. "We're not—we didn't do anything to you."

"Have you seen this face I went to so much trouble to grow?" Bucketmouth says back, turning his head to spit what Harper guesses must be blood, maybe a molar. From John Henry's fists. From all the fists, all the knees, all the boots.

"You had my *sister*," Harper says. "You left me no choice."

"Ah, the backed into a corner defense," Bucketmouth says. "I know it well. You could say it's the one I'm using now. I either take care of you and yours, now that my big secret's out, or . . . well. I'm sure you understand."

"You were doing this long before those holy rollers picked you up," Harper says.

Bucketmouth digests this, says, "Either way, did you or didn't you, aside from using this face all up, burn up all my secret ones too?"

"That was just *me*," Harper says, stepping forward. "You were there, you saw. Let them go, take me, this can be over."

"What, are you some kind of bad-ass hero girl?" Bucketmouth asks. "Seriously, hero girl, why settle for one when all three are just as easy?"

"Try it," Dillon says, swaggering up onto the trailer with all his height, all his shoulders, all his tone.

"Ah, the knight in shining armor arrives to—" Bucketmouth says, but stops from what's got Harper's attention now as well: a motion on the *other* side of the Peterbilt's narrow cab. Something's scrabbling out the open window and tumbling down, falling, crunching and yelping a sharp pitiful little cry out.

A lap dog.

"*Sheba,*" Harper says without thinking, the waiting silence making her voice travel more than she means.

This must be that rank trucker from the gas station's rig.

Bucketmouth fought or killed or wormed his way through all the fists and boots pummeling him and found this trucker stepping up into his old Peterbilt, left him lying in the tall grass, didn't realize the dog was already up in the cab until he was out on the interstate feeling for the tall gears, the better to slap a statie with.

The dog flops over on the asphalt and stands trying to scurry away but its front leg is what that crunch was. It chin-dives, rises shaking, is still trying, still mewling.

"Sheba?" Meg says then, in wonder, and Harper realizes Meg's out of the Park truck. That she heard this random nothing-dog's name. That it kind of means everything to her—is why she's on this crazy ride in the first place.

"*Meg, no!*" Harper screams, but this is already happening. All she can do is try to catch up. She grabs hold of Dillon for traction, pushing him back hard so she can launch forward. It sends her off the side of the trailer too fast. She splats but doesn't slow even a little, doesn't need skin on her knees and hands right now, just needs to get to Meg.

Meg is *to* the scrawny hurt dog now, is on her knees cradling it up. Harper slides to a hugging stop, placing herself between Meg and the footsteps she hears behind her.

She looks up through her hair and it's Bucketmouth, still with Jam's beaten-in, split open face. He's holding a tire beater. Not the kind you get off the rack but the kind that's a sawed-off bat wrapped with electrical tape. Because he left his pistol on that shelf in the store, of course.

"Can't say it wasn't a good ride," Bucketmouth says with Jam's voice—the voice *does* change—and raises the tire beater, Harper's hand and arm coming up like they're on a string attached to that tire beater, and, does she close her eyes? Either her eyes or her mind, because what Dillon says, it comes *into* the darkness she's mired in.

"Hey, numbnuts," he's saying from the far side of the flatbed he's just climbing back up onto. "I wasn't done with you."

Bucketmouth halts his swing, looks from Harper and Meg back to the flatbed, then finally nods, says to Harper and Meg, "Just be a minute, ladies. Y'all keep each other company, all right?" With that he turns around, but a couple of steps later he stops, looks back. "Did you already name that dog?" he asks, impressed it seems. "How can anybody name a dog that fast just from seeing it?"

"Dillon!" Harper calls. "*Run!*"

Dillon shakes his head no, is just standing there on the flatbed waiting like it's a canvas mat in the center of an empty arena.

Bucketmouth appraises him, shifts the tire beater to his other hand, then back.

"I would say this is going to be fun," he says, "but . . ."

He turns back to Harper and Meg, then calls out to Dillon, "Y'know? Think I will start over here, if nobody's particular."

"*No!*" Dillon says, coming to the edge of the flatbed.

Bucketmouth raises a hand to keep him there, his eyes still to Harper and Meg.

"Wonder if that dog will lick up anything I splash out of their heads?" he says loud and clear for Dillon. "Dogs don't know, right? It's just—it tastes good, why not eat it, right? That's not a bad way to get through life, you ask me."

"If you want to—" Dillon starts, but Bucketmouth's already going: "I know, I know. Mano to mano, let's beat each other senseless, blah blah, whoever hits the hardest or gets back up the most times wins, all that boring stuff. Know what, though? I've already been a couple of rounds tonight, with gentlemen significantly more, um, stout than you, no offense."

"You don't know," Dillon says.

"You're right," Bucketmouth says. "And I don't think I choose to."

"You don't have a—"

"There's always a choice," Bucketmouth says with a smile. "And this time, it's yours. Either—either I take two steps forward, bring this down into a skull or two, or . . ." He looks back and Harper takes that chance to lunge up.

She's stopped by the blunt, rounded top of that tire beater pointing right at her forehead, touching it almost, Bucketmouth looking at her down along it with Jam's swollen nearly-shut eyes, Jam's beat-to-crap face.

Still talking loud to Dillon but watching Harper now, he says, "Or . . . you look like you know your way around a load, yes? Like you might have helped secure one at some point in your life? Something about you. I've got an eye for that, see. So, what I want you to do, *Dillon*, is strap yourself down up there."

"How do I know you won't—"

"I give you my word as a weary traveler," Bucketmouth says, still watching Harper, Harper unable to move, as he can flick the tire beater either way, tap her hard on the temple. "The weariest traveler, you might say."

"You'll let them go?" Dillon asks.

"For now," Bucketmouth says, and raises his other hand, doing the Scout's honor fingers.

"Dillon, no!" Harper says, moving as little as possible.

"No, no, stay with us a little yet," Bucketmouth says over Harper to Meg, trying to creep away with the hurt dog. Then, to Harper: "Tell me what your boyfriend's doing back there if you will, Harper."

"You don't get to say my name," Harper says.

"Harper Harper Harper . . ." Bucketmouth says, tasting it and grinning wide. "Do I hear any cams ratcheting down back there?" he calls out to Dillon.

"I don't care what happens to me," Dillon says. "I'm already toast."

"Well that's no fun," Bucketmouth says, then: "If the law shows up before you're done up there, then all deals are off, you understand."

Dillon holds Harper's eyes for a long moment, then nods once and casts around for the dirty yellow strap. He finds it, pulls it, reseats the buckle onto the rail.

"No," Harper says, her throat awash with hot tears.

"Ah," Bucketmouth says about the defeat on her face. "Yes."

Dillon sits down, squirms his legs under a strap and reaches for the heavy ratchet.

"Across the *mid*section, let's say," Bucketmouth calls back.

"But lying on your stomach, of course, facing front. Once we get on the highway it'll feel like you're flying, won't it?"

"Don't," Harper says. "Please."

"I just wanted to get a little further along down the road," Bucketmouth says, shrugging like this is all too bad. "I didn't ask anyone to—"

"You can't do this," Harper tells him.

"What I'm already doing, you mean?" Bucketmouth asks, and chances a look back to the flatbed.

"Please," Harper says.

"Ah, what stage of desperation would this be?" Bucketmouth says. "We start out with denial, then flight, then comes resistance, which you're really better at than I was thinking, then . . . is dealmaking next? Are we skipping something here?"

He looks back to the truck, and all around.

"Oh yeah," he says, snapping his fingers by his head. "Next up, for you, is acceptance. Now, say goodbye."

Harper turns her head from Dillon, ratcheting himself down, and senses the tire beater coming for the side of her head.

She flinches back, looks up to Bucketmouth watching her, holding the tire beater just short of where it would have made contact with the eggshell side of her right temple.

"See you soon," he says, and jogs backwards, sits up on the flatbed and swings his legs over.

Harper rushes after, gets there as he's planting his knee into Dillon's back, watching her the whole while.

"Harp, no!" Dillon says, his face sideways against one of the wide wooden slats of the flatbed.

"*Harp, no!*" Bucketmouth falsettos, and cranks the ratchet once, tightening the strap a few clicks, and then again.

Dillon groans, his face going red.

"Stop!" Harper says to Bucketmouth, reaching ahead but not coming closer.

"This would be where I say that's entirely up to you," he says, and cranks the ratchet again, having to put his weight into it now.

Dillon pukes into the boards he's being pressed against, blood vessels in his eyes bursting.

"When I was in elementary school," Bucketmouth says, his tone all about having all the time in the world, "our classrooms and hallways would get infested at a certain time of year with these fuzzy caterpillars. You don't have them up here, but trust me, they were a plague—a beautiful one, but still a bother. Being kids, we made a game of it, of course. We found that you could step on them from back to front, and shoot all their insides out their head. Whoever got the longest spurt won, right? Too, remember this is elementary. All us young boys, we were interested in the opposite sex, but didn't know how to talk to them, exactly. Our solution? We'd wait until we saw them in proximity to a caterpillar, then we'd rush forward, our hearts full of love, and we'd step on that little caterpillar front to back, gushing caterpillar brains and guts onto the girl's shoes, or, if we really liked her, and it was a really juicy caterpillar, her *shins*. It was the only way to show the depth of our affection."

He lets that sit, then raises the ratchet handle one more time, his hand ready to drive it down, this push being the one that forces Dillon's guts up through his mouth.

"All leading to you wondering how much affection I have for you, right, Harper? Harp? Do I love you enough to send the very best? How far do you think his insides will go if I push this down just—"

"No, don't!" Harper says, backing off.

"This doesn't mean I don't love you, of course," he says, standing, his foot to that cam lever now.

"I'm going, I'm going," Harper says, still backing off, coming down to her knees beside Meg and the ratty little dog.

"Nice seeing you again," Bucketmouth says, raising his hand in farewell. "I'm sure we'll be running into each other again somewhere down the road." With that he walks up the long trailer, jumps onto the tractor, pulls around into the cab and fires the engine up first turn, all this destruction just another day at the office for this rusty Peterbilt.

"What's he going to do?" Meg says.

This time, instead of trying to go through the work truck, he backs deeper into the restroom and hauls the wheel to the right, just nudging the work truck to the side, bumping and grinding through the camper, over the curb, the flatbed rattling, Dillon's face loose against the wooden planks, his chunky throw-up stringing from his cheek to the boards over and over, but he's past caring about that now.

Pulling out of the parking lot, Bucketmouth lets the horn go, raises his hand friendly-like from the window, doesn't tap his brakes in response to the clump of blue and red lights screaming eastbound, on perfect intersection with him.

"Yes, yes, yes," Harper says, standing, stepping forward to help this along.

Just like it looked, the Peterbilt hauling Dillon away should cross perfect with all the emergency vehicles . . . except the cops and ambulances and firetrucks are shooting *over* the bridge for the officer down, and Bucketmouth is ducking *under* that bridge. All it would take is one statie to look down past the railing, see Dillon strapped down tight to the trailer. All it would take is one single fireman high in his truck looking idly over to the rest stop, at everybody standing from the rubble.

Instead, the Peterbilt eases under, its left blinker a dot of white now, the red plastic crumbled off in the restroom.

Harper sags down to her knees.

Bucketmouth makes the turn, belches smoke up into the night, and right as he's about to step up onto the interstate, all his lights turn off.

He's gone.

16

HARPER'S TRYING TO attend to the diagonal cut—more like a burst—on Meg's forehead when Meg says it in her checked-out voice: "He wants us to follow him, doesn't he?"

Harper dabs at the edge of the torn skin and Meg doesn't even wince. The dog is licking delicately at the blood pooled in the hollow of Meg's throat, its eyes on Harper the whole time. Harper can't tell if the dog's asking permission or if she's making sure Harper's not going to dart in, steal some. It doesn't matter. The dog weighs all of two pounds. Harper pushes it away from Meg's throat, tries to clean that up too.

"I thought he would have a different face by now," Harper says. "He still looks like Jam. Just, Jam all beat up."

Meg settles her eyes on Harper.

"We've got to think," Harper says. "We can't outmuscle him, probably can't outrun him, definitely can't outcrazy him, and he probably already knows every move we think we're coming up with. So, what does it *mean* that he still looks the same?"

"That he can't—can't change too much, or that fast?" Meg says with a shrug.

"Or he's a picky eater," Harper says.

"Both?" Meg tries.

Harper dabs at the blood, nods sure, both, could be. And ten other things besides. The phase of the moon, blood type, rate of human digestion, presence or absence of snacks to burn as fuel. On and on. Maybe it only works at highway speeds, even.

"I need to get you home," she tells Meg.

"The one you're running away from, you mean?" Meg says.

"It's not—that's just me and Mom," Harper says. "Nothing about you."

"It's because you're just the same," Meg says.

"I'm not like her," Harper says. "I won't ever be like her."

"'Watch out for boyfriends like Dillon, Meg,'" Meg parrots with their mom's 'talking while doing the hateful dishes'-delivery. "Is he a movie nobody in our family should rewatch the next night, because we all know how it ends?"

Harper licks her lips, looks back to the truck, crunched into the blue Beretta, and tries to figure out whether that's what that last big blowout was really about or not. And also wondering how little sisters can be so perceptive. But, years hiding in the corner, watching, listening? Maybe they are, yeah. Maybe they can be.

Still, "I thought I was smart when I was twelve, too," Harper says.

"Said Mom to Harper, when she was twelve," Meg says right back, and Harper winces to have to remember *that* big blowout.

"I'm trying to keep your head wound from leaking your brain out, here," Harper says.

"I'm using that brain," Meg says with an evil grin, and brings her hands up, picking another dab of glass from Harper's hair.

"Then use it to help us," Harper says. "Why does he want me to follow him? He could have ended it right here if he wanted."

"Something worse, right?" Meg says. "Isn't that the only reason you drag a thing out? Because there's something better for you at the way end of it?"

"Worse for me is better for him," Harper says, sitting back, Meg's forehead as good as it's going to get without a first-aid kit or an emergency room, a time machine or a magic wand.

"So it's all about you?" Meg says, sucking the dot of blood from the pad of her finger from that last shard she plucked from Harper's hair.

"Like you weren't already losing enough blood?" Harper says.

Meg shrugs, keeps sucking.

"And, it's about *me* because I'm not letting *you* go any further down this road, remember?" Harper says.

"It's my fault he has Dillon," Meg says, the dog back in her lap, favoring its shattered front leg.

"It's not your fault," Harper says.

"Y'all were going to have him up there on that trailer until I . . ." Meg says. "Sorry?"

"He was as surprised by Sheba as we were," Harper says. "It's not like that was some big plan he had. He just, like, took advantage. Anyway, I don't say her name like that, you don't come out to save her."

"Why *did* you call her that?"

"Because that's her name," Harper says, nodding down to the dog's tags. Meg thumbs them up from the fur: QUEEN SHEBA on one side, DON'T TREAD ON ME on the other.

"I'm keeping her," Meg says, roughing the dog up between its alert ears.

"Have to ask Mom," Harper says, flicking her eyes away from the pale Buick one building over that she's only just realizing she's been staring at.

She's been here all along.

Mom.

Shit.

Her car's okay, though. She's not in it now, too, meaning . . . restroom? Not coming out until all the crashing and destruction is for sure over?

More important, she hasn't seen her daughters huddled together in the parking lot.

"What?" Meg says, registering Harper's eyes, but Harper—no time to think of a proper fake-out—hunches forward like in pain. It works: Meg stops cranking her head over to clock the Buick, reaches forward to help.

"Just—glass in my hair," Harper grunts, losing her fingers in her hair, where she's pretty sure there really *is* glass.

"Here," Meg says, and starts threading the larger shards out.

"Why aren't the cops here yet?" she says, completely focused on Harper's hair now.

"Busy night," Harper says, watching the door of the Ladies' so closely, now. "Think they're spread kind of thin. And—" making a show of casing the rest stop, because she can't have Meg seeing that Buick—"no payphone here. If they hear about a trucker losing his shit at Wagonhound, it'll be from another trucker, most likely."

"And they don't rat their own out," Meg completes, citing The Gospel of Dad.

"I don't know if Bucketmouth counts as a trucker," Harper says. "But I guess he was driving a truck, yeah, so how would the other truckers know he wasn't one of them."

"Bucketmouth," Meg repeats, sort of tasting it. "That's like —what is it? Buffalo Bill, yeah. From that movie we rented."

"He's made up, just on video," Harper says. "Bucketmouth's real."

As proof, she nods to the destroyed Men's restroom across from them, which it's completely safe for Meg to look at.

"In the movie version, he'd have driven right through that in slow motion," Harper says. "And it wouldn't even mess his grille up."

"So we know he can drive a truck," Meg says.

Harper nods, hadn't considered that.

"I can too, though," she says. Then, quieter, "Dad was going to teach you too. He told me."

"It's a truck-driving contest?" Meg says back.

"Me and him, maybe," Harper says. "Not you and me."

It's always been an unspoken point of contention or jealousy or something, that Harper, just because she was born first, ended up having more time with Dad. More memories of him.

Guilty as she feels for that, though, she wouldn't trade them.

"He can ride a motorcycle, too," Harper goes on, getting her and Meg over this conversational hump. "If he . . . if he lives out here on the road like this, catching rides and, you know, *eating* people, we have to think there's not anything he can't drive, and there's no cab or car or bike he can't talk his way into, onto, whatever. If we think like that, then he can't surprise us."

"Road graders, harvesters, cop cars," Meg enumerates,

narrowing her eyes to try to think of what else could be traveling by interstate.

Harper nods, has to accept this: not only can Bucketmouth change faces on some obscure schedule or mechanism, but every vehicle on the road, it has the potential to have him behind the wheel.

"RVs," Meg adds, still doing that. "School buses. Normal buses."

"Those big things that change the concrete dividers," Harper adds with a grin. Her and Meg have only ever seen those on the news—with Dillon, right?—and this stretch of 80 doesn't have anything like that going on, but still. If you're going to dream, dream big.

That probably goes for nightmares as well.

"Those three-wheeler choppers," Meg says, trying to make this last. "Trains?"

"He's getting away in something right now," Harper says, standing like looking for him. She tips her head to the Ladies', says, "Grab a handful of paper towels for your bleedy head, and we'll hit it."

"We," Meg says, letting Harper haul her up.

"Sisters," Harper says.

"Even though he *wants* us to come out there again?" Meg says.

"He's got Dillon," Harper says back, in defeat. "His game is the only game, for now."

"But he'd come for us, wouldn't he?" Meg says. "If we just . . . *sat* here?"

"Dillon," Harper says, pressing her lips together after saying it, meaning: they have to give chase, can't just sit here.

Meg can't argue with that, just says about the bathroom run Harper's sending her on, "I thought you said there weren't any paper towels in there?"

"I didn't check if there were any pads," Harper says. "We can stick one to your big head."

With that, she nudges Meg off to do this last errand. "I'll extract the truck from your great parking job," she adds, turning back to survey the damage.

"The parking job that saved us all, you mean?" Meg says, leaving for the Ladies' at last, thank you.

"Taking your rat?" Harper says about the dog. "I got a truck to care for, can't be babysitting."

Meg scoops Sheba up—Harper's already calling her that in her head, not "dog."

"She needs to go too, you think?" Meg says with a smile, twirling away with the dog.

"Be safe," Harper calls out, nominally about these paper towels, that restroom, but she means it just generally as well, and for it to last for however many years it's about to be until she sees her little sister again. If ever.

"Bye, girl," she says where Meg can't hear, then makes herself turn away, wipes the tears from her eyes, and steps up through the Park truck's missing door, and then can't help it once she's in the seat—she has to cry, thinking of her mom taking two long steps from the sink to pull Meg to her, hold her and hold her, not let her go all the way back to Laramie.

"You're welcome, Mom," Harper says and fires the truck up, screeches and tears and drags away from the hurt Beretta then pulls out of Wagonhound through the entrance, taillights off. If they even work anymore.

WHEN HER DAD didn't come back from his Tacoma run her sophomore year, Dillon found Harper on the roof of that same apartment complex. They were broken up that May—Dillon had Jennifer Chalmers's initials in fancy white script on the passenger side back glass of his truck, and Harper was making sure to be seen with Randal Sees Bull—but evidently Harper's mom had been calling around for where her oldest daughter might be, and her oldest daughter's main ex-boyfriend was standing around the kitchen, overheard that call.

"What are you doing up here?" Harper said to him without even looking around.

"Don't worry, I didn't tell her where you'd be," Dillon said back, settling into the gravel beside her but not touching sleeves.

"Her?"

"Your mom."

"Good," Harper said. "It's her fault."

Dillon looked over to her about this. She could feel it.

"Thought you might be hungry," he said at last, and pulled a paper-wrapped burger from his pocket. It was from the cooler at the truckstop.

"You nuke it?" she asked.

"A minute longer," Dillon said, leaning forward to connect the burger with her hand. "Knew it'd cool down, getting here."

"Your defroster's broke in your truck now, what?" Harper asked, tearing into the rubbery bun.

"My defroster?"

"You can turn it on high, set your food up there to warm it," Harper said, blinking fast. "My dad taught it to me, said it's how you can still have a hot meal at sixty miles per hour."

"Got to drive with the windows down, I bet," Dillon said.

"Got to do that anyway," Harper said. "Bunk smells like a locker room."

They were her dad's exact words. They were what made her finally start crying, the kind she couldn't stop. When Dillon edged closer like to maybe touch her shoulder, she pushed away, stayed alone.

"How late is he this time?" he asked.

"It was just *Tacoma*," Harper said. "Electronics. It's not even winter, right? What could happen between Wyoming and fucking Washington? Why wouldn't he have called?"

Dillon just sat there, finally extracting another burger from his pocket, opening it for himself.

"Unless you want it," he said about the burger.

Harper just stared at it.

"If—if nothing happened to him," she said, like there was a jury that could hear this logic, make it so, "and we'd have heard about it if it had, then, then, then what does that *leave*?"

Dillon just squinted and chewed.

"It means he saw his exit is what it means," Harper said, wiping her eyes hard. "He saw a way to get away from my mom and he took it, just left his rig somewhere nobody'd ticket it for a few weeks and walked away. I don't blame him."

"He's probably just hung up somewhere," Dillon said. "Maybe the cops jammed him up about something."

"For delivering electronics he has a bill of lading for?"

"I mean, they're *cops*."

Harper couldn't deny that. "He used to always tell me there were aliens," she said then, quieter. "Maybe that's what happened."

Dillon watched her about this until she looked away. "I don't think aliens would take him," he said, then added, "If they've got UFOs, then they're pretty covered for electronics, think?"

"Mom was always saying he was just like his brothers," Harper said then, just all at once. "That he only cared about making enough to get through this week. That he wasn't thinking big enough thoughts, that he wasn't thinking long-term."

"My mom and dad used to fight too," Dillon said, shrugging.

Harper looked over to him, didn't say the obvious: that his parents divorced five years ago, that his mom lived two floors below where they were sitting now, that his dad took every job he could and hadn't turned in an honest logbook for years, just to stay gone as much as he could.

In the truckstops she always moved through like a dream when making a run with her dad, him having to shake her awake to go inside and hold onto her shoulders for the first few steps to keep her upright, all the blankets and caps always had some version of a trucker or a biker merging with an Old West cowboy or Indian, and going kind of grand and transparent in the process.

Was that what had happened to her dad? Had he zoned out coming down a grade and just shimmered away, gone ghost without even dying, without leaving a fiery wreck behind? Was he still out there haunting the slow lane, finally at peace? Was he Phantom 309 now for hitchhikers? If it meant not having to go home and be reminded what a failure he was, then yeah, that might be him, Harper figured.

Fading into the backdrop was all he had left, his only real option anymore if he wanted to stay the same person he'd always been. But he *could* have come home, that was the thing Harper couldn't let go. Not for Mom, Mom hated him, but for his *daughters*. He could have come home long enough to take them with, anyway, couldn't he have? They could live in the bunk, who cared what it smelled like. It smelled like him, and that had to be better than never seeing him again.

"So . . ." Dillon said then, right when Harper's thoughts were really roiling and churning, about to spill over, make her stand up and sling her hamburger off the edge of the building, "so you're gambling on him driving between here and here?" He held up his right finger to mark where the part of 80 they could see started, then his left finger to show where it ended.

"He has to come through there to get to here," Harper said, obviously, ready to fight about this. Looking forward to it, even.

"But," Dillon said almost meekly, squinching his face up like he didn't want to have to be the one to tell her something this obvious, "have you tried, you know, looking for him on the air?"

"On TV?" Harper said, pretty sure this fight was about to be on.

"My dad's home right now," Dillon said, setting his burger down half-eaten and wincing: "Sorry, I didn't mean that—"

"You said we could find him," Harper said, setting her burger down as well.

"We can try," Dillon said. "We can use my dad's CB—*that* air. I know where his keys are."

Harper stood into this new idea, looked around at all the possibilities: someone out there had to know, had to have seen him, had to have heard something. Going CB to CB, you could leapfrog across states in no time, cast a blanket as wide as you could want.

Her dad would be under that blanket somewhere, she knew. He had to be. There was no trucker out there who wouldn't pass along a message from another trucker's kid.

"Well?" she said, tilting her head to the idea of Dillon's dad's truck only a half-mile walk away, and he stood and they walked to the broken roof door together, and he jogged ahead at the very end to pull it open for her like always, and *that's* the Dillon Harper's pulling onto the interstate for now, no door on her left side, blood and pee on the windshield, vomit in the floorboard, tears running back from her eyes, into her hair.

The Dillon she's going after, it's the Dillon who jogged ahead to catch that door for her when she was perfectly capable of getting it herself. But it made her feel special. Just like her dad always did when he was home. And, right before stepping through that open door, to sit up all night with Dillon talking to truckers under the dome light of his dad's million-mile Mack, she'd looked back to the interstate one last hopeful time, just on the chance, and what she saw was their two paper-wrapped truckstop burgers side by side in the gravel, which is how she knew he wasn't going to be with Jennifer Chalmers much longer, that her initials were going to be all over his life.

Like they still are, Harper figures.

Only, now they're carved in, and he's bleeding from them.

Which is pie-in-the-sky hopeful, she knows. If he's bleeding, he's still alive.

But if a monster's a real monster, then it has to be able to sit by you on a flatbed trailer and bite your index finger off, chew the meat from each side of it like a chicken wing while your stump burbles blood out onto the wood slats.

Why wouldn't Bucketmouth want to be a tall, strong eighteen-year-old with sure hands, a quick smile, a devil-probably-doesn't-care reckless look to his eyes?

Trick is, though, the first rule of taking someone's face and life, it's got to be erasing the chance of there being two of you in the same aisle at the truckstop at any point.

Harper puts her foot into the pedal, tries to go faster.

17

THE TRUCKERS ARE no longer blowing their air horns down at her when they sweep past, and there's no more spit cups drifting through the air for her windshield, no more cigarettes sparking into the cab. It can't be because of the arrowhead she burned and rubbed off the passenger door—the Park truck's not limping past anybody in the left lane, so the only eyes seeing that smudged arrowhead are the deer and coyotes out in the pasture, and they don't care.

It can't be the Texas plates letting her slip past either, she doesn't think. Texas plates in Wyoming, where the cowboys are *real*, are more an invitation for abuse than a shield. Probably it's that word of her circulating from cab to cab like a joke or a call to brotherhood or an appeal for justice, it went *with* the group of truckers who are now asleep, or in another state. They didn't hand the instructions about what to do with and to this Park truck back to the next set of wheels rolling in, and so now that be-on-the-lookout-for was getting forgotten. Not forgiven, but there were other idiot drivers on the road to deal with. And schedules to keep. That always has to come first: the schedule. And Harper isn't on it anymore, it doesn't feel like.

At first she thinks this is good, but a few miles to the west she decides that really, the truckers not paying her any attention anymore, that just leaves her out here even more alone, where Bucketmouth can do whatever he wants.

If she ever even catches up with him, that is.

When the temperature needle edges close to the red she flips the heater on, feels not even one speck of that warmth. The brown Audi passes her again and the college kids don't look over this time—it's dark in the Park truck's cab now, thanks to Dillon yanking the fuse—and Harper wonders if they were at Wagonhound when it came tumbling down, are still shellshocked. If not, then they're just in a loop, driving west until the turnaround at the fire then hooking it back this way, deciding twenty minutes into it that the interstate has to be open by now, doesn't it? They're the Moth People, Harper decides. They're just battering themselves against that bright light over close to Laramie, getting singed, then drifting away, coming back for more in tighter and more suicidal circles.

It doesn't matter.

She rolls through the AM for a voice—church, politics, sports, weather, whatever—but the statie evidently took the antenna into the ditch with him. She resigns herself to side B of the Gordon Lightfoot.

"Where are you, where are you?" she says to Bucketmouth, leaning forward like being ten inches closer to the windshield is going to be what makes him pop out in the headlights. But this Park truck's about to boil over, too, and if it does, she's back to riding her thumb, and that's no way to save Dillon. She hits the heel of her hand on the top of the steering wheel in frustration and drifts the truck onto exit 260. There's no lights calling her in, no signs talking about services leading up to it, and the ramp is hardly even maintained, might as well have grass growing in the cracks, but still, she slows, looks left and right, comes to a full stop at the intersection.

Nothing. Wyoming at night. A wide spot in the road, and hardly even that.

The gauge is edging up to 230, is in the red now because it doesn't have fast air cooling the radiator.

"Why do you suck so much?" Harper says to the Park truck—and to herself, she guesses—easing back into that cool wind, then feels bad, pats the dash. This stupid unsellable truck *did* keep them from getting steamrolled on that first ramp out of Laramie, she guesses, which probably used up its last gasp of youth, and it's taken some hits meant for them since then, for sure. The windshield is trash, the door is gone, the rear bumper's crunched up into the gas tank, and she doesn't even want to think about all the body fluids splashed around. Including statie blood, which is just blood, she tells herself. From a person who *was* living, isn't anymore. A person who was just doing his job, stopping who his cop radio was telling him to stop.

Shit.

To say nothing of that explosion at the pullout, all the lives and schedules probably left burning there. And what if there was somebody in that restroom when Bucketmouth pulled it down, right?

Is this all fallout from the fight she had with her mom over Omar Epps, or would some version of this be happening anyway, with someone else? The first read on the situation puts her at the center of the world, which she very much knows not to be true, but the second just accepts that all this bad stuff was unstoppable, so why even try.

But at least Meg's on the way back to Laramie, Harper tells herself. With their mom, sure, but Harper survived her high school years in that house, under that regime. Meg can too. And who knows, maybe it really was a Harper and her mom thing all along. Maybe it'll be better with Meg. Or maybe her mom's learned something, has some regrets, will try harder now.

Harper cues fast through that moany shipwreck song, can't handle it right now, thank you, and then she sings along with the next one even though she doesn't like it. It's not about staying awake, it's about trying to keep from thinking and dwelling and wishing, none of which helps.

All that's going to help is seeing that rusty old Peterbilt and turning the steering wheel that way, dealing with whatever comes next.

"The one that's not here, not here . . ." Harper mutters, coasting through this dead exit, taking the sad excuse for a ramp back onto the interstate.

The truck cools down to 220 again with the wind cooling the radiator, but even at just forty-five, that temperature gauge won't let its little arm fall any lower. The gas tank didn't puncture on that Beretta, though, which is a miracle in itself, since these trucks were built to explode, pretty much. Harper tucks her hair down the back of the leather jacket then zips it up tight to her neck. It's not a ponytail holder, but it's better than nothing. She should have got one from Meg, who wears them like bracelets, like she's the Girl Scout of hair bands, but screw it.

"Where are you, where are you?" she says again, to remind herself.

And if she makes Utah before finding Dillon? What then?

Well, first, half a tank won't get her that far. But, even Rawlins, right? If she rolls into Rawlins, hasn't seen Dillon, what then? Keep driving, or follow the Audi's maybe-lead and just start making circles, showing the truck from all sides to draw Bucketmouth out?

"Tell a cop," she says out loud. Obviously. Except this truck is probably on video shaking a torn-in-half statie off its hood.

If she could just cue forward and backwards like this cassette tape in the deck, she thinks. She'd either jump ahead to after this is all over and her and Dillon could lift a sad beer to it, or she'd go back to right after the big storm-out, and this time she'd take the east ramp instead of the west. Then Kissy and Jam never find her on their way back to Yellowstone. Her sister might still be following her, but—so she watches Harper go one way instead of the other? Who cares. Going east like that, too, Harper doesn't tangle up with the Thunderbird people, which has to be where this all started. If she doesn't take their bottle of water and stupid glow bracelet, then she doesn't feel obligated to follow that big red car out into the pasture, Dillon doesn't hike Bucketmouth's lost duffel bag of baby food jars onto his shoulder, Harper doesn't insist they burn it, along with a few trucks and as many acres of BLM as they can. Wagonhound survives the night as well. And Kissy, and Jam, and the statie.

Kissy maybe finishes her journal and tucks it into a drawer for her someday daughter to find, read on the sly, find out that her mom was once young and stupid too. Younger and stupider than anyone ever. And so in love with Jam, who Harper guesses had to have been strangled out in the bushes, Bucketmouth watching his eyes lose their light the whole while.

This is what her dad always told her was the worst part about driving alone: living in the cab with nobody but yourself to talk to. You end up cycling through the same bullshit over and over.

Harper turns "Sundown" up, is kind of actually starting to tolerate that one.

Halfway between exit 255 and where she knows there's a gas station or a truckstop a few minutes ahead, Harper lets her foot off the gas and watches something slip past on a white stripe.

Not a dead animal, not a cup let go from a window.

She checks her rearview, coasts to a stop, backs up in three hitches, between approaching headlights, then pulls up right alongside.

A boot.

"No," she says, rushing to it, looking up at the coming headlights.

The boot's Dillon's, though. She can tell from how the back quarter of the heel is worn down, from that leg-dragging way he walks when he thinks he's bad, when he's got his gunfighter eyes on. Which is most of the time.

Harper blinks her tears away.

She leans over, hooks a finger through the pull-hole, and rolls out of the way of a car-hauler barreling past, horn blasting.

Breathing hard, gravel speckled all over her, calving off, Harper sets the boot on the seat beside her.

Four or five miles later she slows for what turns out to be the camo cap he had on. It's held to the stripe by a heavy bolt laid crosswise over it.

Harper shakes the bolt off, seats the hat on her head, the brim low over her eyes.

At least the boot doesn't have a foot in it, she's telling herself. At least there's no blood on the inside of the cap. Oh, wait: except Dillon didn't have a cap on when he strapped himself down, did he? Even if he did, it would have blown away just on the on-ramp. Meaning—shit—this is that one Bucketmouth stole from Akal, when he said it was *him* who should be wearing the Realtree.

Harper peels out of it, tosses it through the rear window into the bed. She pulls onto the shoulder to let a rig slam past then gets back up to speed, the temperature back up above 230 now from all the reverse action, which is the opposite of putting air against the radiator, she knows.

Passing exit 235, watching the white stripes closer than she ever has, Harper chances a look down the ramp not taken, sees a boot standing up in the middle of it. She cuts hard right, gouges across the long narrow triangle of grass, the Park truck fishtailing like it wants to start rolling but she turns into it as best she can, rides it out until the tires crash up onto the asphalt of the ramp and she can brake.

To the right is a Shell station. She sees it for maybe two seconds before the dust she dragged up catches up, engulfs her. It takes nearly a half minute to settle. A half minute until she can breathe. Two rigs whine by on the interstate but the drivers must be able to tell she's not a wreck, has done this intentionally. Either that or they don't want to get involved, have already heard over the air that Wyoming tonight is haunted as hell, best just keep on truckin'.

Harper coughs and looks around the Shell station. It's what her dad would have called a cigar box—small, square, temporary. Cigar boxes were his generation's comparison for everything.

There's truck parking behind it because you've got to cater, but only one rusty old Peterbilt, looking back at her with its headlight eyes. One rusty old Peterbilt 281. Translation: this is mostly just a gas station, doesn't have showers or booths, doesn't keep the deli fired up twenty-four/seven. More like sunup to sundown, for the daylight crowd. No lights are even on now. Could be it's closed down, even. The pumps are still there, though. Just, nobody to take any money for a quarter tank.

Harper sits at the turn, the Park truck's engine loping unevenly, gasping for cool air.

Either that Peterbilt she knows and will never forget isn't idling, or Bucketmouth's got all the lights turned off. There's a house with green trees just past the parking lot, which means somebody lives there, and there's an old rowhouse in the parking lot with all its windows gone, turned into empty eye sockets.

Harper tries to make anything out on the Peterbilt's flatbed, can't in the darkness, even though there's a massive white tank behind it like a sideways silo. For gas, maybe? It's too big for propane or butane anyway, she thinks. Never mind that the go-juice is usually in underground tanks.

"Enough stalling," she says to herself for resolve, but kind of in farewell too. This is some version of a trap, zero doubt about that, but what choice does she have? Bucketmouth led her here, sure, but that's exactly what she was wanting.

She dials the Park truck down to parking lights so as not to wake the sleepers in that house, hauls the wheel over to the right, eases down the blacktop and into the crunchy surface of the truck parking. When she's head-on with the middle of the flatbed trailer, she turns her brights on all at once, throwing a line of shadow onto the big white tank.

Just like she didn't want to have to see, Bucketmouth's sitting there alongside Dillon, still has him strapped down tight. He shields his eyes and in that hand is a little knife, the blade huge in shadow against the tank.

Harper steps on the brights button, brings the headlights down to not-quite-so-blinding.

Bucketmouth waves thanks, and then, like he's been waiting for an audience, for the right spotlight, he brings the knife down to Dillon's hand, hits it once with the heel of his other hand, and snatches a flying front joint of an index finger from the air, easy as anything, like he was born to do this.

Dillon's body shudders, some part of his knocked-out self registering the pain, the loss, but he doesn't wake, quite.

Harper surges the truck forward like that's supposed to be any kind of threat but stops just short of the flatbed. Bucketmouth watches this with bored eyes, doesn't even flinch.

He says something she can't hear over the engine so she kills it.

"Gonna need your lighter," he says, over-enunciating, and holds his hand out for it.

She pulls it, holds it out, but he shakes his head no, says, "Heat it up, please? If you really love him?"

Harper pushes the lighter in, waits the twenty seconds, Dillon's finger blood pooling around his hand—she's standing on the rocker panel, can't help looking. When the lighter pops out she hot-potatoes it up to Bucketmouth. He catches it, juggles it to get the non-burny end, then, before its glowing-red coils can ash over, he presses it onto Dillon's stump, holds it there, the flesh sizzling, smoke rising. He breathes its deliciousness in, closes his eyes, then steps back.

They both watch Dillon's hand.

The blood doesn't come again.

"Call me the Florence Nightingale of the road," he says, blowing on the lighter, turning to toss it off the other side of the flatbed then stopping himself: "Boom," he says about the big white tank, wowing his eyes out. Instead he underhands the lighter over the cab of the Park truck, into the bed.

"Resale's better if all original parts are there," he says with a smile, about the lighter finding the truck it was born with.

"Are you done now?" Harper says back. "I've got half the cops in Wyoming here in five minutes. That's how much headstart you've got."

"Half the cops in Wyoming . . ." Bucketmouth says, still Jam under all that damage, grandstanding on the flatbed like it's his own personal stage. "So, what, six officers? Seven?" He laughs about this. "They've got bigger fish to fry tonight, I'm afraid—or, *un*fry, as it were. And anyway, how are you supposed to have called this particular emergency in before it even happened?"

"Handheld CB in the bed," she says. "That statie you clipped?"

"Clipped in *half*, yeah," Bucketmouth says. "And if that radio's still in the bed, then that means you haven't been using it, doesn't it?"

"How'd you know I'd follow?" Harper says.

"Specimen like this?" Bucketmouth says, pushing the toe of Jam's hiking boot into Dillon's side. "How could you not? Good nineteen-year-old stock—"

"Eighteen."

"—liver's mostly whole, long limbs, kind of rangy but with promise once he settles down. More smalltime rodeo hero than underwear model, but he's definitely a product of this great state, wouldn't you say? None of that matters to you though, does it? You love him, don't you? That's why you're here."

"We're not together," Harper says.

"No single people in a fox hole," Bucketmouth says, turning on his heel like a professor on a television show, lecturing. "Though I do wonder where your precious little sister is, now . . ."

"Gone," Harper says. "You'll never get her."

Bucketmouth shrugs, watching some car or rig pass on the interstate.

"Don't they look like they're just going to launch up into the sky?" he says, and Harper risks a look back at the bridge, at the headlights now on the other side of it, headed west.

She comes back to Bucketmouth, says, "Just give him to me, walk away. I won't say anything to anybody."

"Going back to bargaining?" Bucketmouth says, disappointed. "Thought we were past that?"

"I was already running away," Harper says. "Give him back to me, I just keep on doing that. Nobody even knows I was here for all this. If nobody asks me any questions, then I don't slip up answering."

"Spoken like a true criminal," Bucketmouth says. "You've got potential, Harper. You might actually make it out here—" He holds Dillon's finger over his lips, shushing himself, then adds, "I mean, I mean you probably *would* have made it out here on the mean old road. If you hadn't run into someone who's been doing this longer than you've been alive."

"*Why* are you doing it?" Harper says.

"Because it's *fun*," Bucketmouth says right back, a distinct glitter to his eye, "and because why not," and with that squats down to the other side of Dillon, stands with a flourish, presenting . . . a five-gallon gas can? It's one of the old ones, round, metal, and rusted, its yellow emblem long since faded, its spigot stumpy and connected to the handle in some many-jointed way that probably seemed like a good idea in 1942.

Bucketmouth swirls it down to his feet then props a boot up on it, shakes a cigarette up from the pack in his shirt pocket, flicks a match alight with his thumbnail.

"Could your friend Jam do that?" he says, cupping the cigarette and leaning down to light it. "All that potential, untapped."

"What did you do to him?" Harper says. "If you—if you just have to eat a part to steal somebody's face, then . . ."

"Hopeful, good," Bucketmouth says. "We can use that. We can definitely use that."

He breathes in deep, extracts the cigarette to study the red coal at the end of it, then nods, satisfied, and pulls the gas can up by the handle, so the spigot opens into a gaping mouth.

"Careful," he says, splashing some onto and around Dillon but keeping his own boots dry.

"What—?" Harper says, coming down to the ground to rush up there.

Bucketmouth holds the cigarette up, says, "Don't want me dropping this on accident now, do you?"

Harper stops at the thick metal edge of the flatbed, is looking right into Dillon's face.

She thought he was unconscious. He's not. He's just past being able to care.

She hikes herself up, straightens her arms just as Bucketmouth steps onto the Park truck's hood, still splashing . . . it's not gas? It's sweeter, more oily.

"Kerosene," Bucketmouth says. "Doesn't burn fast as unleaded, but burns longer. And, for our purposes here, I'd say it's fast enough."

Harper, not on the flatbed yet, just glares at him.

He nods like that's not unexpected here and sits down on the hood, slides off, still trickling kerosene out.

"I'm not going to let you do this," Harper says, coming back down to the ground, glaring at him.

"Good," Bucketmouth says. "Because, believe me, I don't want to. Fireball like this will draw more eyes than would be . . . *beneficial.* All I want is for us to have a sit-down, like. This is just insurance." He pats the gas can. The kerosene.

"He needs medical attention *now*," Harper says.

"Won't take but this long," Bucketmouth says, and holds his cigarette out horizontal like a timeline, then stabs it into his mouth, fishes the box of Reds up from his pocket, slings it into the scrub without tracking it.

"Matches too," Harper tells him.

"Smart girl," Bucketmouth says, squinting from his own smoke, grubbing the box of matches up too. Instead of tossing them he shakes one out, pins it in the little paper drawer and holds it to the cherry of his cigarette, waits for it to flare up before tossing the lit box to Harper.

She wants worse than anything to slap it back at him, to make him flinch from the sparks then go for his eyes, his balls, his heart if he has one, but an ember might fall into the kerosene he's pouring. The kerosene that leads up the hood of the truck, right to Dillon.

She catches the box, tosses it clear of them and they both watch it spurt flame out both sides when it lands.

"Here I am," Harper says. "Talk, if that's what this is about."

"Over there," Bucketmouth says, pointing with his lips to the rear of the Shell station. "Got a little picnic all ready for us, and just enough of this"—the kerosene—"to get us there."

"One cigarette," Harper says, falling in, keeping her feet and pants legs clear of the splash.

A crotch rocket on the bridge throttles into the brief climb, trying to make more of the rise than there really is, and Harper looks away right as it crests, doesn't know whether it's going to launch into the sky, become a constellation, or crash and burn.

BUCKETMOUTH WORKS THE gas can onto the ratty picnic table sitting bent and ugly behind the Shell station, one of its tubular legs chained to a cinderblock. Not against thieves, but the wind. The tabletop is mounded with salty snacks and candy bars, jerky and peanuts, all evidently carried here by the armful, dumped and spilled. The back door of the Shell station is kicked in, hanging on by the top hinge.

Bucketmouth settles into what's apparently his side of the table, the one that keeps his back to the station, which she guesses he knows is empty. Unlike the parking lot that'll be behind Harper, where people from the house could appear at any moment. She'll see that in his eyes, though, she tells herself.

She sits down opposite him.

"You could have started honking back there, you know," he tells her, like a coach critiquing her game. "Woke the neighbors up, maybe slipped away with your beau while I was talking them down. Or, you know. Getting them *quiet*."

"He's not my boyfriend," Harper says again.

"You just drove a beat to hell truck to a dangerous place with a guy like me at midnight in the middle of nowhere because he's a good friend?"

"It's not midnight."

"More dramatic if it is, c'mon. You got to work with what you got, don't you know."

"That what all this is?" Harper says about the plundered snacks.

"Didn't know what you liked," Bucketmouth says.

"Not hungry."

"That makes one of us," he says, and tears into a bag of Fritos.

"What do I call you? Bucketmouth?"

"*Sir*," he says, then has to laugh. "No, no, sorry. I just always wanted to say that. Um . . . not 'BM' either." He has to stop to chuckle about this as well.

Harper regards him, says, "Are you drunk?"

"On life," he says back with a guilty shrug.

Harper nods to the cigarette he's just holding, not smoking down.

He obligingly takes a drag, angles his mouth up to exhale into the blackness.

"Not often I get to really *talk* with someone," he says. "I mean, without all the buildup on my part, of when am I going to carve a piece of them off. You know."

"I really don't."

He looks back to Dillon like checking on him.

"This your way of telling me you're not going to eat me?" Harper asks. "Because I'm a girl?"

He smiles a tolerant smile, pulls the cover off the gas can's spigot and ashes delicately into it, Harper's fingers spread wide on the table to push away, as if it's possible to outrun the kind of explosion that would be.

"You're Native American," he says, twirling his cigarette hand to indicate her hair, her skin, the whole deal.

"We not good enough for you?"

"Endangered species," he says with a grin. "What can I say? I'm a conservationist."

"More of us than you think," Harper tells him.

"Said the girl who . . . *didn't* want me to take a bite out of her?"

"You just don't want to be a girl," Harper tells him.

"Native Americans—"

"Indians."

"You have natural immunity or something, I don't know," he says. "Your kind is just meat to my kind. And, if it's just about meat, then give me a double cheeseburger at the drive-in, thanks."

"Your *kind*?" Harper asks.

"More of *us* than you'd think," Bucketmouth says, gesturing grandly with his cigarette. "I mean, active and aware, no, okay, not that many. But who knows. It's not like we have a clubhouse. Really, I bet a lot of people can do . . . *this*"—Jam's face—"but they never think to *try*, or it starts to happen and they freak out, wreck into a bridge pylon, fall out a window, choke on a sandwich, hang themself in a closet."

"You mean, they never eat someone's ear, so never know they could have looked like that person?" Harper asks, incredulous.

"I found out in Vietnam," he says, as if Harper might have

asked. "It was a . . . you could call it a bad day, I guess. Like every single other day over there. Except, next morning, I slipped through the lines with a face like Charlie, right?"

"From eating someone," Harper says flatly.

"I wasn't even hungry," Bucketmouth says like this is all history, so hardly matters. "I was in a, like, a hamster tunnel I guess you'd call it, Charlie was all over the place in their black PJs and slope hats, and then my tunnel started caving in from the rain, and from them poking sticks down to find where I was. It was a bad situation all around. But then, doing that Army-crawl up out of that tunnel, hoping for the light at the end, y'know, who do I bump faces with but a gook sent down to flush me out? We got all tooth and nail like happens when you meet a body coming through the rye, and then I just, yeah, I bit his lips, pulled them away, and then I was like an animal, I went for the tongue. I think that was what did it. I spit the lips out, I'm pretty sure—lips are chewier than hell, did you know that? Like jerky that's been soaking in Crisco for a week. But that tongue, I swallowed that right on down, didn't even chew it, it fit perfect down my throat hole, and was still twitching like an eel, helping itself along, and then, like probably had to happen, the tunnel collapsed. By the time they dug me out a few hours later—" He uses his fingers to stretch his eyes out.

"I don't want to hear this."

"For a few years after that, I thought tongues were the magic ingredient," he says. "And that I had to swallow them whole like that. I even got superstitious about if the tongue's taste buds rubbed on mine on the way down. But, really, shit, any little bit'll do, long as it's got some meat to it."

"You took Jam's face, though," Harper says. "Not Kissy's."

"That was her name?" Bucketmouth says, slapping the tabletop with his open hand. "Man. I thought I heard it wrong, that it was 'Kris' or 'Chrissy.' That's the hard part about this, you know? Nobody says anybody's name when everybody knows each other. I thought you were Harp at first, didn't know what it was short for."

Harper just stares at him.

"No," he says, "I'm not what you might call equal opportunity with the sexes. How it works is I turn into whoever right as they are when I carve that piece of them off, yeah? Like, this finger, that ear, it's a biological snapshot of them at that exact moment in their life. Make sense? I mean, sprained ankles or an arm in a cast don't matter, but . . . *permanent* situations. Leukemia, diabetes, lupus, spinal shit—all that junk the body can't kick, that's the stuff that can cross over to me, yeah?"

"Leukemia doesn't have to be forever," Harper tells him.

"Whatever, but, with the ladies? I know y'all's time of the month isn't, like, a condition, but it crosses over too, don't ask me why, I didn't make the rules. But, if I'm going to be wearing someone's skirt, I go through the last two or three trash cans she's passed beforehand. Just because I don't need that kind of hassle."

"Like we do?"

Bucketmouth shrugs.

"Still," Harper says, "people on the road are gonna pick a Kissy up off the shoulder long before they stop for a Jam."

"There's trade-offs, sure, sure," Bucketmouth says, pouring peanuts into his mouth and then gauging the length of his cigarette as he chews.

"Why are you telling me all this?" Harper asks.

"Right to the point, aren't you?" Bucketmouth says back.

"Tick tock."

"Because I never get to unload like this?"

"And because it doesn't matter what I might tell anybody?" Harper says. "Because I don't live through this night?"

"Runaways disappear all the time," Bucketmouth says, just stating sad, general facts.

"Like you'll let me disappear."

He opens his hand to the interstate, offering it to her.

"*With* Dillon," Harper says.

He closes his hand, purses his lips in regretful apology.

"Why do you do all this cat and mouse on the highway bullshit?" Harper asks.

"It's not always the highway," Bucketmouth says, studying the bridge again. "But—you figure it out, I guess. Living like I do, doing what I do, it's good to always have a fast way out. Hundred years ago, maybe I work the rivers, right? I'm the Steamboat Boogeyman, the Canoe Killer. Just, what someone with my . . . my predilections needs is some place where not all the heads are counted. Where every next face you see is anonymous."

"Lonely life," Harper says.

"You can say that again," Bucketmouth says.

"*That's* why you're talking to me."

He doesn't shoot that one down.

"So you just hitch around," Harper goes on, "take a bite out of whoever stops to help you out?"

"Why do you think it's always *me* with my thumb out?" he asks back, leaning forward to look right into her eyes. "Is it because of that movie? Often as not, I'm behind the wheel for these little sorties. Well—" He opens his cigarette hand to the Peterbilt as evidence.

"Sometimes you're the bug, sometimes you're the windshield," Harper says.

"I like that, I like that. Can I use it?"

"That's why you save people in jars," Harper says, figuring this out. "You take a piece when they're in their prime, or . . . when they're how you want them. When they're how you want to *be*."

He looks at his cigarette from the side.

"What does the cinnamon do?" Harper asks.

"It tastes good," Bucketmouth says, obviously. "You should try it, y'know? See if you're like me. Never know until you take that first bite."

"I've eaten chicken," Harper says. "It didn't turn me into one."

"That's cooked," Bucketmouth tells her. "The essential vitamins burn away in that kind of heat. And it doesn't work with animals anyway."

"Happy to go through life ignorant," Harper says.

"For . . ." He makes like peering down at a watch, seeing how much of her life she's got left to be ignorant in.

"Smoke," Harper says, urging him on.

He takes another deep drag, their timeline losing another eighth of an inch.

"Can't believe your friend didn't smoke with this body," Bucketmouth says. "It's glorious, truly."

"So you get new lungs each time around?" Harper says.

"Well . . ." he says. "If I were going to stick with him, they'd be kind of new by the end, yeah."

"The end?"

"It lasts about two weeks," he says, waggling his fingers over his face, "this. Stay any longer, you can get stuck. Just saying this so if, you know, if you do end up going for the lifestyle."

"Stuck?"

"You don't just have to eat a finger or an eye then," he says. "You've got to eat and eat and eat, down to the bone, and crack into the marrow. It's kind of ugly. Guess that's the downside to all this."

"*That's* the only downside?"

"Don't knock it till you've tried it, girlie."

"Harper," Harper says. "It's Harper. We almost done here, or you got more important stuff to be telling me?"

"'Bucketmouth,'" he says, blowing his smoke out in a tight stream this time. "I don't know. Do you like it? Does it fit, you think? I mean, if you're going to be a legend, you want to be a good one, don't you? Have a proper sounding name, all that?"

"Why us?" Harper says, glaring right at him. "Road was full of people tonight. It could have been anybody."

"Would you accept bad luck? On your part, I mean."

Harper shakes her head no, hitching a bag of chips up through the V of her index finger and thumb, flipturning it then starting on the other side. The nerves have to go somewhere.

"Did you not wonder how I had that picture?" Bucketmouth says, not looking away from her.

Harper dials back, back.

Picture?

Photograph. The dead guy. The mummy propped up against the snow fence.

She pushes back from the table, shakes her head no.

"That was *you*?" she says.

In answer he collects Jam's short hair on one side of his head, makes to comb it over to the other side.

The Thunderbird people.

"You were the holy roller," she says. "You—the two of you didn't pick someone up who killed them. You were *already* in the car."

"Sometimes you're the windshield, sometimes—"

"So you knew *then*?" Harper says.

He takes another drag, holds it in, his eyes watering from it.

It makes sense, Harper guesses. The driver, Mr. Combover, that *was* his face that had slapped down onto their windshield, special bird-delivery, but he wasn't stumbling out through the darkness like her and Dillon had thought. He'd been waiting out there without a face, waiting for one of them to be alone. So he could take a bite.

"I should have known," she says.

"*Bam*," Bucketmouth says, pointing his finger right at here. "That's what you all say."

He takes another contemplative drag.

"Want to see something cool?" he asks.

"I just want to be not here," Harper tells him.

Bucketmouth delicately inserts the cigarette between his lips then reaches back to the hinge of his jaw on the right side, his fingers pinching for, for—for a *grip*. Something to grab onto.

He tugs and a flap of skin rips free.

Harper steeples her hands over her mouth, sucks air through her fingers, shaking her head no, please no.

This is happening, though.

Working slowly, breaking it free tug by wet, creaky tug, Bucketmouth peels his cheek off all the way up to the corner of his mouth, showing some molars, then, being careful of the cigarette, guiding it through the lip hole, he keeps going, has peeled the whole lower part of his face off.

"I can usually do it in one piece," he says, Harper watching the words form in his mouth, those words different now, being shaped at the end by lip muscle, not the actual lips. "But your trucker friends at the gas station back there—there was some trauma there."

With that he works his right index finger up under his eyelid and pulls it gently out, pulls the top part of his face off like taking off a domino mask. Now his cheeks and eyebrows and chin and jaw and forehead are muscle and blood shot through with white and yellow.

He reaches into the pile of stolen food, comes out with a little bottle of Visine. He lips the cigarette with raw muscle, the paper sucking up the blood, and tilts his head back, applies two drops to each eye.

When he smiles, Harper gags.

This is hilarious to him.

"I don't mean one piece like whole *body*," he says. "That all comes off too, but that takes a week to get done, usually. Bit by bit." He punctuates it by crumbling a handful of Fritos into his mouth.

Harper can see the chewing in a new and terrible way. She promises then and there to never eat a Frito again.

"What about 'Lockjaw' for a name?" Bucketmouth says then, snapping his mouth open and shut, spilling wet yellow crumbs. "I could learn to like Lockjaw, I think. No, wait. That's tetanus, isn't it? Yeah, I think it is. It is, shit. Okay, I don't want to be tetanus."

"Are we, are we—?" Harper asks through her hands.

"Done?" Bucketmouth says, shrugging, watching more headlights on the interstate. "I've always wanted to do this too, if you've got the—" He eyeballs his cigarette for how much time they've got left in this conversation.

"No," Harper says. "Please."

"Just real quick."

He holds his hands up under his chin, fingers fanned out.

Harper's shaking her head no, no, please.

"How many fingers am I holding up?" he says with a big smile, and—no no no—it's eleven.

Moving slow so she can see every bit of it, he leans forward, takes the eleventh finger, Dillon's, into his mouth, sucks it up.

Harper is throwing up before she's even aware there's anything in her throat.

"Not bad, right?" Bucketmouth says when she's done.

"You're, you're—" Harper says, about the cigarette.

Bucketmouth takes it out, studies it. It is almost to the butt.

"You don't need him anymore now, right?" Harper says, about Dillon on the flatbed.

Bucketmouth looks over there, considers this.

"That's always a quandary," he says. "No, technically, I don't need him to complete this . . . *process*. But?" He inhales the cigarette bright red, holds it up between them. "Problem is, see, there can't be two of us either, can there?"

With that he flicks the cigarette . . . *away* from the line of kerosene he trailed into the parking lot.

Still, Harper dives for it, can't help trying.

Bucketmouth laughs about this.

"I keep my word," he says.

"Now can we—" Harper says, but doesn't get to finish: the cigarette has bloomed into a flickering flame. "No," she says, looking over to the flatbed trailer.

The flame goes wide all at once then, is a line, *another* line of kerosene, one he poured out before she got here. And, kerosene, of course: gas would evaporate. But kerosene's oily, kerosene lasts longer. And she didn't question the harsh scent on the air, since he poured it out while she was watching. Since the can was sitting on the table between them.

The line of orange races in a wide curve towards the trailer . . . and then goes *under* it.

"What?" Harper says, looking to Bucketmouth.

"Wait, wait," he says. "It's just that kind of night, isn't it?"

His face glows orange when the flame ignites the pool he'd evidently poured under the tank. In all that dry grass.

"What's in that tank?" Harper asks.

"Hell," Bucketmouth says, looking for all the world glad that she asked. "But don't worry. It's not the end of the world."

He sweeps away the chips and peanuts and jerky to reveal a fire extinguisher laying on its side. Harper looks from it to the fire to Bucketmouth's anatomy-class face, sees that she can either take that heavy hard fire extinguisher, hold it high and come at his head with it, or she can do exactly as he wants: race with it across the parking lot, try to put that fire out, save Dillon.

"Asshole," she says to him, stabbing her hand down for the dull silver handle of the fire extinguisher.

"That's not how it's pronounced," he says back, watching the fire lick up at the tank. "Think it's more 'Bucketmouth.' You've got to do your mouth where it says 'Buck-et' at first, then, after that, 'mouth.'"

"This isn't over," Harper says, striding away.

"Hope not," he calls after her, and after about three dignified steps, she's running.

Because the flames are surging up under the flatbed, she can't slide under it, and would need both hands to climb over, so she runs around the rear, already turning her head away from the heat.

"Dillon!" she calls out, pulling the pin on the extinguisher, aiming its nozzle down and squeezing the handle.

Nothing.

She looks down to the extinguisher, shakes it, squeezes the handle harder.

A disappointing burp of white foam spurts out, doesn't even have enough pressure behind it to clear the wide nozzle.

"No no no no," Harper says, and drops the extinguisher, sure that exactly what Bucketmouth wants her to do now is clamber up onto the flatbed, try to free Dillon.

What he *doesn't* expect is for her to be able to put the fire out.

Harper runs back around the rear of the trailer, skids to a stop at the passenger-side back door of the Park truck, and hauls out one case of water bottles, then the next. She chocks them under her arms, galumphs back to the tank, empties a bottle each onto her pants legs and sneakers then wades into the flames with the cases, rolls them under the tank one by one like grenades.

For a few seconds there's nothing, but then the fire melts

through the plastic and the water splashes out, turns almost instantly to steam. If anything, the water just somehow feeds the fire bigger, send its orange fingers even higher up around the side of the tank.

"*No*," Harper screams, having to back up from the heat. Having to imagine whatever combustible stuff's pressured up in that tank. The explosion is going to take this whole lot out, is going to be visible for miles.

Now she has no choice but to try to get Dillon away from it, whether that's what Bucketmouth planned for her to do or not.

She hops up to see over the flames and tank, make sure the kerosene on the trailer hasn't caught a spark yet, and, and: *Bucketmouth's* up there with Dillon?

"Get him out of there!" she calls to him.

Bucketmouth, just a silhouette, watches her through the flames.

"*Please!*" she screams then, and Bucketmouth finally nods, steps forward with that same knife, only has to touch the blade to the very edge of that dirty yellow strap to snap it, it's ratcheted so tight.

At which point Harper's right pants leg bursts into flame.

She falls down instantly, rolling and patting, and by the time she comes up she's twenty desperate feet out in the pasture. She rubs her calf and shin and ankle, searching for hidden embers. She leans around to see one, threading her hair out of the way, and suddenly her leg goes black. Not from burn or ash, but because—because she *had* been lit up by headlights. And now she's not.

"What?" Harper says, standing, looking through the smoke.

Bucketmouth. He's driving away in the Park truck, Dillon slung over the hood like a gutted mule deer.

"No," Harper says, shaking her head. He's—Bucketmouth, he's supposed to fire the *Peterbilt* up, leave in that, and she's supposed to go after him in the truck he's now driving.

This isn't how it's supposed to work.

Harper runs around the edge of the fire after him but gets there too late, can just grab a handful of gravel, sling it after them, none of it even pinging in the bed.

The Park truck gentles around the turn, taking the ramp slow to the west, so as not to sling Dillon off.

Yet.

"What are you doing?" Harper says, and squats down on her toes to push her fists into her temples, *think*.

What she needs to do first is get the hell out of here, she knows. Before that exploding tank turns this place into *Hell*.

The second is . . . she doesn't get to two.

By the toe of her right sneaker is . . . another finger?

She narrows her eyes to look back to Dillon's hand from before, try to remember how many fingers *he* was holding up. She starts to pick the finger up, save it—for what?—but then can't quite get her own fingers to touch it.

Which is when a window in the house goes yellow.

18

THE OLD PETERBILT fires up first try, the hoods on each side clattering with all the exhaust leaks. Harper releases the parking brake with her left hand, clutches in, works through the low gears to be sure she has them down.

Sort of? Maybe?

Her dad said learning to shift, it's more about doing it wrong about eight hundred times, until there's only one right way to get it done. And it's not about thinking, it's about instinct, it's about feel, it's about being one with the road, the engine, the grade, the load. At any point in a run, she could ask him what gear was he in *now*, and he could never answer, even in general ranges. He would look down at his right hand like just being reminded that it was part of him, and kind of smile in wonder at it.

Harper eases the clutch out, trying to get a sense of where it breaks over, hands off to the engine, and the Peterbilt jumps forward, almost stalls before she catches it. She checks the mirror on the far side, trying, she guesses, to maybe gauge or guess when that big white tank might finally blow. The flames flickering under its wide belly make her forget everything she just figured out about the gears.

"Calm, calm, it hasn't blown yet," she tells herself, and makes herself slow down, take stock of this cab all over. A faded eight of clubs tucked up into the speedo. Toothpicks lined into a crack in the dash. An old election bumpersticker on the inside of the windshield, probably being used as Band-Aid for a crack or hole in the glass. And, in the passenger floorboard, two dog pans. Instead of a passenger seat there's a wooden box with a dog bed nestled inside.

Meg will need these, Harper thinks, her hand running through the gears again, getting them down without her head running interference.

In the house now, more of the windows are going yellow. Because Harper's had the engine rumbling too long, isn't just someone cruising through to see if this joint's open.

She eases forward again, has enough of a feel that she's pretty sure she can do this, but then she stomps the clutch and brake in when a rotating yellow light cycles in from the east. At the top of the bridge it becomes a bright white tow truck, one of the big-big ones that go fifty thousand pounds—they have to, to pull a semi tractor up from a muddy ditch. Probably every one of these in Wyoming is zeroing in on the burn to drag rigs up from the ashes, try not to cross their cables.

Harper lowers her left hand to the light knob to get this chase started—the Park truck's going to overheat inside five miles—but of course it's a dry pull, since the headlights were trashed back at Wagonhound, are probably still inside that destroyed camper.

It's good the truck stays dark, as it turns out.

A door's just opened in the house, and it filled with shapes for a moment, with people roused from sleep, about to break into emergency mode once the smoke in the air registers for them. The time to decide is *now*, Harper tells herself.

She works through what she can think of: Bucketmouth had this all planned out the whole time. He never intended to give Dillon back to her. He always planned on ditching her with the Peterbilt, taking off in the faster, more nimble vehicle. Or, maybe he's ditching her with the big rig because it just demolished a rest stop, might be on some sort of rampage, just plow through the next traffic slowdown, tossing civilian cars to either side like nothing—which is to say, as far as Wyoming troopers are concerned, shoot to kill.

She's still playing into his hand, isn't she? *Shit*. She's still walking right into where he wants her to be. This must be what he does, to cover up: leave a big mess behind, frame someone else for it. A patsy to take the fall, complete with a story even she would never believe—"I was chasing the *real* bad guy, it's not me, he's still out there, you've got to let me go after him!"

If Harper gets back on the interstate in this Peterbilt, then, because she's not like him, doesn't know how and where and when to hide and probably can't drive as well anyway, she's caught inside of ten miles, will either have to shift to a taller gear, drive for the horizon, damn the roadblocks, which will confirm all the reports on this truck, or she'll have to pull over, step down for the cavalry to take her in. And Indians, never mind if they've never been on a horse, they know better than to let the horse soldiers get them.

Harper turns the truck off and steps down from it, walks immediately off the bright surface of the pale parking lot. Voices are approaching. Footsteps are crashing through the brush. An actually charged-up fire extinguisher is foaming and spraying, making that big hollow sizzling sound. This ugly-ass truck isn't supposed to be there, the people have to be saying. And there's not supposed to be *any* flames around that tank, ever. And, once they get that far, the back door of the Shell station probably isn't supposed to be kicked in either.

Harper ducks deeper into the leather jacket, the collar coming up around her ears like it knows what she needs, and she thrusts her hands in the pockets, keeps to the dark brush until she finds the road, which she crosses for more of that lush darkness, to cut over to the on-ramp.

A hundred, hundred and fifty yards down the interstate, her shadow jumps out in front of her.

Like she meant to be doing in the first place, before all this started, she hikes her thumb out.

THE NEXT HOUR is the best and the worst at the same time. It's the best because the red piles of gore spread out across the asphalt are consistently mule deer and coyotes, never Dillon, like she keeps squinting against. It's worst because car after car, rig after rig, they just keep sweeping past, sucking her hair over into their draft, leaving her to breathe their rancid exhaust. Twice there's been beer bottles whizzing by her head—they don't even shatter in the ditch, just thunk in a way that makes her skull feel like paper—and once some college kids in a Taurus station wagon pull over, make her jog the polite jog up to them only to have them flip her off, peel away, throwing gravel at her.

So this is the life, she tells herself. This is what I wanted.

The jacket's probably not helping her any, she knows, but it's too cold to lose it.

For a half mile or so she gives up, walks deep in the ditch by the sheep fence, her hands balled in the jacket pockets. But then the grass starts getting taller . . . because of the concrete tunnel boring under 80, which is in a low spot, of course. She doesn't know if it's for deer to cross without getting splatted or if someone is really hopeful about how much rain this part of the country is going to get someday, but, just like when she was a girl, she stakes it out for a couple of minutes. Not because she really believes a Bigfoot is going to silhouette its shaggy self at the other end of the tunnel, but because her dad always *thought* that was going to happen. That it happened all the time, just, nobody ever thought to look. It had to be how they avoided the headlights though, right? They can't go over, so they go *under*.

Harper, five years old, had nodded yes, yes yes yes. It made perfect sense.

Now she's not looking for Bigfoot so much anymore, though. Just her dad, please.

She's still that kid in that Alabama song, waiting by the phone. Roll on, Daddy, till you get back home. Sure, your rig did eventually show up, its load long plundered it had been sitting so long, birds living in the cab, but it wasn't the truck she was praying would come back. It was her dad.

She maybe cries a bit here. Not for herself, she doesn't think, and not even for Dillon, really. For her dad. Because it would have been so perfect for him to just appear, a shadowy form at the end of that long white tunnel, his hair long, his clothes ragged, but he'd smile, she knows. From seeing his daughter after all these years. He'd smile and open his arms for her, and as she ran to him she'd be shedding all the bad years, leaving them behind her.

She maybe watches more than a couple of minutes, but when she stands she's what she needs to be: hard, tough, leather. Her eyes are flint and her heart's steel, and her lips are always going to be pressed tight together.

That's the kind of girl who survives a night like this. That's the kind of Indian who makes it out of the twentieth century.

When tires wind up behind her again she dutifully hangs her thumb in the wind, and only looks up when the asphalt in front of her washes red with brakelight.

She ups her pace, isn't going to jog like a fool this time, but then the taillights and cargo doors and stripes register for her: an ambulance.

She veers off, swishes through the grass, steps over the fence, is running hard out in the blackness.

Medics have radios too. They know all the cops, all the firemen, have got all the same alerts and warnings.

From out in the night she watches the ambulance. The medics are standing against their bright white cargo box, looking for her. Calling, but their voices are lost. Both women, one of them Indian, if Harper's seeing right. Indians make the best medics, everybody knows, because of that old-time medicine. But still.

She shakes her head no like she's having to convince herself to stay hidden here. To not trust anybody with a lightbar. Two, three minutes later the medics finally climb back in, use their blinker to get back on the road even though it's only them.

Harper stands when they're gone enough, angles back over to start this bullshit all over.

Note to self, she says: look before you extend that left arm. Or, better yet, only try to thumb down the tall headlights, the big rigs. Because the angle she's taking is meant to connect with the right swerve the road's taking, she's pulling her boots through the tall grass for longer than she meant, until—

The Park truck.

It's just sitting there.

Harper squats, watches it, then slowly, carefully, circles around it until headlights from the interstate show her its silhouette in snatches.

"Hey!" Harper calls out to it. "You! Bucketmouth!"

No reply, and she's pretty sure it's not like him to keep quiet.

She feels around for a rock, lobs it onto the hood, no response. Just the rock, clattering off.

She approaches from the side, on the chance the truck's going to start up, either drop into low or reverse, to run her over.

It doesn't, "Can't," Harper aloud when she's finally to it.

It's been left behind.

She runs her hand along the bed rail, over the two doors, the cab empty, then pats the front fender.

"You were a good pony, weren't you?" she says.

She pops the hood, touches her palm fast to the radiator cap, and it's still hot like she knew it would be, but it's not scalding hot anymore. Meaning Bucketmouth and Dillon are miles ahead by now. Well, unless they're walking, Bucketmouth carrying Dillon, or dragging him by the foot.

But, no: carrying him.

It's a good way to get a ride.

Harper grits her teeth, nods to herself, and jogs to the shoulder, is ready for this chase again, now that she has the scent.

The chase doesn't agree, though.

The next two rigs just whine past. The second for sure sees her, since he drifts over to the passing lane to give her room, not blow her face-first into the ditch, but he doesn't let any speed off, doesn't even consider stopping.

"What the hell?" Harper says, getting more and more pissed.

She knows taking riders is against the rules for most companies, and that independent drivers have probably been burned enough by hitchhikers to know better. But still. She's not like that. And she won't call to tattle to Dispatch about catching a ride with one of their drivers. Promise.

An hour without a ride, now. Maybe an hour and a half, even. She stops to skirt a splatted antelope, but then goes back to hold her palm to its forehead, to send it on its journey better. If it's an Indian thing, it's one she's making up, but it still counts, she's pretty sure. The next stop is to play detective: the ditch is still torn up, from a *heavy* rig stepping over into the ditch, but then also making it back out. Which doesn't track for a tractor-trailer, as you never risk pulling this far from the road, just set up cones or flares on the shoulder if you need to, but . . .

That big white tow truck that was booking it this way, maybe? It had an eighteen-foot utility bed it looked like, like most of them do, but's still stubby enough to go four-wheeling like this, and's probably got a 12.7-liter turbo driving the wheels, which is torque to burn, practically a drag-truck compared to all the other rigs out here.

Dredging up the specs of this maybe-truck only makes her miss her dad more, though. He drove a wrecker for a season, when she was in kindergarten and he was trying to stay close to Laramie, and he never lost his love for those custom rigs, would walk Harper all through their features when one was nosed into the truckstop, and then keep talking about them all through burgers and chili and cokes, telling tall tales about what-all impossible things he'd seen them do.

Harper finally shrugs about whatever happened here, shrugs past, hands in pockets, only to stop when a passing station wagon lights the toe of a human foot out in the grass.

"No," she says.

But yes.

It's a dead dude. One for some reason wearing flip-flops and gym shorts with a pearl-snap shirt, unsnapped.

Harper takes her hands from her pockets, narrows her eyes at all the darkness around her, then finally edges in, nudges the guy's calf with her toe.

Nothing. Definitely dead, she can't tell how.

She spins away, doesn't need to get involved, but then . . .

She makes herself stop, her back ramrod-straight, lips peeled back from her teeth in frustration.

"Stupid, stupid," she's telling herself. But she does it anyway, goes back, toes the grass aside to count the dead guy's fingers on both sides.

They're all there.

Meaning?

"Nothing," she tells herself.

There's dead people all up and down this road tonight. And all she's concerned with is the living one called Dillon, thanks. The one who's moving away from her miles at a time, while she's just hoofing it.

Another half-hour creeps past, she's pretty sure.

It's so stupid how, before she started thumbing for real, the night had been clicking forward one single second at a time, each minute packed with wrecks and bodies and monsters, and now these last couple of hours have just been a long, never-ending smear of nothing, the clock hands hardly even moving at all, wherever they are.

For maybe a quarter mile, a pair of eyes pace her out in the pasture. The next rig's headlights show it to be a grinning coyote, tail low. The next time Harper thinks to look for it, it's gone.

Is she not getting picked up because she doesn't have a bag, maybe? Does that make her suspicious? Do the drivers think she's some girlfriend or wife who got pissed at her husband or boyfriend, made him let her out so she can stalk the side of the road? It can't be her hair this time, she knows, or her skin. It's night. She's not Indian in the headlights at seventy miles per hour. She's probably barely even female.

Finally, what feels like a lifetime later, she walks onto a rig pulled over onto the shoulder. No taillights, just a line of angled-out cones leading up to it, telling her this *isn't* whoever was four-wheeling back there.

Still, "Great," Harper says. A trucker with engine problems isn't exactly helpful, is it?

She walks out into the grass, on the dark side of the truck, and there's no light from the cab. The fiberglass hood's pulled forward like she was expecting but there's nobody up in that rocking chair. She climbs up, knocks on the window, tries the door almost on accident, to keep from falling. It's open.

"Hello?" she calls in, ready to run.

Nothing. No one.

It smells like cigarette smoke and body odor. And the keys

are in the *ignition*? Granted, this eighty-thousand dollar tractor probably doesn't start right at this moment, but there's probably keys to the trailer on that ring, and some sort of cameo picture Harper knows it's none of her business to look at.

She shuts the door, climbs down, walks around the front of the truck, nearly breaks her ankle on the gouges in the ditch: tires. Deep, double. *Here's* that big white tow truck, then. The one this trucker must be riding in now, for whatever reason.

"Good for you," she tells him.

At least someone found help tonight.

Harper keeps walking, then, not quite far enough she can't see the broken-down rig anymore, she stops, looks back to it, a particularly evil thought bubbling up.

In five minutes she's there again, pussyfooting it across the tow truck ruts. She doesn't clamber into the cab again—not that a snack wouldn't be nice, a nap even better—but picks around behind the sleeper. Not for boomers, not for chain, not for shovels or a pry bar. She digs past all those, feels around the air hoses, finally finds what she was hoping for: a little two-gallon gas can, emergency red.

It's full but she pours it out, doesn't need the gas this driver was carrying just to give the hapless unleaded crowd ten or fifteen miles down the road. What she needs is that bright red can.

Before leaving she does haul herself back up into the cab, to paw around for a notepad, a pen, to leave an IOU in front of the gauge cluster. The pen is easy—the visor, always the visor—but she can't find the logbook anywhere. Not even a battered metal clipboard, which you always have to carry for the loading dock to sign on.

"Sorry, sorry," she says, broaching back through the curtain, into the musty bunk.

She finds the light third-try, lucks onto a paperback right off, and tears a mostly blank page from the back, is writing her note on it when she realizes she's being watched.

Slowly, pen still to pulpy paper, she looks up.

It's the driver.

He's staring at her from the hindmost corner, where he's been stuffed.

Harper jumps and pushes, gets nowhere in the blankets.

The driver doesn't move.

Harper gets conscious about her breathing, is still pushing as far away as she can.

"Sir, sir, sir?" she's saying.

Nothing.

Moving jerky, she pulls the paperback to her, lobs it back at the driver. It hits his face and his expression doesn't change. A dark line of blood seeps from his right nostril, though, around his mouth, and hangs onto his chin, waiting to gather enough weight to drip down onto his chest.

He's dead. And hidden.

Shit. Second one of these inside of a mile? But why, what's the gain? *Think*, Harp, she tells herself.

But the dead trucker won't stop watching her with his dry eyes.

She balls her note to him up, doesn't turn her back to him the whole way out of the cab, fully expects him to be coming for her.

She falls to the ground on the passenger side, is immediately looking back up to the open door.

Nothing clambers out after her.

She stands, guides the door shut, not just her hand shaking but her whole body, pretty much.

Fifty yards down the road, her breath hitches and suddenly she's crying.

"I don't even know you!" she screams back at the rig.

It just stares at her with its dark headlights.

She sets the gas can down, throws handfuls of gravel back at the windshield.

The one rig that passes during this episode rides the far left edge of the bumper lane. He blinks his lights in understanding, though. Or apology. Something.

Harper sits down for what feels like ten minutes, and when she finally can, she stands, is walking with purpose now, her steps long, the plastic gas can bumping on her left thigh, to keep it in obvious view of the road.

This time she doesn't even have to stick her thumb out. The third truck that sweeps past, its Jake Brake engages just past her—she's thudding down a slight grade—then it pulls over a quarter mile up to wait for her.

Without a grimy bag over her shoulder, she's become a woman whose car ran dry. Now she's just hiking to the next pump, maybe even has a kid or two back in the car she had to leave behind.

Who wouldn't stop?

19

THE DRIVER IS doctoring his swindle sheet when Harper finally steps up to eye level with him.

He looks over his reading glasses, waves her on in but the door won't open. He clicks something on his side and it doesn't just unlock, it pops open.

"Fancy," Harper says, out of breath.

"Takes a while to get her stopped, sorry," the driver says back.

"Thanks for stopping at all," Harper tells him, settling into the passenger seat, taking stock of the cab to make sure there's nothing hinky.

He's bald, sun-faded denim shirt with the sleeves cut off, armful of ink, droopy eyes, gunfighter stache. For a shrieky moment Harper wonders how it works with Bucketmouth—if he changes into the person he was at the moment he got a piece off them, does that mean he gets their facial hair too? Their haircut?

"Saw the colors," he says about the patches on her sleeve.

She looks down to them for the first time, licks her lips, telling herself to lie, that lie already forming in her mouth—her old man's waiting in Rawlins, is probably cooking back this way already—but isn't that the wrong foot to start out on, when he's the one already being cool?

"Not mine," she admits, looking out over his hood so as not to put him in a position. So as not to challenge him.

"Not yours?" he asks.

"Found it," Harper says.

He tucks his logbook away, watching her closer now.

"Where's your car?" he says, his tone a little fake now, like he can feel this all going downhill.

Harper shakes her head, doesn't have a good answer for that either. At which point he looks all around her, mostly on the floorboard.

"Gas can?" he tries, the look on his face showing how ready he is to have been taken, here.

"That was just to get somebody to stop," Harper says, her eyes getting a shine to them, she knows and hates. She's never been one to cry when the cop comes to the window, has never used tears to get what she wants, considers that the cheapest of the cheap, and insulting besides. But her eyes are doing shit without her, here. It's from telling the truth, she thinks. It feels good, even if it trashes her only chance at a ride.

"Guess it worked, yeah?" the driver says about the dummy gas can.

Harper nods, doesn't strap in. It's another thing her dad told her: unless you trust this buckle not to have been messed with, not to need a coat hanger or something to pry open, don't belt yourself down tight. He'd heard some crusty old story about a trucker who would trap hitchhikers like that. Not to do anything bad to them necessarily, but because he thought he was a comedian of the road, and liked to try his bits out on a captive audience for a thousand or two miles. At which point he'd let the hitchhiker out not just in a different state, but in a different state of *mind*: shellshocked from bad and constant standup, blinking in the ditch, finally laughing, but just for that experience to be over.

This guy doesn't seem funny like that—*un*funny like that—but you never can tell.

"I can get out, you want," Harper says, her finger to the door just like Dillon's was, once upon a statie's life.

The driver considers this, considers it some more, then checks his mirrors, says, "Where you headed, then?"

"California eventually," Harper says. "Maybe Seattle. Got some stuff to do on the way, though."

"Always rats to kill," the driver says, setting his shifter, easing them ahead, the whole rig shuddering.

"What you hauling?" Harper asks.

"Tortilla chips!" the driver says with fake cheer. "Unless I pull up alongside some hoss carrying queso, at which point it'll be love at first sight . . ."

Harper smiles into her chest.

Fifteen or twenty trucks left her standing in the ditch the last hour, hour and a half, and it's the gay driver who actually pulled over to help. But she shouldn't judge, she imagines. Maybe all those other drivers were gay as well, and this guy's just stopped for her because of who he is.

Not that Wyoming is any kind of good place for him to be stopping, of course.

"Just to be sure there's no funny business," the driver says then, and reaches behind the console, comes up with what he evidently keeps clipped in a holster back there: a stubby-thick snub-nose.

Harper rubs the side of her face, trying to hide that pistol from herself.

Is it the same one Bucketmouth left on that shelf back at that Akal place a lifetime ago?

Impossible, she tells herself. The world is full of snub-noses like this. The road's a dangerous place.

"Got any good stories from the ditch, then?" the driver says, leaning over the wheel to stretch his back.

"Just horror ones," Harper says. "What do these patches mean?"

She looks down along the sleeve and the driver looks with her.

"It's like—you know Russian tattoos in their prisons? They tell a story, are an autobiography you write on yourself, maybe a wall of caution signs too. This is like that."

"This one?" Harper says, touching the red wings.

"You don't want to know," the driver says, and pops a knife out from the left side of his belt. "Couple of those a lady maybe shouldn't be advertising around, though."

He flips the knife around, offers it across to her.

"Probably just shave em all off," the driver says. "Bikers are all twitchy about if you earned them, could get you in a pickle."

"Like Boy Scout badges," Harper says, digging the point of the blade in for the thread, trying not to snag the leather.

"Boy Scouts in Hell, yeah," the driver says with a smile, and watches the road and his mirrors for the few minutes it takes Harper to get the patches off, stack them on the console.

"Got a trash?" she says.

He slides them into the cupholder, says, "Coasters now, yeah?"

"So 80's open back there?" she says, tipping her head behind them—east.

"You know about that?"

"You're not my first ride," Harper lies, wincing inside from it.

"Down to one-lane, but yeah," the driver says. "We were all ducks threaded on a string for a while there, though."

"That like sardines in a can?"

"Lot more quacking," the driver says, giving his horn a perfunctory tug.

Harper grins, leans back in her seat a touch. More mentally than with her body, really. Being in this truck, it's . . . it's not quite like her dad showing up at the other end of that concrete tunnel, but it's got that feel, anyway. Like home.

"Hungry?" the driver asks, reaching back, coming up with a tube of Pringles.

It's another thing Harper's been warned about, of course: taking food. When she peels the top, though, this tube still has the pressured-up foil at top, just like new tennis balls.

"Thanks," she says.

He nestles a cold beer down into the cupholder for her too, letting one of the patches soak up the water from the cooler.

"You're of age, right?" he says. "I don't mean—I'm not trying to—"

Harper cracks the beer open well below window-level, says, "Old enough, yes."

He studies her and she can tell that *he* can tell she's probably not twenty-one, but he lets it slide, says, "You know how the captain on a ship can marry people, and how, in international waters, there's no drinking age?"

She chews, sips, nods.

"This is my ship," he says, reaching forward to pat the dash.

"Never been in one this new," Harper says, taking it all in.

"Be paying on it for a good twenty years after I'm dead and gone," the driver says.

"I just—you're my second ride, so far," Harper says, barely remembering the other ride she's supposed to have had. And also that she's Ava, from Utah. In a brown Audi. And she was never at Wagonhound, and she didn't start any fires, and she ate an exploding hamburger, and and and . . .

"Sure about this-all?" the driver says. "Being on the road, I mean? The life?"

Harper shakes her head no, fills her mouth with salty goodness.

"I don't have any money to pay you for these," she says, trying to hide her hungry chewing.

The driver doesn't care. He shifts down to pass a slow RV with a shaky wheel, pours on the steam to get around them before they wobble into his lane.

"Can you imagine if they had highways just for freight?" he says, daydreaming out loud.

"Like train tracks, you mean?" Harper says.

"Still got to get those heads of lettuce from the station to the grocery sto—" the driver says, flinching back halfway into it.

It's an empty snack-size bag of Fritos slapped to his windshield from whoever's ahead of them now.

"Classy, dude," the driver says to the big white tow truck

in front of them, and does his windshield wipers twice to clear the bag.

"Wait," Harper says, setting her beer down blind, feeling for the cupholder. She tries to crank the window down, can't find the handle.

"Gonna be sick?" the driver asks, thumbing a button on his side double fast. Harper's window glides down and she shimmies up and halfway out, reaches around, just snags the Fritos bag whipping back and forth under the wiper blade, her hair everywhere.

She sits down with it and the driver's watching her for what's next.

"You like a, a anti-litterbug, what do they call them?" he asks. "Conversationalist?"

"No," Harper says about the bag, and looks up to the tow truck ahead of them. "Can you pass him?"

On the silver-foil inside of the bag, just barely, there's a smear of blood. It's from eating one-handed while driving. Shaking the bag straight and then tilting it up, pouring the Fritos down to your waiting mouth.

"Was going to anyway," the driver says, downshifting. "Looks like he's just trolling, waiting for the next call."

"If he was, he'd have picked that rig up a few miles back," Harper says, thinking out loud. "He backed up to it but then just left, did you see?"

Harper can feel the driver watching her while reaching for a lower gear.

Smoke and effort billows up from their stacks and they ease around the bright white tow truck, where Harper can see it's a Freightliner, shiny-new and solid as a battleship, right at eye level with them, hooks and chains and rolled-up tarps all over it, pulleys and winches, tow bars and boom arms, feet it can lower to anchor itself, to do some real lifting. It's so clean it can't be Bucketmouth, Harper's telling herself. Trucks with bad intent, they're—they're like that Peterbilt, they're rusty and evil looking. Not spotless and showroom-floor.

The yellow light on top of its cab is still revolving slow like a prison searchlight, just keeping things safe.

"Got be nice to these guys," the driver says, leaning over to raise a hand in greeting now that the cabs are about to be even with each other. "Never know when they might be pulling your ass up from—"

Bucketmouth looks over from that cab, a toothpick chocked between his lips, his face still raw and bloody as a nightmare. He tips the cap he's now wearing then looks over again, realizes who's watching him, her hair floating all around her.

He nods in greeting.

"Who's he think he is?" the driver says about Bucketmouth's pizza face. "Fred—"

"Where is he!" Harper screams between the two trucks, having to sit sideways to try to get her question all the way over there.

Bucketmouth leans towards her, cups his hand around what's left of Jam's ear.

Harper slings her beer across. Bucketmouth leans back, lets the can zing past into his cab. He leans over, picks it up while it's foaming, tries to get an airy slurp off the top before holding it out the window, dropping it into that rushing space.

"What the fuck are you doing!" the driver says to Harper,

reaching for her and losing his straight line a bit, the tortilla-chip truck veering across the stripes, bringing Harper close enough to Bucketmouth that they could clasp hands if she leaned out a bit, reached.

"Where is he!" Harper screams again.

Bucketmouth swirls his fingers around his head, brings them to a point on his own not-yet-done face, like telling Harper to wait a few, she'll be seeing Dillon here directly.

The driver reseats himself, finds his own lane.

"*Ram him!*" Harper says, coming around to give the driver her full attention.

"What the—?" the driver says, and Harper lunges across, grabs onto the steering wheel, pulling the truck sharply over again, this time enough that its front fender taps into the front bumper of the tow truck. Because it's a new truck, isn't metal, the big blue fender bends in, comes loose, goes under the rig with a terrible and fast crunching, sucked into a vortex.

Bucketmouth's smiling, damn him, his tow truck keeping a straight and steady line.

"Lady, you got to—!" the driver's saying, but Harper's looking for what else she can throw.

She calms when she realizes.

The driver sees it on her face and they both dive for the console, for behind the console.

The tortilla truck slings back and forth, pops out of gear, and when the driver grabs the wheel and the shifter for control, Harper comes up with the snub-nose.

She turns sideways in the seat, aims out the window into the cab of the tow truck. Bucketmouth sees this and locks his rear tires up so her shot goes sailing over his hood.

"Slower!" Harper calls back to the driver, and instead he gives it some pedal.

She turns around in the seat, levels the snub-nose on *him*.

"I'm so sorry," she says. "You don't understand. He's going to kill my boyfriend."

"*He* was your other ride?" the driver says back. "What did he do?"

"He's the one who started that fire!" Harper says. "And—and he destroyed a rest stop back there!"

"Like, the Men's room, you mean?" the driver asks, checking his mirrors.

"Like the walls and the cars and the people!" Harper yells, already turning back, having to hang out to see the nose of the tow truck. "Slower, slower!" she calls back to the driver.

"Holy—" the driver says, a new terror washing over his face, and Harper checks the mirror on her side, sees the tow truck coming across from the far shoulder—it veered away so it could come back in at a sharper angle. She grabs onto the open window and the left arm of her chair right at the moment of impact.

The tow truck slams their trailer, taking out that whole flimsy wall. Tortilla chips everywhere. The snub-nose jounces from Harper's right hand, falls silently to the asphalt, is gone just as fast as the tractor's fender was.

"What the *hell* is going on here!" the driver screams, shifting *up* now, to try to shake this crazy tow truck.

"No, no, slower, we need to—" Harper says, reaching for the wheel again, but the driver pushes her back hard now.

Instead of coming to a stop at the door like she expects to, the driver thumbs a button on his side and the door opens, lets

Harper fall through, and out, and down, her hands grabbing for whatever there is: a bracket on the gas tank.

Her hair's brushing the blacktop now, the heat off the stack baking the skin of her face. She pulls her head up, terrified of getting sucked under the blurry wall of double tires chewing up the road right behind her.

"Stop, stop!" she yells up to the driver, but her voice is ripped away as soon as she opens her lips. In front of her is the huge naked front tire, its fender gone, its tread liable to knuckle up a piece of gravel and sling it through her face at any moment, and behind her—she looks—the chrome bumper of the tow truck is coming, headlights off, hood trailing remnants of the tortilla truck's trailer.

Harper shakes her head no, no, that she wants a do-over, that this could have all happened different, and then she feels the rig she's hanging onto shift up, the road passing beneath her even faster now, leaving Bucketmouth behind for a moment. Or at least matching the tow truck's speed.

The tow truck's stacks belch smoke in response.

Harper looks above the tank for something to grab onto. The door she came out is shut from the wind, and its chrome grab bar is so high up there.

Instead, she works back on the long tank, hooks her fingers into some cabinet door of the sleeper she can just grab into, hopes it's locked, that that handle won't flop open, spilling her to the ground.

She pulls up with it, pressing as hard as she can into the side of the sleeper, and, reaching and reaching with the left toe of her sneaker, she *just* manages to get to the diamondplate step she's so thankful for, that a lot of rigs don't have. She slaps her hand around the corner of the sleeper, finally connects with a chain. One she knows is just hanging on a bar, isn't meant to support a person's weight. But there's no other choice. She lets go of the handle, swings out on the chain, is in open air now, flopping back, just holding on, whipping in the eighty-mile-per-hour wind.

She kicks forward against the sleeper hard enough that she swings around, falls into the brake lines and uses them to moor herself but they're slick with grime and she's still falling back, back. What she finds instead of the slick brake lines is the pigtail, pulsing with electricity for the trailer. Because pigtails just have a Bessie lock or some bullshit to keep them in place, not glad hands like make sense, and because that Bessie lock doesn't always get put back on—who would ever pull the power cord?—the pigtail slips right out of the plug and the trailer behind her goes dark. Harper drops the pigtail, grabs onto a boomer clanging against the back of the sleeper. It holds, lets her hand over hand her way in, out of the worst of the pulling wind. But the tires and the road are still right there under her, a mis-step away—there's no catwalk on this truck, what?

She sits down hard, grabbing onto everything she can, gambling it won't let her down too.

There's bright red alarms going off in the cab now, she knows. Has she dislodged or snagged a brake line, making this a runaway truck, now? One out here in the flats, where there's no sandtraps to try to climb? Think, *think*, she tells herself, trying to remember what the blue and red lines do, what her dad was always narrating, each hookup, each drop-off. One's service, one's parking, and . . . and if she pulls the parking one, the red one she's pretty sure, then the trailer thinks it's in the lot, so it locks up. Which, at highway speed, is instant disaster, a moment of smoke billowing up from the tires and then—she doesn't even know, can't imagine. But she knows that, where she is, she won't have to imagine. She'll be in the teeth of it, the thrashing metal of it.

Up in the tractor, the driver lets off the gas, engages the Jake Brake—it's so *loud*, being right here—but then he surges forward, the tow truck probably filling all his mirrors.

Harper crawls forward to sit against the back wall of the sleeper, her knees to her chest. She knows that if Bucketmouth rear-ends them hard enough to break the kingpin connecting the trailer to the tractor, then the front of the trailer will surge forward, pancake her between. But there's nowhere else to sit, no way else to be.

She collects her hair, wraps it around her left hand to keep it out of her eyes, and, moving steady and intentional, the tow truck pulls up even with her, knows right where she is.

Bucketmouth nods hello to her with his bloody face then keeps easing forward like showing her his new tow truck foot by shiny white foot.

When the shadow of the boom passes—it's the only part painted glossy black—he clicks every light on the beast on. Including all the ones shining on his hooks and chains and tow bar at the end of the boom, still folded up neat, a tarp burrito'd to it.

Bucketmouth eases forward a few more feet and Harper thinks he's getting position to swing over into this lane, end this once and for all, bounce her under the trailer, but then he just holds steady, pacing them, the tortilla truck driver probably not sure whether to try to run or hit the Jake Brake again. It's a standoff at eighty miles per hour, and climbing.

But then Bucketmouth engages something in his cab and the tow arm folds out parallel with the road like the two forks of a forklift, and Harper thinks she gets it: he's going to accelerate in front of them, raise that boom arm, get the tow bar level with the rig's windshield, then slam on the brakes.

She pushes against the sleeper to a standing position, bangs her open hand on the metal, trying to get the driver to understand, but then Bucketmouth isn't accelerating.

Harper holds onto the base of the blue line, her hair whipping out straight horizontal, and tries to see whatever Bucketmouth's showing her.

The boom arm. The tow bar. The tarp-burrito strapped to the underside of the two forks of the tow bar.

What?

Those are—tow bars, they're made to slide under the front of a rig, and sometimes that means maybe a foot clearance, getting past the fancy bumper. So they'll lower all the way to the ground, and usually have to. Why would any tow truck operator mess that up by strapping a tarp *under* those twin forks?

Harper's answer comes a moment later, when Bucketmouth nudges the tow bar lower, low enough that the front lip of the tarp makes contact with the asphalt blurring past.

It's enough to unravel the burrito, show the meat inside: Dillon.

And he's awake.

Harper stands holding on tight to the brake line, shaking her head no, screaming at Bucketmouth.

There's nothing she can do, though.

From the cab, Bucketmouth lowers the tow arm a half foot,

then three or four inches more, so Dillon's socked toe is right at the blacktop.

"*No!*" Harper screams, unable to even hear own voice.

Dillon wriggles in his straps but there's nowhere he can go, no way he can hope to stop this.

He's looking right down at the asphalt now.

Bucketmouth kills all his lights again, plunging Dillon into darkness. But Harper hears metal moving over there. The big piston of the boom, relaxing.

A light comes on on the side of the truck, shining down over the wheel, then it goes off and the one Bucketmouth meant comes on, spotlighting Dillon.

He's inches from the asphalt blurring by under his face, is jerking and jerking, trying to get away from it, but even if he could shake free, it would just be to fall.

Harper shakes her head no, no, and then, years before she's ready to say goodbye, the lights go dark again. When they come back on, Dillon's had his whole frontside scraped off. Blood and viscera string back from him, most of it burned black by rushing contact. Even the front half of his feet are gone, the heels still so perfect in their white socks.

Harper lowers her face, lets her hair go, and when she looks up a minute later, not wanting to see, she's alone.

Bucketmouth is gone again.

The truck she's in eases over into that lane, its trailer not trailing chips anymore, just sparks, and Harper looks to her left hand, death-gripped onto the red line, realizes that if she would have thought to crank that glad hand connection up, the trailer that's a wall behind her would have locked up, slowing the tractor she's standing on, and . . . and this tortilla-chip truck would have slowed, taking away Bucketmouth's audience—*her*. And? And maybe Dillon lives a half-minute longer?

Unlike Harper, probably, trying to hold onto that red line, whipping its metal head back and forth.

There's nothing she could have done, no. Nothing except—except not tilt that couch up into the ceiling, scream at her mom, and stalk off into the great unknown, pulling all her friends with her, because if she's trashing her own life, then she's not going down alone, is she?

She almost has to laugh about it, about the futility of it all. She huddles behind the cab, sobbing, screaming, chest hitching, and feels the big truck starting to slow to check the damage.

Check the damage and call in the law, hand her over. It's not like this *isn't* her fault.

And? Why not go to jail for a few years, right? What's left for her out here? May as well ride out the coming nightmares in a cell instead of a ratty motel over a bar. May as well go live with the killers and criminals, since that's what she is now. She can't beat Bucketmouth. He's been out here doing this too long, knows all the ins, every out, and all the shit between, knows it well enough he can have fun with it.

Harper nods to herself that no, she's not running off into the pasture before the truck's all the way stopped, but then she looks over into the passing lane, at the car steadily pacing them, honking one long continuous honk.

It's a pale Buick, Meg hanging out the passenger window.

Harper shakes her head no but her mom surges ahead, is even with the tractor for a half mile, trying to get him to pull over, but the driver up there's been spooked, probably isn't sure who's good, who's not.

The truck gears down to accelerate away from whatever this is starting to be.

Harper pulls herself up with the brake line, the lazy spring up there bouncing her, and leans out into the wind to track the Buick.

Maybe a half mile up, it screeches to a stop, parks itself sideways in the road, across both lanes.

"No, no," Harper says, the Jake Brake so loud and all at once, the tractor's brakes trying, the trailer pitching in, but they're not going to make it, they're not going to stop in time.

"No no no no!" Harper screams, then sees her shadow shoot out in front of her, meaning . . . meaning another truck is coming in, doesn't get why this truck is slowing, up here—but then, no, that's not it, Harper knows. The trailer's brake lights are dead! The truck back there isn't going to see them in time! It's going to jam this trailer behind her up against the sleeper, crushing Harper flat in the process.

She steps out onto the bobtail frame, sees immediately what she needs: the pigtail line, flopping in the deadspace between the wheels, its rubbery head catching the asphalt and bouncing up, bouncing up.

Harper drops to her stomach, holding her hair back with one hand, her other reaching for the line. She gets it, loses it, reaches farther, her hair probably in the tread of the whirring tires now, and then she has it, is pulling back, rolling to safety.

She fights the wind up to the sleeper, lifts the flap to plug the pigtail in, and . . . the rubber's all chipped. It won't fit. Harper tries again, insisting, trying to get all those little brass pins lined up. Same result. She drops to her knees, inspects the rubber plug, finally puts it to her teeth and tears the offending rubber away, then forces it in, having to use all her weight.

The lights come on behind her, and the best sound in the world is the rig back there hauling on its horn, its tires locking up, its trailer probably swinging around to jackknife, Harper doesn't know, is curled against the sleeper with her eyes squeezed shut, her fists by her temples like that's going to stop all this from crushing her flat.

It's weird, she thinks, that she can smell that driver back there's tires, but then of course the tires she's smelling are right here—the tortilla-chip truck's locked up too, to try to keep from slamming through that Buick up there playing chicken.

At what has to be the last moment, the driver, not stopping in time, veers over into the ditch, the truck losing weight on one side, trying to roll over. If it had a real load, it would definitely already be on its side, bulldozing earth and grass before it, but what chips are left, they still weigh nothing.

The truck finds its center again, settles, then coughs once, dies.

"Harper, Harper!" Meg's screaming, the rear passenger door open.

Harper steps down into the ditch and the world under her feet is still rushing past at eighty miles per hour, fast enough that she falls to her knees, the heels of her hands. She's shuddering, can't breathe right, her mouth opening and closing like a carp pulled up onto shore to drown in the air.

"What the everliving fucking—!" the driver's saying through his open door.

And he's coming down after it, isn't the nice guy he was. Who would be.

Harper shakes her head no, no, is already rolling away,

scrabbling up onto the blacktop, lunging across the lane and collapsing through the open door of her mom's car.

"I'm sorry, I'm sorry, I'm sorry," she's saying into the bench seat, the Buick already accelerating away from what's about to be the worst pile-up on 80 in years, probably.

"Did you see, did you see?" Meg's saying over the front seat, reaching down to pat Harper's back.

"You good?" their mom asks in her all-business voice, like this was just an everyday thing that just happened.

Harper shakes her head no, she isn't, and when she leans forward, it's into her mom's back, to lay her head there, be safe at last.

20

BECAUSE THAT BIG white tow truck can be a couple miles behind as well as it can be waiting up ahead—with headlights off, it's invisible, it's everywhere—Harper doesn't let her mom pull them over to the shoulder.

"But you were—" her mom tries, and Harper understands: she was riding on the non-passenger part of a rig barreling down the interstate, she almost died, she might be hurt somewhere she doesn't even know yet. More important, just to be not moving for a few minutes, to rest, to breathe, to settle and reset, take some bearings, stop shaking, let the tears finally come . . . her mom's right about all of it, doesn't even need to say it, can say it all just with her concerned eyes in the rearview mirror, with her right hand on top of Harper's on the back of the front seat.

Harper can't stop, though.

Waiting in her head for the next quiet moment are all of Dillon's last moments.

She swallows them down as best she can, shakes her head no, waves her mom on, on, go, keep moving.

Her mom looks to Meg, who nods yes about this, so she gets the Buick back up to speed again.

"But the first turnaround," she promises.

"Cops," Harper manages to get out.

"She's saying we need the police," Meg clarifies.

"What is going on, girls?" their mom asks, and the way she skips the contraction says how deadly serious she is. How this is the end of whatever bullshit they're going to try. The end before it even begins.

A sign for the Fort Steele rest area smears by.

"There?" their mom asks before either of them can come up with an answer for what's going on tonight.

Together, they shake their heads no.

"Why?" their mom asks, not liking this.

"Rest stops fall down," Harper says.

Meg nods solemnly, stroking Sheba's head.

"Then I think I will just—" their mom says, slowing again to pull over on the shoulder.

"We can't stop, Mom!" Meg says.

"He'll find us," Harper adds, already looking behind them.

"He?" their mom says, then to Harper: "He where you got the jacket?"

Harper looks down to it, kind of amazed to still be wearing it.

"What were you thinking?" her mom asks the two of them. "Two young girls out on the interstate at night? Did you know there's all manner of danger out here tonight? I was stuck in line for that fire for I don't know how long, and then—some trucker blew his lid at that other rest stop, I guess."

"Wagonhound," Harper says.

"How do you know its name?" their mom asks, watching Harper in the rearview again.

"I used to always have to stop there to pee," Harper says, trying to hide her reflection. "With Dad."

"I'm just lucky to have found you at all."

"You weren't supposed to," Harper says.

"I'll always come after you, Harper," her mom tells her. "I don't care what you say to me, what you break in the house. You're my daughter."

"That driver almost had to hit y'all, Mom," Harper says. "I don't know how he stopped. If it wasn't—"

And then she realizes: it was a new truck, wasn't it? Meaning that pigtail's electricity, it wasn't only for the lights, it was also for the electronic braking system, wasn't it?

Meaning, it was *Harper* who almost killed them.

No surprise.

"But he did stop," her mom says. "It wouldn't have mattered if it was a train either, girlie. I would have stood in front of that for you too, I hope you know that. That's what mothers do."

Harper tries to blink the heat from her eyes.

"Kissy," she says, her voice cracking at last. "And Jam, and—and *Dillon*, Mom."

"Dillon will always be around," her mom tells her. "His kind . . . he's made of Laramie, won't ever be able to leave, not really. And I'm sure Kiss and James will show up just before winter. Yellowstone doesn't need as many workers once tourist season is—"

Harper interrupts by sputtering into tears again. She buries her face into the backseat.

"What's got into the two of you?" she hears her mom asking Meg.

Meg doesn't say anything in reply. Because it's Harper's friends, Harper's news, Harper's secret.

Harper's *fault*, Harper corrects, inside.

"And I don't know if the cops are going to help us, Harp," her mom announces. "I think they take the side of truckers when there's a kid trying to stow away on their truck. Trying to get him in trouble might even get you on their radar, right?"

"It's not him, Mom," Meg says.

"Then who?" their mom asks.

Bucketmouth, Harper doesn't say. This monster of a man who eats parts of people and then tears his own face off, grows another one. He doesn't like Indians, though, Mom, so we're safe from him in that regard, anyway—safe from getting eaten, anyway.

Harper sits up all at once, realizing something.

"What?" Meg says.

"He doesn't . . . he can't do that thing he does with, with *us*," Harper says. "With Indians."

Meg considers this but doesn't fill in any of the blanks for their mom. Not out loud.

And then the Buick's speed sags.

Fort Steele. The rest stop.

"We don't have to stop or anything *scary* like that," their mom says, making fun of the idea. "But this is as good a place as any to turn around."

"Mom, no," Harper says, leaning up to touch her mom's shoulder.

"Harper, if you don't tell me—"

"Straight," Harper says. "Please. Please. Listen, I'm sorry I broke the plates, I won't ever watch that baseball movie again, whatever you want. Just—not here. Keep going."

"Why?" her mom asks again, that easy turnaround still drawing the Buick that direction, her foot already off the gas to ease them over into the exit.

"Rawlins," Harper says. "I promised myself I would get to Rawlins."

"Any promises for after that?" her mom says, turning around, face to face.

Harper shakes her head no, and, in response, her mom re-centers them in the westbound lane.

"So I'm helping you keep a promise to yourself that you made when you were mad at me?" her mom asks, raising her eyebrows in the mirror about it.

"Promises to yourself are the most important, right?" Harper says, settling back into the seat, the Buick gathering speed again.

"It's called discipline," her mom says. "And this isn't exactly what I meant."

"It's a start," Harper says, and watches the dark pasture for a glint of chrome, a flash of white.

"What's in Rawlins?" their mom asks a couple of miles later. "I've been there, you know. It's not exactly a resort destination."

"Isn't there that DPS station or whatever on this side of town?" Harper asks.

"Why are you so interested in the police tonight?"

"We're Indian, Mom," Meg says. "That's rule number one, right? Always know where the cops are?"

"So you can know where *not* to go, yeah," their mom says with a sort of pressed-lip grin, switching hands on the wheel to regard Meg.

"He'll follow us there," Harper says.

"Dillon?" her mom asks. "Are you still hung up on him, Harp? He's just going to . . . never mind. Some things you have to learn for yourself, I guess."

He'll just grow up to be like your father, she was going to say. Hauling just enough loads to pay the bills, never enough to sock anything away.

It's almost comforting to Harper, really, her and her mom falling back into their old arguments.

She breathes in deep, lets it back out.

"How far to Rawlins?" she asks.

"Twenty minutes?" her mom says.

"Staties are at the first exit, right?" Harper says.

"They don't like to be called that," her mom says.

"Troopers," Meg fills in.

Harper leans forward, hangs her arms over the front seat, says to Meg, "Turn that on?"

It's the CB their dad wired under the dash that time they drove to Yellowstone for their big family vacation, so he could ask about the traffic ahead of them. He said it felt weird to be on the road without his ears on.

Their mom had hated it, hated that he could essentially leave the car anytime he clicked the mic open.

It hadn't been the best trip. But they had gotten headsup about a blowover ahead of them, which had felt to Harper like looking into the future, seeing over the horizon.

"It still works?" Meg says, twisting the power on.

The mic hisses static.

"The antenna," Meg says, and is halfway out the window working on it at sixty miles per hour before their mom can stop her.

Meg comes back breathless, windblown.

"What are you two trying to do?" their mom says.

Meg hands the mic back, looks to Harper to answer for them.

"Save our lives, I hope," Harper says, and closes her eyes, speaks into the void.

"BREAKER BREAKER," HARPER says on channel after channel, because they don't know where he might be listening in. "Come in, Lockjaw, calling Lockjaw, this is Big Sis. Paging Dr. Tetanus, somebody looking for a shot of conversation, here. Bucketmouth, Bucketmouth, got your ears on, come back."

After which, each time, she holds the handle up, eyes closed in prayer. If this doesn't work, then . . . what? Wait for that white tow truck's grill to fill their rearview? If he gets that close on the open road, though, then it's all over.

Some chatter comes back, but it's just asking questions, and asking if she's on the right channel, and how old she is, and isn't, which her mom scowls about, as it just confirms her estimation of all truckerkind.

Wash, rinse, repeat, channel after channel, mile after mile, until, finally, a mic opens up, sucking in the static. No voice comes through but there's ears on the other end.

"There you are," Harper says.

The mic opens and closes in what feels like grudging hello. The way you acknowledge something when you know there's people who can listen in.

"Guessing you don't look like any certain boyfriends by now, do you?" Harper says.

Meg furrows her brow about this but Harper shakes her head no, she can't explain.

"It's because he's *Indian*," she says, her lips right to the mic. "Did you think Indians can only have dark skin, long hair?"

Bucketmouth opens his end, leaves it open, then closes it.

"Sorry about that," Harper says. "Would have told you, but, you know. Had some other things to be dealing with, you could say."

"Harper, what are you—" their mom says, the mic open, and Harper curls around it, away from her mom.

This time a chuckle comes through the static.

"Rawlins," Harper says to him. "Take the first exit. You'll see me."

"And why would I do that, Big Sister?" Bucketmouth says at last, his voice low and creaky—*not* Dillon's. Not anybody's, the way he's talking.

"Because I've got something you want."

The open air sucks in, holds, goes away.

She's got his attention.

"*Bucketmouth*," she says, not to him but about him. "I know where your name comes from."

"I told you, it—" he starts, then seems to remember he's on open air, here. He clicks back off in what sounds like frustration.

"It's not fish," Harper says.

"Bullshit," he says back. "Over."

"You're either there or I'm gone forever," Harper says. "I don't know what you're going to look like next, but I know how you work, can tell the world. This is your one chance. Take it or leave it."

"Rawlins," he finally comes back.

"First exit," Harper confirms, and lowers her face into the top of the front seat.

"I don't know what this is about," her mom says.

"It's almost over," Harper says back.

It's really a prayer, she supposes.

THE NEXT CALL is from the one working payphone at the truckstop just east of Sinclair.

While it's ringing Harper gets herself breathing hard.

"911, what is the address of your emergency?" the dispatcher says instead of hello.

"He just—he's the one who hit that state policeman!" Harper says in her best practiced shriek. Luckily, she's been practicing all night.

"Ma'am, ma'am, okay, I need your—"

"He's driving this, this big white tow truck, like for eighteen wheelers!"

"Ma'am, if you can just—"

"He's at Rawlins in a few minutes, the first exit westbound."

She cringes, was trying to talk stupid, not good.

"How do you know this, ma'am? Can I get your—"

"You've got to stop him! He said he's coming to get the rest of the cops!"

With that Harper hangs up, holds the phone there long enough for anybody standing close by to keep walking.

She turns to Meg, right beside her.

Meg nods good, good.

Their mom is at the pump, filling up for the drive back to Laramie.

"She's gonna ask," Meg says.

"We'll tell her later," Harper says. "We tell her now, she checks us into the hospital because we're crazy."

"You sure about this?" Meg asks.

"Mom?"

"Him."

Harper studies her mom, working the gas spigot back into the side of the pump, taking two tries to get it to hang then threading her long hair out of her face, just looking out at the interstate like studying it.

For maybe the first time, Harper wonders if her mom's looking for her husband out there the same way Harper and Meg are always still looking for their dad. It's something about the way her body's both turned to the road, but also turned away—it's a posture, a way of being, that somehow means something's missing. Some*one*. Does her heart beat harder when she hears a tractor coupling to a trailer through the thin walls of their house? Did she already know that CB still worked, because she listens to it every time she's alone in the car? Does she see her husband every time she looks into the faces of his daughters? Is that why she's so hard on them, because she's forever mad at him for not coming back?

"She's not going to like this," Harper says to Meg.

"Go," Harper says, and steps into the truckstop behind her little sister, casing every face in the place.

He's not there. All these faces have skin, or are covered in beards. And none of them are tracking her and Meg.

They meet their mom at the register, Meg with an apple

and a tall blue Icee, Harper with a microwave burger.

Their mom nods, pays for all that and the gas.

"You girls are going to bankrupt me," she says, her usual line.

Harper smiles, puts her burger in the microwave for two minutes and looks past it, out the window.

A big white tow truck is coasting past the pump island for the cars.

Her heart beats once, hangs there when the truck slows, but then it eases forward again for its own pumps, disappears behind a brown Kenworth W900 at the first island, its forty-eight foot trailer painted up with a stagecoach robbery mural.

Harper lowers her head to hide her face in her hair, and, finally, when her burger dings, she breathes out again, draws in with a gasp.

"You ever going to tell me what this is all about tonight?" her mom says, standing right beside her.

Harper nods yes, yes, says, for her mom and Meg both, "I'll be out. Bathroom."

It's not because she needs it, it's so they won't be a mom and two sisters. Still, she makes hot eyes to Meg, directs them outside so Meg will get it, and then takes Meg's hair, pushes it up.

Meg gets it, wraps her hair into a sloppy bun on top of her head, and, on the way out, peels a pair of stoner shades from the spinning rack, has them on like they were hers all along.

"Good girl," Harper says, already shrugging out of the leather jacket, dropping it down on the newspaper rack.

A solid sixty-count later she's pushing through the door after them, telling herself not not *not* to look over to the left, and someone nudges the back of her left arm.

Harper spins around, ready to run, ready to scream, ready to die, but it's just a biker.

He's holding the leather jacket out to her.

"Think you dropped this," he says, and they both look down to the dark places on the jacket's arm, where the patches just were. Where they most definitely aren't anymore.

"Thanks," Harper says, all eyes in the place on her now.

She turns, pushes through the door at last, and makes her way to the Buick, only looks over to the left about eighty times.

"What?" Meg says when Harper gets in, immediately goes to the rear floorboard.

"*Drive*," Harper says to her mom.

Her mom doesn't give her away by looking over the back of the front seat, just eases away, and Harper, traitor to herself that she is, is more thankful for her than anything in the world.

"We don't have to watch that movie again, Mom," she says from under the leather jacket, in case maybe her mom didn't hear her say that earlier.

"I watched it," her mom says back, checking if she can turn onto the road. "That black player, he's easy on the eyes, isn't he?"

"I hate you, Mom," Harper says, her lips pressing together right after.

"Hate you too, love," her mom says back like they never even fought, like their couch is in the same place it always was, and eases them away.

21

BECAUSE OF HARPER'S call, the line for Rawlins starts about a half mile out.

"No no no," Harper pleads, leaning over the front seat again.

"Seatbelts," her mom says, checking the rearview.

Harper does too.

It's just a normal Mack dumptruck, a woman in an orange vest behind the wheel, drinking from a tall green thermos.

Meg belts in and Harper does as well.

"They're only supposed to have a roadblock for *him*," Harper says. "Not for—not for everybody."

"Because that's how roadblocks work," Meg, ever the little sister, says, looking back to punctuate it with her eyes, her Icee-blue mouth kind of undercutting it all.

Harper flips her off close-range.

"Girls, girls," their mom says, then, half in jest: "Don't make me stop this car . . ."

"We're already stopped," Meg says, obviously.

The headlights pile up behind them.

Meg dials through CB-land, finds news of the parking lot this leg of 80 is now.

"What's a checkpoint charlie?" Meg asks.

Harper opens her mouth to answer but her mom's already there: "What your sister engineered up here, evidently."

Harper looks behind them again. Bucketmouth should be ten, twenty, maybe thirty vehicles behind them, shouldn't he? It's all just headlights, though. He can't be in front of them anyway, or there'd be no need for the roadblock.

He can bring that big white tow truck around in the passing lane, though, can't he? Just hammer on down past the exit, then circle back? How do roadblocks ever even catch anybody?

"This where Dad used to think Bigfoot lived?" Meg asks then, bringing Harper back.

"Bigfoot?" their mom says, looking between them.

"He—" Meg starts.

"I know, I know," Harper says.

"He said he saw him running into a tunnel just east of Rawlins," Meg recites from their meager store of family lore. "Right?"

Harper unfocuses her eyes enough to dredge that bedtime story up: her dad jamming gears out of Rawlins, everything around him grand and dramatic, just an hour and change from his baby girls and his beautiful wife, but . . . is that *Bigfoot* in his headlights? Was he over on the golf course chasing deer, eating flowers? At which point their dad's fingers would find their ribs—Meg's mostly, since Harper was older—and Meg would scream and laugh, and they'd all get in trouble for not going to sleep, for not being reasonable, for laughing until they were crying.

"Must be," Harper says.

That story always ended with Bigfoot running back to his side of the road, out of their dad's headlights, their dad acting out those large steps in the girls' small bedroom, then diving down into a tunnel that went under the interstate. How her dad played that in the confines of the bedroom was wriggling under their two beds as best he could, coming up between, roaring his Bigfoot roar.

Harper hasn't let herself think of that in years.

"Do you think it's really there?" Meg says.

"Bigfoot's a he not an it," Harper says.

"The tunnel, I mean," Meg says.

Harper looks left and right, can tell . . . maybe? . . . that the grass is a touch taller just behind them. Like water's been going more that way than other ways?

"Why would he make a story up about a tunnel?" their mom says, shutting this down because when they're talking about their dad, she's always way on the outside, the bad guy.

"There are tunnels under the road," Harper says. "I saw one earlier."

"Where?" Meg asks.

Harper shakes her head that it doesn't matter, and then it's their turn to process through the checkpoint.

The city bear leans down, looks in, casing all these Indian faces.

"Little far from the reservation, aren't you, ma'am?" he says to Harper's mom.

"This used to *all* be our land, you know?" her mom says back. Harper and Meg lock eyes and shake their heads: this statie doesn't know what can he just opened, does he?

"Ma'am?"

"This used to *all* be Indian land," their mom repeats, clipping her words more than usual, doing her hand over the dash to show she's talking about all of America.

"Ma'am, we just need to—"

"But then men with hats like yours, guns like that one, they came and they took it all away," their mom goes on. "Far from the reservation? First, the reservation system is broken, and second, this is *all*—"

"Okay, okay," the statie says. "These are your daughters?"

"Oh, so now we're talking about stolen children?" their mom asks right back, ready to go. "Do you know how much it used to cost to adopt an Indian baby when I was a girl?"

The statie looks at her, looks at Harper, looks at Meg, sees the family resemblance, the complete absence of smiles, then stands, waves them past.

"Yay, Mom," Meg says.

"Don't try that," their mom tells them.

"Because they can shoot you?" Meg asks. "What about you?"

"Let him try," their mom says back, and Harper looks over to the brand-new DPS facilities that probably weren't there when her dad was making up his Bigfoot story.

"There," Harper says like just thinking of this. "We can watch from there."

Her mom, close-lipped, playing along with a game her shoulders are telling them she knows is stupid, loops them around, parks out at the edge of that parking lot, turns the Buick off.

"How long till he comes through, you think?" she asks.

"He?" Harper says.

"Your boyfriend."

"Not long enough for us to explain it," Harper says.

Her mom nods like she should have expected that.

Meg crunches into her apple and her mom studies the line of headlights for Dillon, completely unaware that there's probably some of him in the tread of the Buick's tires.

Harper squints her eyes, trying to push that image away.

"What's he in?" her mom asks.

"Big white tow truck," Harper says.

"Kiss and James with him?" her mom asks, blind to the knife their names are. "They were looking for you, you know."

"He went by Jam, I think," Meg offers.

"Before signing on with Yellowstone, you mean?" their mom asks back.

Harper's watching a big tow truck silhouette edge forward, just one vehicle back from the checkpoint now. Twenty seconds later it's there, and the staties converge, pistols drawn.

Harper opens her door to see better, stands behind it.

"Run, run," she whispers across, one-hundred-percent ready to see Bucketmouth gunned down. Instead, a black driver steps out, hands high. He drops to his knees, places his forehead to the ground without being told to. Because, Harper knows, he doesn't want to get shot.

"That him?" Meg asks.

Her answer is one of the staties shining her light onto the door of the tow truck, showing that the paint's not white but yellow. The statie's noting the company the truck tows for.

"Shit," Harper says.

"Language," her mom calls out.

Harper looks farther down the line, doesn't see any booms silhouetted against the far lane.

"I don't understand," she says.

"I understand this stake-out needs some facilities," her mom says, standing.

Together her and Harper look back to the dark DPS building.

"It's after five," Harper says.

"Cops sleep?" her mom says back.

"Me too," Meg says, coming up through her window to drum on the roof of the Buick.

"Again?" Harper asks.

"Forty-four-ounce Icee?" she says back.

"Go, go," Harper tells them.

"You too?" her mom asks. "Hour and a half home."

"I'll pee in a cup," Harper says.

"Not in my car you won't."

"Seat, then," Harper says, then, about the roadblock, "I've got to *watch*."

"They're not going to let us in," Meg says, down in the parking lot now, carrying her apple core by the stem like it's suddenly radioactive.

"This used to all be Indian land . . ." their mom says back grandly, tragically, like an elder about to go off for six directionless hours, and Harper shakes her head in wonder, steps aside to let her pass.

"Don't go anywhere," her mom says, then raises the keys to show Harper that isn't really an option anyway.

"Thanks for the trust," Harper says.

"Thanks for the great track record," her mom tells her, and's gone, Meg trailing behind.

Harper settles in behind the wheel to be sure not to let Bucketmouth slip through the checkpoint, but now that the big tow truck's pulled to the side, its driver cuffed in the back of the car, she can tell they're pretty much just waving people through, are only still doing this because they haven't gotten official orders to stop. But their heart's not in it so much anymore.

"Thanks, guys," Harper says, and looks down to the blinking lights of the CB, the volume dialed all the way down, the red wire connected straight to the battery, Harper knows, because that's how her dad always did things.

Three cars later, one of them an ambulance that the staties just wave through, a hunting truck pulls up. Harper can tell it's a hunting truck because it's painted camo, a home job. And because it's missing all four doors.

Harper stands fast from the Buick.

It's the Park truck, stripped down and covered back up. And the driver, he's wearing camo too, and evidently has a face of some sort under that same camo cap, isn't just muscle and bone and teeth.

The statie steps back to study this truck and shakes his head in appreciation, or amusement, like this isn't something he wants to get involved with writing up tonight.

He waves Bucketmouth through.

"*That's him, that's him!*" Harper screams, rattling the chain link fence, kicking it, then going back to the car, honking and honking.

All the staties look over to her and she points ahead to the Park truck, points with both arms, with her whole body.

The staties look to each other, shrug, and turn back around.

The Park truck, though. Bucketmouth went back for it, left the doors in the pasture, went after it with a couple spraycans of paint, and poured water into it for one last ride.

Coming up the ramp now, he slows enough to lift something black and blocky from the seat beside him. Then he unwinds a spiral cable, holds the mic up for her to see.

The dead statie's radio rig. Right there beside him for the stop.

Harper fumbles at her CB, finds him on 19 saying "Big Sis, Big Sister, Harpo Marx, looking for you out here, darling. Big Sis, come in, I'm here wait—"

"I'm going to tell them now," she says back.

"Tell who what?" he says so innocently. "I just want to have a face-to-face sit-down, over. Well, emphasis on *face*, over again."

Harper tracks the Park truck's one good taillight to the intersection.

If she doesn't pull him away somehow, he's coming right to her, she knows. And her mom and Meg have to be almost done inside by now.

"Meet me *under* 80," she says all at once.

"Under?" Bucketmouth says back playfully.

"You just drove over it," Harper tells him. "I'll be there when you figure it out. But not for long."

"Sorry, Big Sis, I don't quite—"

"Turn left *now*," Harper says, watching his one taillight.

His blinker comes on flashing white through the shattered red and the truck eases over to the left.

Good, good. Perfect.

"I'll be there," Harper says.

"Copy that," Bucketmouth says.

Harper sets the mic down, checks the rearview, fully expecting to see her mom and Meg walking up.

Nothing. No one. Yet.

"Shit," she says, and stands up, closes the door quietly, just pressing it shut at the end.

She stalks off, comes back five steps later to pull the leather jacket up through the rear window, wrap herself in it against the cold.

22

HUNCHED AGAINST THE curving west wall of the tunnel under 80, the smell of dead animal and must in every breath, Harper catches herself wondering about the Bigfoot story her dad used to tell her and Meggie.

It was just for fun, of course. They even knew that then.

But can a story become real? Because, right now, there *is* supposed to be a monster ducking into this concrete tunnel with her.

The dead animal she stepped through to situate herself here was a dog, Harper's pretty sure. Maybe a coyote. Probably it caught a bumper in the upper world and dragged its way down here to lick its wounds, die in private.

When Bucketmouth kills her, will anybody find her bones, or will some other dogs drag them off? Will the coyotes pull her apart, snap at each other over the choice bits?

It's better than the other option, though. It's better than Bucketmouth getting his teeth into her mom, or Meg. That's the one thing Harper wants to extract from him before it's all over. A guarantee that he won't come for them, ever. That it can stop with her, here, now.

The other option is to end him, of course. But how? She can't outmuscle him, can't outfight him. She could slap him with a fast-moving bumper like he did with Kissy, like he did that statie, but he's not going to let himself get tricked up onto the blacktop, Harper knows. If anything, she'd be the one standing in those sudden headlights.

If she had a knife she could use that . . . maybe. But he'll have a knife too, she bets. And maybe another gun. If he stashes little jars of body parts up and down the ditch, then he's probably got weapon caches too. Or, no: he's wearing that camo now. Not just the cap. That has to mean he jumped a real hunter, right? Even though it's not hunting season. Meaning he must have knocked on the door of some small house a mile or three off the highway, and then plundered the closet, the shop, taken his time in the mirror, the bodies of a family sprawled over his shoulder.

It doesn't matter.

Harper feels around for a sharp piece of rebar, a bottle to shatter a jabby edge from, but all she finds is grime and plastic cups and, for some reason, balls of yarn. She turns one of the balls of yarn over and over in her hand, imagines all the kittens of Rawlins, Wyoming gathering here in secret, for some serious play. It makes her smile, and that feels good and then bad, because she can't help but suspect it's the last smile she's going to get.

She cracks the wristband alight at last, shakes it brighter, needs the light to see what color all this yarn is, like she can't get killed without knowing.

Purple, one ball of gold.

With the weak glow of her wrist, she can see a pile of

blankets a body length farther down the tunnel. Some hitchhiker's slept here, or waited out the rain. She doesn't shake the ratty blanket, doesn't want to know if bones might spill out. She doesn't need to see any skulls right now, thank you. If she's in a mausoleum already, she'd rather not have to know that.

Finally she extracts the baby food jar from the leather jacket's secret pocket and studies it with her wristband, stares into these two swimming eyeballs, one blue, one brown, like scooped out of a dog's skull with a grapefruit spoon.

Who *is* he now? Not Dillon, he can't be Dillon. But, is there a breakover point, by blood quantum? Are half-bloods safe, quarter-bloods a maybe, just have to bite and see?

Think all you want, she tells herself. It doesn't change one single thing that's happened, or's about to, does it?

She sets the baby food jar between her feet, considers breaking it for the shard of glass it'll give. But that shard wouldn't even go deep enough to nick anything vital, would it? It would just make him mad, which would probably prolong whatever complicated death he's got planned for her. She didn't see into the bed of the Park truck, after all. He could still feasibly have the half of Dillon that didn't scrape away, could make her—just spitballing, down here in Hell—he could make her fold him over, sew his ragged edges together, knit his head together without the face, fold the shoulders across to each other.

Thing is, if it saves Meg and her mom, Harper might just do that if he wants it done, she knows. Whatever it takes.

But, a face-to-face sit-down?

Why did he want that back there, at that gas station? Why is he saying yes to it now? Doesn't he just want her gone so she won't tell anyone about him? Sure, he's a cat playing with his mouse, but it's been ninety miles, a few different trucks, four or five hours, and who knows how many bodies. The cat in him should be tired of the game by now, just want to curl up somewhere, sleep for a day or two.

Harper shoots her wrist out to keep that circle of green light in view, not sit in the absolute deepest darkness with this smell, those bones, that blanket. These two human eyeballs swimming in cloudy cinnamon.

She holds them up again, considers them.

"I'm sorry, Bible lady," she says to the blue one, and shakes the little jar gently like a snowglobe, the powdered cinnamon going cloudy, the brown eye floating around to look out at her now, like just realizing she's out here past the glass. "Who were you?" she asks it.

All she knows for sure, if Bucketmouth was telling it true, is that Brown Eyes was most likely a white guy, and probably a healthy one, at least at the moment his eyeball was scooped out. Otherwise Bucketmouth might be crawling into a body festering with cancer, or trying to heal a broken leg, or—

"Big Sister, Big Sister . . ." a male voice says from the north mouth of the tunnel. "You were listening back there, weren't you? You know I was born in a tunnel. Did you think I could die in one as well? I like your thinking, girl."

"It's Big Sis," Harper says, taking his silhouette in with a glance and then choosing to stare instead at the chipped concrete wall opposite her. "In Arapaho it's Nah Bee."

"Na-bi?" he says.

"My mom was trying to teach my sister to call me that when we were kids," Harper says with a shrug. "It means 'my big sister.'

My dad thought it sounded good for a CB handle. White people always think Indian words sound ancient and cool."

"Na-*bi*," Bucketmouth repeats, something familiar to his voice—no, to his mis-pronunciation? "It does sound pretty all right."

"*Nah* Bee," Harper corrects, just like her mom used to do with her dad, but it doesn't matter. Not at this stage of things. She's not her mom, and—

Harper stands all at once, her head thunking into the ceiling, her scalp scraping, hair snagging. She smooths it back, holds it tight to her scalp.

Why in God's green earth is she thinking of her dad now?

Bucketmouth feels his way down, is close enough to smell now. Close enough to smell like blood.

"Who?" Harper says about that blood, resigned.

"I never ate your boyfriend's finger," Bucketmouth confesses. "I didn't like being nineteen even when I *was* nineteen. Remember I was saying how, if I was smart, I'd hide emergency rations up and down the highway?"

Harper shakes her head no, no, please.

"It's three years ago," he says. "Winter, but between snows. 80's open for once, so all the trucks that were stuck in the barn, they're out and galloping, you know how it is. One of them picks up a lonely traveler who has to be cold, limping there on the shoulder like his right foot's frozen in the boot. Call it Christmas spirit."

"No, please," Harper says, her eyes heating up in a way she promised herself she wasn't going to let happen.

Bucketmouth takes her wrist in his big hand to *make* her listen.

"Things go the . . . what I guess you would call the *predictable* way," he says. "At least, predictable if I'm the one thumbing a ride. Is it a crime if a mountain lion kills a pretty deer just to not starve? That's all it was, Big Sister. Never mind if that deer has a spotted fawn or two back at the homestead, all—"

"*No!*" Harper says, trying to pull her arm back.

"What you don't understand," Bucketmouth says, "it's that I either take someone in my signature fashion or I'm Mr. Bloodyface. And nobody picks up hitchhikers with bleeding faces, believe me. And then I really do get frostbite."

"Please, just—"

"Anyway, I still had a few days with the face I was wearing, so I stashed a bit of the old man by a certain utility pole, one just up the road from here. For times of emergency, like tonight. Maybe you knew this gentleman of the road?"

With that he pulls her glowing wrist to his face, and under that green glow is, is: her *dad*, after all these years, all her praying, all the deals she's made with the world, in secret.

Harper jerks and pulls and kicks.

Bucketmouth smiles, drinking this in.

"You wanted to know why I didn't finish it back there when I could have," he says. "It was for this, Big Sister. Little girl. That trucker who picked me up, once he got comfortable enough with his new, ahem, traveling companion, he showed me school photos of his two beautiful daughters. Had them right there on the back of his visor. I recognized you the moment when I stepped up from that big red car, Harper, all the way back in Laramie. You could say I'm what you might call *good with faces*. And, damned if I didn't know exactly where this night could take us, if we did it right. And hasn't it all been worth it, for this reunion you never thought would happen in the real world? It's so rare I get to participate in the little rituals like this. It's always bite this, kill him, kill her too, run here, hide that, burn this place down, drive drive drive. You miss out on the normal parts of life, though. And you start to actually miss them. They're boring, sure, but they make it all complete, like. Without them, it's . . . it's like you lose your tether to the human world, does that make sense?"

"*Fuck you!*" Harper screams, pushing him into the west wall of the tunnel. "You're not him!"

"Of course not, of course not," Bucketmouth says, coming forward to hold her by the shoulders, offer his fake consolation. "Nobody could ever replace a father, and I would never presume to. But I did think to bury his commercial license along with his pinky finger, so, yeah. I might deliver a load or three, these next couple of weeks. Our little interaction, this, you and me here, it's going to last me for a while, I think. Give me a lot to . . . to think about. I'm going to miss you, Big Sister. Or, I mean—former Big Sister?"

"What are you saying?" Harper asks, her face going even colder, her heart pausing between beats to listen.

Bucketmouth holds his right hand out, showing the topside and then the palm, like just seeing them himself.

Slowly, Harper guides her green glow over.

Blood. His hand is black with it, along with long strands of matted hair. The blood and hair go up his sleeve, into the camo.

"Your mom actually hit me," he says, touching a place on his jaw. "*Hard*, I mean. I think she thought I was actually him, coming back at the most random time. Just sitting in the backseat of that eggshell Buick."

"No no no," Harper says, falling to her knees.

"I didn't know what you might have told her," Bucketmouth says with a shrug like he regrets this just as much as she does. "Police will listen to a hysterical mother years before they'll listen to her runaway daughter. You left me no choice there, sorry."

"But, but . . . Meg?"

"Ah, *little* sister, yes," Bucketmouth says. "A dilemma, I agree. Actually, she's hogtied down at the end of the tunnel, gagged pretty tight, too. Out of the way of any headlights. I wasn't sure if she was a problem to be solved or a bargaining chip, so I hedged my bets, figured I could solve her later if I didn't spend her now."

Harper's watching that end of the tunnel now.

"Meg!" she calls.

No answer. She pushes away to go there, see for herself, but Bucketmouth has her by the upper arm already.

"Like I was saying," he says, and makes his non-bloody hand into a blade, holds it tight across his own mouth to show, "I gagged her tight. And you could say I've got some experience there."

"Let me see her!"

"What would I get from lying?" he says back to her. "I didn't lie about your mom just now, when I could have, when it would have made you more . . . *docile*, if you didn't know the truth."

"You want me to keep having hope, so you can crush it."

He shrugs, says, "You've got an evil mind there, Harper. I like it, I like it."

"How would she even have been a bargaining chip?" Harper says. "What could I have that you can't just take?"

"I thought you might have found your way to a gun," he says, and pats his chest with both hands. "I'm charming, kind of wily, know my way around these roads, but I'm not bulletproof."

"You're a monster is what you are."

"Said the deer to the mountain lion. That's not what the mountain lion says to itself, though. The mountain lion just says 'I'm hungry.' Guess I better go do what I do."

"What do you *want*?" Harper says, offering herself. "Take me for her, there's your bargain, your deal. I'm the one you want."

"But you said it yourself," Bucketmouth tells her. "I've already *got* you."

"I—your stupid name," Harper says. "I know where it's from, what it means. You don't have that, do you?"

"Ah yes," Bucketmouth says. "That niggling little mystery."

"If I tell you, Meg's safe?"

"Got to see what I'm buying, I think. Be bad business otherwise."

"It's what truckers call someone who won't shut up on the CB," Harper says. "It means you're someone who loves the sound of their own voice."

Bucketmouth lets this settle, finally looks up to her, nodding appreciation.

"It fits, doesn't it?" he says. "Thank you. I wasn't expecting everything to tie up so neatly tonight. Now if only I could figure out what 'band camp' meant to you and yours."

"How do you know about that?" Harper asks before she can stop herself.

"Your boyfriend was saying it when I was . . . cinching him to that tow truck for the big . . . you know." He scrapes his right hand down over the road of his left. "What does it mean to you?"

"It's where we kissed for the first time," Harper lies, hoping it can become true as well. That Dillon's somehow waiting for her by cabin 6, his clarinet hidden behind—no, drums, he would only ever bang on drums, and never with the music the rest of the band was playing, always to his own irrepressible beat.

But then his face scrapes away, the nasal cavities bare, the sinus cavity open like a mucousy geode.

"I'm sorry," Bucketmouth says, touching her cheek with the fingertips of his right hand. Leaving blood, probably.

"No you're not," Harper tells him. "When you're done with me, you're going to kill Meg. If she's not dead already. You don't make it as long as you have by leaving survivors. I'm not stupid."

He shrugs, guilty as charged, his eyes locked on hers, like drinking this up.

"While we're being honest," he says. "That big white tank I set the fire under back at that podunk gas station? It was empty. Been empty for years."

Translation: she should have hit him in the face with the butt of that fire extinguisher. She *could* have, and maybe ended it right there.

"You know what?" Harper says. "Do what you want. It doesn't matter. You can't take away the—the good parts. You can kill Dillon in front of me like that, but I still remember the first time he held my hand. And my mom, you'll never be as tough as she was. And you don't even deserve to wear that face."

Harper reaches out to scratch it off but he catches her glowing green wrist, stops her.

"I really do regret this," he says, his other hand popping a knife open. "I'll make it quick. You deserve that. You've earned it."

"*Meg, run!*" Harper screams, her voice filling the whole tunnel.

"Don't worry about the ropes!" Bucketmouth calls after in Harper-falsetto. "Just shake them off, they're no big deal, he doesn't even know how to tie knots! Because he's never done anything like this before!"

This is hilarious to him.

While he's laughing, Harper brings her knee up with everything she has, to drive his balls up into the back of his throat, make him choke on them, but he sees it coming, sidesteps, and—

"What is *this*?" he says, holding her in place but squatting down.

The baby food jar. Harper must have tinked it over when she stepped into him.

She tries to kick it away, deny him this last morsel at least, but he sees that coming as well, doesn't even have to look up to keep the eyeballs safe.

"You saved one for me?" he says, letting the cinnamon settle so he can see who it is.

"Not on purpose," Harper tells him.

"*No!*" he says then, for the first time truly offended by something, looking fast from the jar to her. "You're not supposed to mix them! God, no, that—*you don't mix them!*"

Harper considers this, shuffling back through this whole night in an instant, through everything he's said, trying to pick out something she can maybe use. There's nothing about mixing or not mixing body parts, though. Just . . . rule one: no Indians. Rule two: nobody who's in a bad-to-him state. Three: any part'll do, not just tongues. Four: cinnamon because it tastes good. The cinnamon and tongues and Indians don't matter right now, though, do they?

The other one, though . . .

"The other jar cracked," Harper says, "it was leaking that cinnamon toast water all over the seat, so I poured them together. Sorry if I ruined the shit out of them."

She makes another stab at the jar, trying but not trying to slap it down.

"No no no," he's still saying, curling away, protecting the eyeballs. "If they—if they stay like this too long, it ruins them both. They mix together, and you end up looking all like . . . droopy, melty, hangdog."

"Little Preparation H under the eyes," Harper tells him.

"You laugh," he says, looking up to her, "but that works. But—it doesn't matter. They have to mix together for more than just two or three hours. We're talking days. Seasons. These are still good, if we can get them apart again." He casts around for some other place to stash one of these precious eyeballs.

"You said earlier you thought I could make it out on the road," Harper tells him, watching him close to see if this registers.

He nods, nods, isn't really paying attention, is frantic about preserving these stupid eyeballs, about restarting his precious little stash. But then he hears what she's said, looks up to her.

"I think I can make it out there too," Harper says. "And you also said there's more of your kind than anybody knows, because none of us normals ever . . . ever do what you did in that tunnel. We never have to see what we're really made of. What we can *be*, if we just . . . take that first bite."

He nods again, slower. All she's doing is repeating what he's already told her. Confirming it. Reminding him of it.

"Let Meg go," she says then, "if she's even really alive down there. Let her go, promise you won't do anything to her, and—and I'll try."

She nods to the jar to show what she means.

"*Are* there girl ones of you?" she asks.

"I—I don't know," Bucketmouth says, in wonder.

"How does your kind procreate?" she asks.

"We're cuckoo birds," he says. "We grow up in your houses, your living rooms, your breakfast nooks. And then one day we bite into the right piece of meat and everything changes."

Harper shrugs, smiles, says, "I was running away when you found me. I can keep running away, with you to teach me what's what."

"But you hate me."

"Because I'm not *like* you." Harper looks to one end of the tunnel then the other, and back to Bucketmouth, having to scream and scream in her head that this isn't her dad she's lying to. "But maybe I can be, right?"

Bucketmouth looks at the two eyeballs swimming in their cinnamon water.

"You're trying to . . . I don't know," he says. "Trick me somehow."

"What do you have to lose?" Harper asks. "How can it be a trick? I eat that"—she gags a little, gets it under control—"and I either turn into whoever that is or I don't, and we're back where we are right now."

He nods to himself, thinking this through, it looks like.

"Negotiation phase," he says. "Bargaining."

"Either way, you win," Harper says. "If I'm not like you, then you've tortured me more, made me eat an eyeball."

He kind of likes that.

"You'd turn into a—into a guy," he says.

"Always wanted to pee standing up," Harper says right back. "Maybe not get whistled at trying to walk across the damn parking lot."

"And she goes free?" Bucketmouth says, tipping his head to the idea of Meg.

"Now if she goes to the cops, she's turning them on to *me*," Harper says.

"If you change."

"But you've got to eat with me," she says, stepping in closer. "I don't want to go through this alone my first time."

"This face," he says. "It's—it's not even thirty minutes old."

"You look like my dad," Harper says, and nods to the jar. "Anything's better than that, if we're walking out of here together."

He smiles a bit at last, says, "That was just for shock value. Guess I've used that up already right?" He raises the jar to eye level again, studies its contents. "And it would be a waste to have these and not use them . . ."

"So do we have a deal?" Harper asks. "I do this, Meg's free."

"If you're *not* like me," Bucketmouth says, watching the end of the tunnel as well, "and—and I have to do what I do to make sure you don't go whispering about me to the state police, then you won't know what happens to her, will you?"

"At least there's a chance this way," Harper says. "At least there's a sliver of hope. I didn't come down here to die. I came down here to figure out how to live."

Bucketmouth paces, studies the eyeballs some more, whips his head back to Harper to say something but doesn't.

"I knew you were different," he says at last, excited about this prospect.

"Let's see how different," Harper says. "Must get lonely out there all by yourself, right?"

"You'll try to kill me, first chance," he says. "I took your mom away. Your dad. Your best boyfriend."

"But I won't come at you before you show me how it all works," Harper says back with a smile. "If I'm going to survive, I need to know what you know."

"If it takes."

"If it takes."

"'Silver-Tongued Devil!'" he says all at once. "*That's* what they should be calling me up there"—the interstate. "It's rude to just . . . do what I do with no pre-amble, isn't it? You can't talk a person to death, no, but you can talk them right up to it."

"Liquid lungs," Harper says.

"What?"

"Motormouth, verbal diarrhea, ratchet jaw, a real rattle trap. Babbles like a brook. Flies in his brainpan—"

"Because his mouth is always open," Bucketmouth completes, smiling so wide now. "At least word of me's making the rounds, right? Worst thing is to be ignored."

"Are we doing this or not?" Harper asks, stopping the bullshit.

"I shouldn't," Bucketmouth says with her father's mouth. "Three times in one night. It's gonna hurt in the morning, believe you me. But—hell. Yes, deal. Your sister will be safe."

"How long does it take to know?" Harper asks.

"With these, how old they are, 'aged' I should say . . . about ten minutes," he says. "Your face starts to itch, like, on the *back*side. Like tiny bugs are crawling all around back there. But you can't cough them out, can't scratch them away. That's how you know it's working."

"Guess I'm not just running away from home anymore," Harper says, delicately taking the baby food jar from him. "This is running away from myself, isn't it?"

Bucketmouth nods, his eyes watching hers so close, for the slightest indication of deceit. Moving slow, she twists the top off, the cloying sharp scent of cinnamon infusing their air.

"Preference?" she says, ready to pluck an eyeball up.

"What color are my eyes now?" he asks.

"Didn't you look in the mirror?"

"It was dark."

Harper leans forward, looks into her dad's blue-blue eyes, says, "Brown. Dark. My mom used to call him Brown-Eyed Handsome Man, after that song."

"Give me the other one then," he says, and tilts his head back for her to feed him.

Harper gets the brown eye out first, dollops it back in, fishes the Thunderbird Lady's up, careful not to burst it. It's slimy and it feels somehow uninflated, and is leaving clear slime on her fingertips.

"Sure?" she says.

"Hit me," he says, and tilts his head back farther, opens his mouth, then comes back up, mister paranoid, taking the jar from her, shaking the eye left behind up. It's brown.

He nods, lets his mouth drop open and watches the blue eyeball all the way past his lips, his hand guiding Harper's wrist the whole way to be sure there's no funny business.

"Watch this," he says, talking thick, and ovals his lips, giving Harper a window on his tongue smushing the eyeball forward through his teeth, the blue disc of color coming slow past his left canine.

He slurps it back in, swallows it without chewing.

"Like . . . you know how you can separate an egg white from the yolk?" he says. "This is like doing that to an oyster. All you're left with is the protein, none of the taste."

"Why did you—" Harper says, unable to get her words to follow her thoughts. "With Dillon, why did you cut his finger off, then?"

"And not his eye, you mean?"

Harper nods.

"Are you stalling?" he asks.

"Maybe," Harper says.

"It's your first time," Bucketmouth says. "Maybe . . . this might help."

He takes the jar, shakes it for the remaining eyeball and pinches it out delicately, inserts it into his mouth and bites through it with pornographic slowness, the pupil bulging out like a cartoon. Then he mushes it between his lips, keeping all the juices right there. He takes Harper by the back of her head, pulls her into a forced kiss, passing the jellied eyeball from his lips to hers—from her *dad's* lips to hers.

Because he can probably still throw his eyeball up if he figures this out, Harper lets this happen, her mind screaming, her fingers straightening hard, her throat trying to gag, her soul shriveling up in the corner.

She comes down, her saliva rushing.

"Swallow, swallow," Bucketmouth says, and massages her

throat with both his thumbs, his long fingers cradling her head.

Harper counts to three in her head, closes her eyes and swallows hard, trying not to think about egg yolks or oysters or that clear sac she saw a kitten born dead in once, and never told anyone about.

They sit down facing each other, their legs parallel but opposite, their backs against different sides of the tunnel.

"Ten minutes," Harper says.

Bucketmouth wipes his lips, nods, watching her.

"About one good cigarette," he says, patting his chest, not finding his pack.

"I can go get one?" Harper says, setting her hands to push up.

He applauds the effort, shakes his head no.

"Was that a dog I walked over back there?" he leans forward to ask, like he doesn't want the dog to hear.

"I think it was a coyote maybe," Harper says. "Is Meg really out there?"

"Scout's honor," Bucketmouth says.

Harper nods, feels her gorge rising. Bucketmouth leans forward to pat her back but she waves him off, gets through it herself, keeping her lips pressed tight together.

"It'll—it'll be better being someone else," she says when she can. "The girl I was, her mother was killed by this mad dog killer on the road."

"Her dad too!" Bucketmouth adds, so chipper about it.

"And her best boyfriend."

"Zhzhzhzh," Bucketmouth says, trying to make the sound of Dillon rubbing away on the asphalt, and then miming it out again with his hands.

"That was pretty fucking brutal," Harper says.

"Life on the road is hard," Bucketmouth says with a shrug. "Especially *on* the road like that . . ."

He tries not to laugh but it spurts through anyway.

"So why fingers?" she asks.

"Not always," Bucketmouth says. "Don't know where they might have been."

"I found his in the parking lot."

"And you didn't figure it out then?"

"That you had an *extra* human finger on you, that you'd dug up on the way there? That you would get some big rush from eating my dead dad's finger across the table from me?" Harper says. "No, I didn't jump to that obvious conclusion."

He laughs, is loving this.

"Fingers, eyes, ears, it doesn't matter," he says. "Nipples are good, kind of rubbery like octopus, but I never go below the belt. This one guy I—in Kansas. He had *milk* in his"—he touches his chest—"Can you believe that? It was sweet, and tasted sort of . . . *blue*, I guess."

Harper breathes deep, trying not to start the gag cycle again.

"But, you're smart," Bucketmouth says, nudging her knee with his. "You should have figured it out already."

"I'm not thinking too well right now," Harper says.

"Maybe it's working, then?" he says, leaning in to look into her face. "I take the fingers because I like them to watch me eat a piece of them. If I take one of their eyes, well. Then they can't watch so well."

"Figured it'd be something like that," Harper says.

"I am as the good Lord made me," Bucketmouth says.

"Got any beef jerky on you?" Harper asks back, trying not to sound like she's stretching this out. "We're going to need the calories, right?"

"The highway's full of snackfood items," he says in a corny PSA voice.

Harper smiles a drunk smile, leans her head back, counts to a hundred and eighty in her head, which is three minutes more. When she looks again, he's just watching her.

"You really are glorious," he says. "You're—if this works out, then you're the perfect one for me. I could never change into you."

"Even if you did women."

He nods.

"Why are Indians immune?" she asks.

"Not immune," he says. "Just . . . they're kind of like indigestion."

"But why?"

"I've thought about that," Bucketmouth says, eyes closed. "The ones of you still around, you made it through smallpox, right? When I got that vaccination as a kid, my mom says I nearly died."

"Your mom?"

"I don't know if she was like this or not," he says. "She never . . ." He opens his hand over the jar.

"It didn't even taste like anything," Harper says. "Just cinnamon."

"People taste the idea, I think," Bucketmouth says. "I mean, they don't actually *try*, but when they think about it, it's the idea that grosses them out. They judge without having any basis to judge."

"How long?"

"Four, five more minutes? It's not exact."

"I think I can feel something," Harper says, holding her hand out, spreading her fingers.

"It's in your face," Bucketmouth says, touching his own.

"You can feel it already?"

He nods.

"So it's started?"

"Started," he says, lost in the painful pleasure of it.

Harper touches her own face, is terrified of any tingling. Which of course makes her skin come alive.

She jerks forward, all ten of her fingers to her face now.

"Really?" Bucketmouth says.

Harper looks to him, her eyes heating up, and honestly doesn't know.

"It has been a lonely existence," he says, leaning back to luxuriate in this moment.

"Will I remember who I am?" Harper says.

"Can't forget," he says, flourishing his fingers over his own face like magic. "You've seen this before," he adds then, "but it kind of . . . accelerates the process, I don't know why. Making room, I guess. Like a snake shedding its skin."

He angles his head over to tighten his neck skin and feels around for a grip on the hinge of his jaw, peel this face off like the last one, and the one before that. But . . . his fingers aren't working? He looks at them like they're traitors, and then tries to snap, manages it once, can't get it to happen a second time.

"What is it?" Harper asks.

"My . . . I don't know," Bucketmouth says, trying to stand up against the curved concrete wall, his legs weak as well. Not his own anymore. He pinches at his thigh, pinches and twists, evidently isn't getting any pain fed up to his nerve centers.

He slumps back down, can't even get his hands up to his face now.

"What did you do?" he asks, his words slurring.

Harper stands, crosses to him, kneels down face to face.

"Breaker, breaker," she says into her right hand, her left cupped over the side of his head. "Anybody out there with ears on, maybe knows what would happen if certain mad dog killers were to, say, eat a part from someone who was paralyzed, come back? Anybody know what eating the meat from a person with a spinal injury might do to someone like him, over?"

His head flops over weakly, drool leaking from the corner of his mouth.

"Over," Harper adds, and does the dead key sound herself, drops that imaginary mic.

"Who, who?" he says.

"You've got some time," Harper says, looking on the ground to his left. "Figure it out. You're smart."

She finally finds the knife.

She pushes the point into the flesh of his forearm, blood welling up all around it. He doesn't jerk from the pain. He can't jerk. There isn't any pain.

She turns the knife over so the edge is down, drags it along his arm all the way to the hand, leaving a long line that opens like a lipless mouth.

"That's so the dogs will smell you," she says. "Or the coyotes. I don't know. Did you know a turtle will scavenge? They do. It's fucking weird, man."

His eyes are cloudy now.

"But maybe you just lie here for a few days," she says, angling her face over to line theirs up. "Sun won't get to you down here, dry you up. And if you figure out how to make a noise—are you trying right now?—who knows, if you figure out how, maybe all the truckers up there will stop, turn their engines off, stick their heads out the window, figure out where you are."

She squats down right before him, says, "But probably not, yeah."

His breath quickens.

"I'm just going to go down there"—the mouth of the tunnel—"see if my sister's really there or not, cool?"

His breath gets even more frantic, his eyes wet.

She watches him, drinking every drop of this up. "She better be there, too," she says at last. "I've . . . I never told you about when I was fifteen, did I? This was when my dad didn't come back from his Tacoma run. And then he kept on not coming back. I went up to the top of this one apartment building, told myself I could close my eyes and listen hard enough to hear through all the other trucks. But I never did, right? And when I came home the next morning, my mom made me waffles, and her hands were shaking." Harper wipes her eyes, doesn't let that stop this from happening all over again. "I think—I think she'd been sitting in the car all night, talking to him on the radio. To the idea of him. And, and *he* was the one who made waffles for us. But now Mom was doing it. And, and she remembered. When she put the syrup on, she did it like—like clock hands, with little dots for all the numbers, the same as he always did, and two lines for what time it was. We sat there and we ate those waffles and we didn't say one goddamn thing, and ever since that morning, it was . . . I don't know if you know what this is like or not. But you can't, can you? You were never a little girl. Wait, were you?"

He doesn't answer, just wheels his eyes all around.

"Until then, *I* was, anyway," Harper goes on. "I thought the world was . . . fair, I guess you'd say. That daddies always came home. But, know what? That day, that morning, part of me hid inside, I think. The little girl part. The me that still hoped, that still knew he was out there somewhere, that he had amnesia, that he'd tried to save somebody from bad people and was all caught up in that, was just trying to fight his way back."

Harper stares up into the curved top of the tunnel, says, "I came up with so many scenarios of what could have happened, what could *be* happening. I couldn't even watch movies at the theater in a normal way anymore. I always knew that rig I was hearing rumble past outside, that it was him, that I was missing my chance."

She settles her eyes back on Bucketmouth.

"I need to thank you now," she says, staring right into his soul. "Until now, I haven't been able to—to move forward? To keep growing up like I should have, I guess. Because I wanted to still be the girl he would recognize when he came back. You can't understand this, I know. But I've got to say it." She leans forward, his head in both her hands, and she puts her lips right to his forehead, says, crying now, "Goodbye, Daddy. I'm sorry you didn't ever make it home. I waited and I waited for you, but now I don't have to anymore. I know you're somewhere with Mom now, if Indians and white guys get to go to the same place."

With that she kisses her dad's forehead, keeps her lips there, trying to make this last and last, and at the end of it she wrenches his head around hard, snapping the neck.

"That's just in case," she says, standing, and, walking toward the mouth of the tunnel then—it's not quite a light, but it's better than this—she stops, the sole of her sneaker not all the way down. There's a caterpillar under it, stopped too, waiting.

Harper considers, considers, then swallows hard, puts her foot down somewhere else.

Two steps later she's running, her sister's name on her lips.

ACKNOWLEDGMENTS

I KNOW INTERSTATE 80 going across Wyoming better than I really want to. In 2015, when Lance Olsen was teaching somewhere else, or maybe galavanting around the world, I taught a semester for him at the University of Utah in Salt Lake City. My kids were still sort of young, but one of them was just old enough to drive—by a few days, I think? Maybe a month. Anyway, we loaded our whole little house into a storage unit, into my office on campus at CU Boulder, and the essentials we were going to need for the fall we loaded into a 1972 Cheyenne, into a 1969 C-10 four-speed, and into our Subaru. The two pickups had their beds mounded and tarped over, and, being just half-tons, they were sitting down on their frames, about. I have a photograph somewhere of our little convoy. Neither truck looks that road-worthy, and the new driver of us was driving the Subaru—the one that kept between the lines the best. This wasn't the first time I was shooting west on 80—the first time had been in the blowing snow in a rental car, with my sister Jenny in the passenger seat, trusting me, still a Texas driver then, to be able to do this—but this was the first time I could see this Wyoming over the ditches.

It's the one I tried to write into *Killer on the Road*.

Over that fall, I ended up driving back and forth between Salt Lake City, Utah and Boulder, Colorado more than I intended, and then, in the snow again, probably about February, my son and I came back to Utah to get the Cheyenne I'd had to leave there. It was a beautiful truck, even had those sport mirrors, all the original trim, stock wheels and hubcaps, but man was it contrary: fuel lines rotted from sitting too long, carburetor that had come from the factory with the wrong jets, and on and on. It wasn't really the best idea to try to shoot 80 between storms in a halfway working truck, but we did it all the same, my son following in the trusty Subaru. A few hundred miles shy of home, the transmission started to slip, then grind. I'd pull over, let it cool, get a few more miles out of it, and like this we got to Cheyenne. Seemed fitting, being in the truck I was in. Had to pull it the rest of the way home, then pay more for a rebuilt transmission than I'd paid for the whole truck. So it goes, right? So it always goes, with the trucks you keep your heart in.

All that time sitting in the ditch waiting for the transmission to cool, though, I could feel this novel uncoiling inside me. I didn't have Bucketmouth yet, but I sort of had Harper, I think, in that I'd already written Nona in *Demon Theory*, Izzy in *The Last Final Girl*, Denorah in *Good Indians*, Char from *Babysitter*, and I was soon to write Jade Daniels. Harper, to me, she fits right in with them. Get her into a corner, I mean, she'll show her teeth, fight her way out, and then fight the whole world while she's at it, just because.

These are the kind of people I prefer to believe in. They're also where I keep my heart.

As for where Bucketmouth finally came from, it's all the rest stops along 80, it's the big rigs slamming past, it's the gas stations out there like they're fading in from 1982. Bucketmouth comes from the loneliness and wind, the cold and the vastness. He comes from "Wyoming" is what I'm saying. Seriously, go drive 80 if it's not closed for wind and snow. 70 down here in Colorado's a gamey proposition most of the time, but 80, it'll plain eat you.

That's where I get Bucketmouth from—that feeling, standing alongside the road, that I could just disappear into all of this.

80 wasn't done with me, either. My son ended up at the University of Utah a few years later, so I was making that drive again, and again, but it was charged differently, now. When you're going to a kid of yours, that changes everything, doesn't it? It did for me. And it made coming back east so much more difficult. I felt like I was in some weird space between two homes, and the result was that 80 became a sort of liminal, weird space for me.

I haven't been all the way up and down it now for probably five years now, I guess? It tracks; I think I wrote *Killer* in . . . 2018? Ellen Datlow had asked me for a novella after *Mapping the Interior* did what it did, and since it only took four days to pull together, I figured, sure, yeah, I've got four days, why not do another novella right fast? Easier said than done. Next time I looked up, it was four weeks later, and I had either this novel or *The Babysitter Lives*. So I sat down to write a novella, please, and . . . four weeks later, it was either this one or *Babysitter*. So, I guess because of that "third time's a charm" lie, I tried one more time, and, bam: *The Only Good Indians* at the end of the next month. I was failing hard to write a novella. But then, finally, I managed to do one: *Night of the Mannequins*. Phew. Sawyer Grimes saved me. I mean, in the good way, not the way he tries to "save" his friends.

So, no, I haven't been back down 80 lately, but neither has 80 left me. I've been down a lot of bad-idea roads, done some pure-stupid drives—on the reservation once, deep in a white-out in November, my dad drove him and me around the barrier keeping people concerned with living off of Looking Glass, easily the most dangerous blacktop on the rez, and we left our tire tracks on all that deep snowpack for the next hour, just creeping along, somehow never sliding off the mountain like we were supposed to—but there's something meaner about 80. If you've tried it when it's angry and indifferent, you'll know. It's always better to get a motel room, wait it out. Or maybe just go up to 90, or down to 70. Or just go home, keep living.

In Tony Earley's story "The Prophet from Jupiter," he says that "in North Carolina, even in the mountains, it takes more than a month of your life to live through August." That's how 80 is: white-knuckling it through a storm, it takes years off your life that you can never get back. But you're happy just to still have a life, too. Many don't.

This is the interstate where Dark Mill South left his victims propped behind snow fences, facing north.

Chances are I'll go back there again, in story. 80's got its hooks in me, for better or for worse. And, in November 2019, it nearly kept me, when I slid off the road just north of Casper, had some unpleasant adventures in the ditch at sixty miles per hour—wild enough that a lot of truckers stopped in wonder, all aghast and laughing and looking at me from different angles, because this wasn't the kind of thing people live through. I very nearly didn't. I don't think I should have, really, and I don't know why I did.

I miss the truck that happened in. It was a 2004—the first one of mine with a CD player. I felt so modern having one at last, never mind that all the rich high schoolers in Midland, Texas already had CD players in the late eighties. Not me. I had to wait until I sold those two old Chevrolets, got that 2004 FX4 off an old man, and cleaned all his shell casings out from under the seat.

So, 80, it's a drive I know.

As for all the trucking stuff in *Killer*, though, man, where to even start with that. One of my stepdads was a trucker, some months—Darren in *Mongrels* drinks his same strawberry wine coolers—and I'd go tooling around with him on short runs, get to know the road from a rocking chair like I'd need to, for this book. Only longer run I ever went on was with my granddad on my dad's side's twin brother, out in . . . Sacramento, California I think it was? Somewhere close to Yosemite. We were hanging out there one summer when I was fourteen, and it was so weird for me, this great uncle's face matching the pictures of my granddad, which was pretty much all I had to go on for him. This great uncle's job was making runs into Yosemite every night, to resupply their concessions, I think? I went with him this time, high up in the cab, him telling me stories about mountain lions he'd seen, me just soaking all this in. I was wearing a choker that summer, so I could be a real Indian. A choker and a headband, and I tried hard to not smile very much, so everyone would know I was tough. I was probably really too old—and way too tough—to have to try not to cry when my great uncle handed me a ham sandwich he'd brought for me that had surprise-mustard on it, but . . . well, I'm not proud. I'll probably still cry if I get mustard in my mouth.

Darren would too.

But, talking trucking stuff, I'd grown up on *Smokey and the Bandit*, *B. J. and the Bear*, *Convoy*, C. W. McCall, Red Sovine, so . . . isn't that all the research you really need to write a novel like this?

Turns out, no.

After *The Buffalo Hunter Hunter*, this is probably the novel I had to do the most digging to write. Just because all the trucking stuff, it had to be at least close to right. While writing it, I did find a place I could ride my bike to that was stacked with tractors and trailers, anyway. I'd pedal there, crawl all over them, trying to understand how this and that worked, always ready to run if anyone saw me out there. And the videos I watched, man. So, so many. Probably the most helpful text was Finn Murphy's excellent and fascinating *The Long Haul: A Trucker's Tales of Life on the Road*. I think about that one a lot, still. There's a dude in there who never sleeps. He's maybe the most interesting person I've ever chanced across on the page. Well, him and Tom Bombadil.

Anyway, though I wrote *Good Indians* the last of *Killer* and *Babysitter* and *Mannequins*, it came out first of all of them. And then suddenly I was on this publishing waterslide: a trilogy, a standalone slasher, *Babysitter*, and a historical, epistolary vampire novel three months ago. Along the way, though, my heart sort of broke for *Killer*. It was because King's *The Outsider* came out. Even worse? *The Outsider* is flat-out amazing, is easily my favorite of his over the last . . . twenty years, say? I could live in this novel about, yes, a monster-of-legend who can taste the blood of someone and then, you know, become them.

It's good that all those other books of mine hit the shelves before *Killer*, I think. Who can compete with King? And, if people think I'm just aping *The Outsider* here, well . . . at least I had a good model, yes?

But I should also thank all the road movies I'm such a fool for. *Forsaken*, *Joy Ride*, *Road Games*, *Roadside Prophets*, even *Cannonball Run*. *The Hitcher* of course. And I consider the two *Reekers* to be road movies too. And there's so many more I keep close to my heart. I think why I'm so forever smitten with road movies, horror or not, it's that the cars and trucks and rigs and motorcycles always get some good camera time, some good—on the page—description. That's maybe my favorite thing with writing: getting to talk cars and trucks. One of the publications I'm proudest of, I mean, it's in *Street Trucks*.

Too, though, and I'm not exactly sure the how of this, but . . . back in, I don't know, 2015, maybe? My son and me are up on the rez hunting with my dad, and there's just been this huge snowfall, so hardly anybody's able to get up the logging roads into the high timber, where the elk might be. This year, though, I had this stupid-tall Jeep Wrangler with monster tires on it, so of course I figured we could crawl our way up the mountain.

Maybe a half-mile up, those oversized tires turned out to be balloons floating on top of the snow, pretty much. They threw pretty white roostertails everywhere, but we were stuck, deep. We got out, dug under this and that tire, jammed branches and logs everywhere, and, finally, my dad said he would stand in front of the Jeep's aftermarket bumper, rock it while I went back and forth from first gear to reverse, and maybe we'd get lucky.

It wasn't a bad idea, exactly. Or, it wasn't bad until, just like we were hoping for, the Jeep's spinning tires finally caught enough to launch it forward. Great, wonderful. Except my dad was standing right there. That big ugly bumper launched him back into the trees, like off his feet and cartoon-flying through the air, and I thought for sure he had to be broken—he wasn't, but he wasn't particularly pleased with me, either. Watching that bumper hit him, though, fold him over, throw him up and back, that was so clear in my head, writing *Killer*, here. You can imagine what it's like to pop someone with thousands of pounds of moving metal like that, but until you've actually done it, and to someone you care about it, I'm not sure you really understand it.

Sorry, Dad?

We did winch ourselves out, finally, didn't have to sleep on the mountain that night, which was good, and I'm not trying to say here that I'm glad it happened, hitting you like that. But, too, I'm not sure I write this novel if it doesn't happen?

Thanks also to James Andrew Cowell here at CU, for the one little bit of Arapaho in here. Thanks to Court Merrigan, one of my little brothers' friends, for some indirect help. Thanks to Paisley Rekdal, for the same thing I thanked her for in *The Buffalo Hunter Hunter*. Thanks also to Jim Shooter, for having Captain America and Wolverine going into this falling-down compound in *Secret Wars*, to free the prisoner bad guys, keep this huge building from killing them. When Harper went back for all those truckers after she'd accidentally lit their parking area on fire . . . she was Cap, she was Wolvie. I don't have that moment without Jim Shooter.

Thanks also, as ever, to BJ Robbins, for getting this to Joe Monti, who, as usual, identified the weak parts, didn't tell me how to fix them, just that they needed some fixing. Thanks to Caroline Tew, for being part of all that, and to Christine Calella and Savannah Breckenridge for making sure this title, this cover was on all the shelves, all the lists, in front of all the eyes.

And all the thanks to my wife Nancy, for giving me, what, four months to write this and *Babysitter* and *Mannequins* and *Good Indians*? Four months where, like you always do, you kept my world working, and let me hide in stories. But, I don't always hide there. I also like to live in this story you and I are in. The one where it wasn't just me shooting up 80 to get to our son, but us. The wind was ridiculous, kept wanting to turn us into kites, and none of my radiators were as good as I hoped, and the big rigs were buffeting us across the lanes like playthings, and the ice was, you know, ice, but I had your hand to hold across the console. It should have been on the steering wheel, but you're more important. If we did have to go sailing across the ditch, to cartwheel end over end into Wyoming? I wanted to feel your hand in mine in those last moments. But we lucked through time and again, and each trip, we'd stop at Wagonhound and we'd stand in that bitter-cold wind together, and we'd know that we were in this together, and no matter which way the road turned under us, no matter what big rig was bearing down on us, it would be you and me, Nan.

It still is. It always will be.

ABOUT THE AUTHOR

STEPHEN GRAHAM JONES is the *New York Times* bestselling author of *The Only Good Indians*, *My Heart is a Chainsaw*, and *The Buffalo Hunter Hunter*. He has been an NEA fellowship recipient and a recipient of several awards including the Ray Bradbury Award from the *Los Angeles Times*, the Bram Stoker® Award, the Shirley Jackson Award, the Jesse Jones Award for Best Work of Fiction from the Texas Institute of Letters, the Independent Publishers Award for Multicultural Fiction, and the Alex Award from the American Library Association. He is the Ivena Baldwin Professor of English at the University of Colorado Boulder, USA.